THE APOLLO DECEPTION

Recent titles by Mitch Silver

IN SECRET SERVICE
THE BOOKWORM
THE APOLLO DECEPTION *

* *available from Severn House*

THE APOLLO
DECEPTION

Mitch Silver

For Ollie

This first world edition published 2019
in Great Britain and 2020 in the USA by
SEVERN HOUSE PUBLISHERS LTD of
Eardley House, 4 Uxbridge Street, London W8 7SY.
Trade paperback edition first published
in Great Britain and the USA 2020 by
SEVERN HOUSE PUBLISHERS LTD.

British Library Cataloguing in Publication Data
A CIP catalogue record for this title is available from the British Library.

ISBN-13: 978-0-7278-8975-1 (cased)
ISBN-13: 978-1-78029-661-6 (trade paper)
ISBN-13: 978-1-4483-0359-5 (e-book)

All Severn House titles are printed on acid-free paper.

Severn House Publishers support the Forest Stewardship Council™ [FSC™],
the leading international forest certification organisation.
All our titles that are printed on FSC certified paper carry the FSC logo.

MIX
Paper from
responsible sources
FSC® C013056

Typeset by Palimpsest Book Production Ltd.,
Falkirk, Stirlingshire, Scotland.
Printed and bound in Great Britain by
TJ International, Padstow, Cornwall.

Luna is a stern schoolmistress;
those who have lived through her harsh lessons
have no cause to feel ashamed.

– Robert A. Heinlein, *The Moon is a Harsh Mistress*

PROLOGUE

Trangie, New South Wales, Australia

July 21, 1969

Una Ronald's eyeglasses with the black plastic frames are about to fall off. They've slid down her rather long nose while she's been sleeping, and now that she's shifted to her side, they're poised to drop to the floor beside the bed. Her husband, Jock, is snoring next to her like the Aussie lumberjack he once was. Meanwhile, history is about to be made on their brand-new AWA twenty-one-inch 'Deep Image' Solid-State television.

It's 5:16 a.m., and the tired anchorman is saying, not for the first time, 'Ladies and gentlemen, the Australian Broadcasting Corporation tonight is proud to—' when he is loudly interrupted by his broadcast partner.

'Gord, we've got pictures!'

The man's interjection wakes the sleeping woman with a start, her glasses giving in to gravity. Squinting nearsightedly at the TV, she tries to wake her husband.

'Jock, this is it!'

The big man simply rolls over. So, she turns back to the TV, leaning over and groping for her glasses on the rug without taking her myopic eyes from the screen. Adding to her focal problems is the billowing dust from the lunar surface that all but obscures the grainy black-and-white images from the Eagle's camera, dust kicked up by the lunar module's retro rockets.

The second newsman can barely contain himself. 'We're first in the world with these pictures, Gord, coming as they do from our own Parkes Observatory right here in New South Wales!'

Soon, the sound of Neil Armstrong's voice cuts through the crackle of hundreds of thousands of miles of static. 'Houston, Tranquility Base here. The Eagle has landed.'

Finally feeling the rims of her spectacles, Mrs Ronald puts them on in time to see something strange: rolling into the lower left-hand side of the picture and nearly hitting one of the Eagle's extended legs is a bottle of Coca-Cola. And then it disappears.

Could it be? She wipes her lenses on her nightgown and peers through them once more. No Coke bottle. Just the surface of the moon and a hatch that's opening high in the lunar module for one Neil Armstrong, whose next step really will be history in the making.

She reaches for the telephone to call someone. Anyone.

ONE

Tumulty's Tavern, New York City

March, 2019

Gary Stephens shuffles the pages of player stats in front of him, deep in thought. For luck, he leans down to pat Armstrong, his bulldog, lying placidly on the floor beside his chair. The lighting in the bar is low to non-existent, and Gary, thirty-nine and a director of TV commercials, has to squint.

Tumulty's is a Ninth Avenue leftover from the days when the Upper West Side was Manhattan's Wild West and the Irish Westies ruled the streets. The beer taps aren't retro, they're old: Bud, Schlitz, and Pabst Blue Ribbon, installed back before craft beers and IPAs and blueberry ales. Which is just the way he and his friends like it.

Tonight, their Rotisserie baseball league is holding its pre-season auction around three tables pushed together at the back of the place. Even though a late March snowstorm dropped three inches of the white stuff on the city this afternoon, the Mets and Yankees and the other twenty-eight teams start playing for real on Monday. So, Gary and his fellow fantasy league owners have to follow suit.

The lone waitress, with *Wanda* embroidered on her blouse, approaches the group carrying a tray of beers. She hands them out and asks, 'Have any of you considered food?'

Gary looks up at her from his clutter of papers.

'Tell me, Wanda, should I go twenty-two dollars on Yoenis Cespedes? He's missed more than half the season each of the last two years.'

'Really?'

'Yeah. Bad wheels.'

She smiles. This banter between them goes on all the time.

'Tell me about it. I'm still driving a Cutlass Ciera. Hey, why not save three bucks and get the fish and chips?'

Bill Pinzler, an intellectual property lawyer and the owner of the reigning league champs, the Needlers and Pinzlers, breaks in with a bid of his own. 'Twenty-two dollars on Cespedes. *And* the fish and chips.'

She writes up his order as Bill's husband, Colin, acting as the league's auctioneer, counts down. 'Twenty-two going once, going twice—'

'Twenty-three!' Gary has to have his favorite Met.

Under his breath, Bill stage whispers, 'You are such a homer.'

Colin starts in again. 'Going once . . . going twice . . .'

Gary turns to Wanda. 'And I'll have the bacon cheeseburger, medium rare.'

Simultaneously, the waitress and Colin pronounce, 'Sold!' Colin continues with: 'Twenty-three dollars to the Even Stephens,' as he enters the player's name and the amount of make-believe dollars on a spreadsheet.

Massive Paul Steinmetz, a house mover and sometime actor, has been watching the Mets' last Florida exhibition game on the bar's television. Now he taps Gary on the shoulder.

'Gar, your new boy just smacked one.'

As Gary shifts his attention to the TV, a *NewsBreak* graphic interrupts the game and an unseen announcer intones, 'We go to Bob Prior in Washington.'

The Rotisserie owners aren't happy.

'Damn it, no politics. Back to the game!'

The TV cuts to a generic correspondent in generic suit and tie standing in front of the White House. 'The Chinese government today announced plans to put a man on the moon.'

There's more groaning from the crowd in Tumulty's. 'C'mon, who gives a rat's—'

Gary does. With eyes locked on the TV, he says, 'Guys, hold it down!'

Now the tube is showing the Chinese press conference, complete with photoshopped flags of the US and China side by side on the moon's Sea of Tranquility. The newsman speaks over the images.

'The surprise mission is slated for July, eighteen months after China successfully landed an unmanned spacecraft on the far side of the moon. Its avowed purpose is to underscore the "peaceful intentions of the Chinese people and their goodwill toward America."'

Gary muses to himself, 'Well, I'll be damned.'

Bob Prior is back onscreen, reading from notes. 'The President's statement, released moments ago, says, "We welcome any advance in man's march of progress and in solidifying our warm ties with the people of China."'

Then he looks up with a wry smile. 'This, of course, despite the convictions of seventeen Chinese nationals for hacking into US databases and the expulsion of fourteen Americans from China in retaliation.'

He continues, moving to the next page of notes. 'The President's statement goes on to say, "I'm reversing the course my predecessor's administration undertook in the name of his so-called Space Force, when he pulled us out of the United Nations Outer Space Treaty. Today, America seeks not to dominate space but to share it peacefully. To that end, I urge the Congress to re-ratify the UN treaty and—"'

Hissing and booing from the bored Rotisserie players in Tumulty's, joined by the smattering of other patrons in the bar, drowns out the rest of Prior's announcement. The network's *Newsbreak* graphic returns to the screen as the unseen voice says, 'We'll have more as the story develops.'

The TV returns to Yoenis Cespedes dusting himself off on third. The Rotisserie guys approve. 'Awright! Finally!'

Gary turns to Steinmetz. 'Can I borrow your phone?'

The house mover gives a can-you-believe-this-guy? look to the others at the table. This has happened before to every guy at the table; Gary, the much-sought-after TV director, refuses to carry a phone.

The big man shrugs in resignation and hands over his cellphone. Gary punches in numbers.

TWO

The Harlem River

S till vigorous at eighty-one, Gary's father, Charlie Stephens, is kayaking under the stars twenty or so yards down from the Macombs Dam Bridge that spans the Harlem River. When his wetsuit starts to vibrate, he stops and unzips his pocket.

His son's voice on the phone says, 'Pop, it's Gary. Guess what? The Chinese are going to the moon! It's on TV!'

A tractor-trailer rumbles by on the bridge above.

'Who? What?'

Back in Tumulty's, the Mets are rallying. Gary raises his voice over the bar's noise. 'The Chinese government. Instead of another satellite, they'll be sending a manned rocket to the moon. You're back in business!'

Charlie lets his kayak drift with the current.

'Me? I don't think so. This retirement bit is too much fun. Besides, NASA is all out of money.'

Gary's still enthusiastic. 'If not NASA, the networks. Nobody does video simulations like you do.'

His father paddles once to avoid a channel marker.

'Did. Like I *did*. It's all up to you now, kiddo.'

The younger man's voice on the phone is incredulous. 'Me? I do commercials for dog food. And yogurt.'

To Charlie's left, Yankee Stadium is all lit up, getting ready for the season. He remembers going to a doubleheader there with his own dad.

'As I said, I'm retired.'

'Just wait till CBS or ABC start calling.'

'Then I'll do to them what I'm doing to you. Bye.'

Charlie presses the end button, and the call is over. Smiling, he lets the kayak float under the stars. A moment later, the full moon overhead is eclipsed as he drifts under the Madison Avenue Bridge at East 138th Street.

Looking up at the iron girders and trusses of the nineteenth-century structure gliding away behind him, the retiree doesn't notice the canoe that pushes off from behind the bridge's stone footings near the far shore. The two men paddling it, their black wetsuits zipped all the way up to their chins, silently overtake him.

When they come alongside, the shorter man, a dark watch cap pulled down so only his eyes are visible, takes hold of the kayak by the bow. The much taller one, his shaved black head reflecting light from the channel marker, grabs the stern. Together, they begin to tip it over. Charlie only has time for a quick yelp.

'Hey, what—'

Encased as he is, Charlie goes over with his boat. He uses his paddle to try to right himself, but together the men are too strong. Though the kayak rocks violently back and forth, he can't come up for air.

Eventually, the rocking ends and his paddle pops to the surface and floats off. The men glide away as quietly as they came, and the overturned kayak drifts down the river under the moon.

THREE
US Capitol, Washington, DC

May 7, 1958

The last of the eight senators returning from their lunch break seat themselves in order of seniority and political party at one end of the ornate meeting room of the Special Committee on Space and Aeronautics. Chairman Lyndon Johnson waits until the massive oak door at the far end is closed and the Congressional aides and reporters in the gallery have taken their seats before gaveling the day's session back to order.

The tall Texan has to hunch down slightly to speak into his microphone as he addresses bald, bespectacled Dr Franz Faber sitting across the way at the witness table.

'Welcome back, Dr Faber. Before lunch we were discussing the staffing of this proposed agency, and I asked you why so many of your recommendations have German names. Do you recall the question?'

Faber's lips move, but his reply can't be heard.

Chairman Johnson says, 'Sir, you will need to turn your microphone back on.'

There's general laughter in the room as Dr Faber looks for the on-off switch. After a moment his lawyer, sitting beside him, reaches across and turns it on.

The chagrined witness leans forward and says in a thick German accent, 'This is better, yes?'

'Yes, much better, sir.'

Faber, not a public speaker, sits uncomfortably at the edge of his chair in order to reach the microphone.

'Then may I to make clear? I do not suggest for Dr von Braun and our group be named to this new agency. Rather, we remain in the Alabama and with the new NASA I liaise, if that is in English a word.'

Silver-haired Stuart Symington, the senior senator from Missouri, quips, 'French. Close enough.'

There's more laughter among the onlookers. Symington's Republican counterpart, the equally silver-haired Senator Everett Dirksen, waits for the mirth to subside before speaking.

'The underlying question is, uh, still on the table, sir.'

The man at the table is puzzled. 'Question?'

Dirksen continues, 'Why so many Germans?'

'You ask, sir, why are we German?' Dr Faber appears confused. 'Because, um, we were born there.'

This time, even some of the senators are laughing. Symington, whose legislation they're discussing, hastens to add, 'And because, uh, let the record show, that Dr Faber and his colleagues at Peenemunde, among them Dr von Braun, surrendered to our army in May 1945, rather than to the Russians. Isn't that right, sir?'

Faber, dabbing at the sweat on his forehead with his handkerchief, says with gratitude, 'Just so,' before slumping back in his chair.

FOUR

The Stephens brownstone, West 85th Street

Armstrong the bulldog, leash in mouth and more than ready for a walk, pads over to where Gary is working in the video edit suite on the ground floor of his brownstone. The room is dominated by a digital console and oversized screen, with a small recording booth off to the left. A racing bike leans against the far wall under the caricature an art director drew of

Gary, tethered at an ankle and filming upside-down out of a Piper Cub doing a barrel roll. It's signed in marker pen by all the agency and client people who were on the Aetna shoot.

The console holds a row of gold-plated Clio statuettes, advertising awards given for work on Ford cars, Dannon yogurt, Miller Lite beer, and two different brands of dog food. Below them are side-by-side framed snapshots: one of his dad working at an earlier version of this console, the other of Carla and Jill, Gary's late wife and daughter, taken when Jill was nine. A carved wooden sign left over from when his father had the place hangs on a nearby wall amid signed glossy celebrity photos. It reads, *C. Stephens & Son/ Ask the World of Us.*

The dog bumps him in the leg with his head, but Gary does his best to ignore the animal as he works at the outmoded KEM flatbed film editor he's pulled out of storage. Multitasking, he holds his studio phone to his ear with one hand, listening, while the other absently twirls a frayed cord with a couple of small keys – one brass and the other silver – around his wrist.

The room's giant screen shows what the KEM, sitting alongside the room's modern digital board, is playing. It's an old strip of 35 mm film of astronaut Neil Armstrong stepping out of a flight simulator.

Gary speaks into his phone, 'Yeah, who drowns in Manhattan?'

He looks at the keys as they make another circuit around his wrist.

'Know anyone who wants a like-new, one-owner kayak? Anyway, thanks for coming to the service, I appreci—'

The dog bumps into Gary with more force. His owner hits Pause on the machine. 'Look, Jon, I gotta go. Or rather, Army does. Thanks again. Bye.'

With the call over, Gary glances at the frozen frame of the astronaut before he kneels down and takes the leash from the bull-dog's mouth.

'See that guy in the funny suit? His name's Armstrong, same as yours.'

As he attaches the lead on the dog, Pippa Stephens Greenwald, his married older sister, enters the studio from the street door and takes in the scene. She has a large black leather book under her arm.

'Morning, Gary.'

'Hey, Sis, you're early. Twins OK?'

She puts the book down on top of the edit console.

'You mean the ten-year-olds who think they're twenty? Perfectly fine. Except I was just informed they like the nanny's mac n' cheese better than mine, so I'll have to come up with something else tonight. Speaking of which—' she takes a piece of paper from her pocket and holds it out – 'the last time I looked in your refrigerator you were out of everything. If you're taking Army for a walk, here's a grocery list.'

She hands him the paper, then runs a finger over the console. 'Don't you ever dust?'

Gary sighs. 'How many more days of free nagging do I get?'

'Roger's back from Rome Thursday. So, how's it coming with the backlog in Pop's storage room?'

Gary looks down at the pile of silver film cans on the floor.

'Half the labels have fallen off.' He nods toward the heavy book on the console. 'What's with the tome?'

'Condolence book from the service. We need to start on our thank-yous.'

Gary speaks to the anxious dog. 'What, Army? You have chores, too?'

Army barks just once.

To his sister, Gary says, 'That's a yes.'

An hour later, man and dog are heading for the 79th Street Boat Basin on the Hudson River. Army pulls Gary, who's trundling two bags of groceries in a wire shopping cart, past a City Parks sign with an arrow that reads, *Kayak Launch*. They make their way along a floating dock between the cabin cruisers and houseboats. The wharf ends at a wooden cabin with a sign that reads, *Canoes/ Kayaks*.

A young woman with a safety pin through her left eyebrow is entering something in a computer on the other side of a plywood plank counter as Gary walks in. The printed plastic card on the counter reads, *Angela R., Watercraft Facilitator*. She wears a faded cotton T-shirt revealing tattooed arms muscular enough to heft a canoe and possibly fling it over to New Jersey. She hits a computer key with finality before turning to her visitor.

'Yes?'

Gary nods toward the plastic card. 'Am I speaking with the Facilitator?'

The woman appraises him with a slight smile. 'I liked it better than Boat Renter. Now, how can I help you? I'm about to close up for the day.'

Gary digs into his pocket and pulls out a slip of paper. 'From the police.'

The woman glances absently at the chit. 'Yeah, we got a kayak back from the impound. If you come back . . .' Then she looks up, sympathy in her eyes, and extends a calloused hand. 'You're Charlie's son. I'm so sorry.'

He shakes her hand. 'Thanks. I . . .'

Surprisingly, she doesn't let go. The cord and the keys Gary still has on his wrist dangle between them. 'Your pop was a good guy. To lose him to a fuckin' heart attack . . .'

Gary extricates his hand and takes a three-by-five card from his pocket. The two largest words on it read, *For Sale*. He slides it across to Angela. 'I'd like you to post this somewhere.'

Her brow furrows as she reads. 'I wouldn't if I were you.'

'No?'

'It's not enough. A LiquidLogic Stinger goes for $1,300 new.'

Without asking, she takes a marker, crosses out Gary's price on the card and writes in a new, higher figure. 'There. You'll get that, easy, for a first-class kayak.'

She detects something – doubt maybe – in Gary's expression.

'Your dad was first class all the way.'

A little taken aback by her intensity, Gary struggles to wriggle the cord with the keys off his wrist. 'And these were in his wetsuit along with his waterlogged cell. One of them yours?'

She picks up the silver one and notes the tiny number engraved on it. 'Ah, four nineteen. This way.'

Pinning the For Sale notice on a corkboard, she leads Gary and Army to a row of bus station-style lockers, saying, 'Came out of the Port Authority.'

In locker 419 is a nicked-up kayak paddle beside a second wetsuit, well used. The suit is draped over something bulky. Lifting it she reveals seven large 35 mm film cans. Surprised, she looks at Gary. 'His work?'

He reads the labels on the side of a can. 'From fifty years ago. Why on earth . . .?'

He lifts the lid to find little rolls of 35 mm film. 'Guess I'll have to come back for them.'

Angela picks up the other six heavy cans, muscles flexing.

'Got your car here?'

Gary smiles. 'Just a grocery cart.'

He leaves the dock a minute later and walks Army past the Boat Basin Café and toward the West Side Highway underpass leading to 79th Street. The film cans are in the cart with the groceries riding on top.

Standing in a cordoned-off work site on a ramp high above the eatery, a big guy with a shock of bleached white hair has been looking out at the Hudson with field glasses. Now he lowers his binoculars to follow man and dog as they make their way toward the pedestrian walkway beneath his feet. His smile betrays one dark tooth.

Down below, a poodle strolling by with a couple of middle-aged women catches Army's attention. The bulldog jerks at his leash, trying to turn and follow the other animal, pulling Gary up short in the process.

A second later, maybe two, a huge sandstone block – one of the thousands being used to patch the crumbling highway – drops thirty feet and crashes down onto the walkway where Gary just was.

FIVE

The Stephens brownstone

The news is playing at a low volume on a wall TV. Three hours after it happened, a reporter for one of the local channels is standing beside a pile of sandstone blocks at the 79th Street work site, thrusting her mic into the face of the man she's grilling. That man, in a suit and ugly tie and wearing a hardhat, has a superimposed title running across his chest that reads, *Joseph*

Gargano, Reconstruction Associates. He appears to be defending himself.

Gary picks up the TV remote and turns off the set.

Pippa reaches for the remote, saying, 'We were just coming to the good part, you and Army.'

Gary beats her to the electronic instrument and sticks it in a drawer.

'Again? You've seen me shaking like a leaf twice already, on nine and eleven.'

'But it was a near-death experience!'

'It was an accident. I'm OK. Army's OK. Can we get back to work?'

Pippa's phone rings. She looks at the screen. 'Brenda. Wants to know how you are.'

'Tell her I'm fine.'

'I'll tell her you're cranky.' His sister starts typing a text with her thumbs. 'In other words, back to your old self.'

'Exactly.'

Gary reaches into the shopping cart, now that the groceries are in the fridge, and lifts the top film can, which is nearly as big as a manhole cover, from the stack of seven. The yellow tape on the edge of the can reads, *Project 11, #4, 5-12-69, Property WDP.* Unrolling a random strip of film from the dozen inside, he holds it up to the light as his sister looks on.

Pippa says, 'You're gonna need Pop's bin.'

He picks up another strip and eyes it even as he yanks his head behind him. 'Storage room.'

Pippa comes back wheeling a canvas-sided bin with a metal frame and a row of hooks on top. She rolls it past Army in his dog bed.

'Is it too early to ask?'

Gary squints at a third short strip from Can 4. Holding it up to the light, he sees a couple of odd black shapes on a blue background. Without looking back, he says, 'Way too early.'

Then he turns to face his sister. 'But you can ask it anyway: "What's a bunch of half-century-old film odds and ends doing in a locker by the river?" And: "Who or what the hell is WDP?" No idea. Yet.'

She's been studying the heavy cans in the basket. 'Then you better start with the first one.'

She hands him a can while reading aloud, 'Project 11, #1, 4-30-69.'

An hour later, with the sandstone block to-do behind them, brother and sister are working like the well-oiled machine they once were. Gary, in white cotton gloves, runs each strip, some several yards long, others only inches, through the flatbed. On the suite's big screen, the word 'Record' in red flashes at the bottom.

Then he marks the strip at one end with a grease pencil. Pippa hangs each one on a particular hook, depending on Gary's marking, over the canvas bin by an end sprocket. There are dozens of film 'ends' hanging from the hooks.

Pippa talks to the back of her brother's head as he works. 'Ever think we'd be handling celluloid again?'

Without turning around, he answers. 'Not in a million . . . hey!'

Up on the screen there's a close-up of Charlie Stephens's thirty-ish face as he adjusts the lens of the camera shooting the film.

A startled Pippa blurts out, 'It's Pop!'

When Charlie steps aside, there's a football field-sized soundstage behind him where dozens of stagehands are wrangling some kind of huge floor covering into place. Like the grounds crew at Citi Field wrestling a tarp on a rainy day. They lower it, looking at Charlie, who's clearly the boss. He motions and they move it a few inches. We get glimpses of a pockmarked, painted, hard rubber tarp before the filmstrip runs out.

Gary hurriedly sets up the next strip of film to run through the KEM. It shows Charlie, his shoes swathed in cotton booties, standing on the floor covering, which looks like the surface of the moon. A camera on a large crane is off to one side.

Pippa says, 'I don't remember this one. Do you?'

Her brother, too, is puzzled. 'For Cronkite, maybe?'

He looks at his watch and gets up hurriedly. 'Take over. I've got . . . something.'

'A date?'

'A drink.'

'With my friend Pamela? You called her?'

'She called me.' He points to the landline on the console. 'On that very phone.' Then he adds, 'It's just a drink.'

Pippa takes her brother's place as he reaches for the leash.

'You taking Army?'

He shrugs. 'You said she's a dog lover.'

She gives him a baleful look. 'Give this one a shot, why don't you?'

Gary straightens up. 'You mean, "Stop comparing them to Carla." I hear you.'

He kisses the top of her head as she runs another strip.

'I'll be at Tumulty's.'

Army pulls Gary toward the door as the suite's screen shows a travel shot along the out-of-focus surface of the pockmarked moon.

Gary and Pamela, an attractive woman of about his age, sit at a table with drinks. She stirs hers as Army lies on the floor between them. The evening news, as usual, is playing on the TV behind the bar. A little tentatively, she begins.

'I guess your phone's blowing up.'

'Nope. Not a single call.'

'Texts, then.'

'Zip. It's the beauty of not having a phone.'

'You're kidding!'

He holds his hands out wide. 'Search me.' Then he adds, 'I don't know if it's not having a phone, or not having friends.'

'Now I know you're kidding, a guy like you.'

'What *about* a guy like me?'

She looks him up and down, appraisingly. 'Pippa said you're sort-of good-looking . . . check. A guy in his thirties . . . check.'

'Just barely.'

'Still. With most of his hair . . .' She reaches out and trails her fingers through his mostly dark hair. 'A few of them gray, but so what?'

Now she assumes the tone of a statistician. 'Six feet tall, one-fifty, one-fifty-five or so . . . you're what we girls call a catch. Straight, no visible scars.'

He smiles sheepishly. 'They're all on the inside.'

'Oh, right.' A sympathetic expression appears on her face. 'She said you were a widower. I'm sorry.'

He says, 'No, I didn't mean . . .'

His date puts a gentle hand on his. 'You must miss them terribly.'

He moves his hand from under hers to run it through his hair. 'Look, I'd rather not . . .'

He stops what he's doing and stares at the behind-the-bar TV over her shoulder. A follow-up to the Chinese moon story, it shows old NASA footage from the POV of the lunar module Eagle on its approach to the cratered surface. Something about it rivets his attention.

'Gary, I'm sorry if—'

He gets up and throws bills down on the table. 'I gotta go.'

His date half-rises. 'Was it something I . . .?'

Gary isn't listening. Army is up and ready to leave. 'I'll call you.'

He and the dog are out the door by the time she picks up her purse.

Under her breath she says, 'Don't bother.'

SIX

Arlington, Virginia

A videoconference is underway in one of the nondescript office blocks that ring Washington. Several people are dotted around the small, darkened room in theater-style seats facing a large flat-screen image of the man with the bleached hair.

'So, you let him slip through your fingers.'

The person who makes the accusation is a middle-aged woman with a lit cigarette in her mouth despite the twin neon *No Smoking* signs over the exits.

On the screen, the man's face reddens. His voice booms out of a speaker on the right-hand wall of the room.

'No fuckin' way! This isn't on me. That goddamn dog.'

A second, much younger woman says, 'How else would you describe it? We send you out to do a simple retrieval—'

'*Simple*? If it's so simple, *you* try doing it!'

The redheaded man wearing a seersucker jacket and a bowtie in the third row says, placatingly, 'Now Karl, simmer down. Nobody's criticizing. Accidents will happen. Let's look on the bright side, we finally found the material.'

Sullenly, Karl says, '*I* found the material.'

'And you let it slip through your fingers.' It's the chain-smoking woman again. 'And now your little escapade is playing round the clock on every TV station up there in New York.'

'Listen, lady, the only thing that slipped through my fingers was a fucking brick the size of your head! A brick you couldn't have lifted two inches off the ground! I'm the one who said the son would lead us to the film, and he did. So, get off my back!'

Someone else, someone with a Southern accent, says, 'This isn't getting us anywhere. The question is, what do we do next?'

An unusually tall woman, sitting several seats down from the redhead, says, 'The old man left behind a ton of film. Maybe we've got time; maybe they won't screen it for a while.'

The man with the Southern drawl says, 'You wanna take that chance, Marion?'

The woman defends her position. 'What other choice do we have, Raheem? Even if, or when, they do screen it, they might not know its significance.'

The smoker turns around to address the others. 'I'm with Raheem. We have to assume when they see what's on the film, the brother and sister, they'll know what it means. I suggest we proceed accordingly.'

'Then . . . like father, like son?' Karl, with a querying look, puts into words what several of them have been thinking.

The woman with the cigarette quickly stubs it out on the arm of her theater seat. 'Out of the question! One is an accident. Two are a pattern.'

The man with the bleached hair won't give up. He raises his hand on the screen as if in class. 'The guy's sister has kids. I could—'

A different voice, one with a pronounced accent from somewhere in Asia, also comes from the speaker, cutting him off. 'No, nothing involving your police. Not when we're so close.'

The man with the bowtie directs his next statement directly to the speaker on the wall. 'What time is it there? It's 0200 hours? Go to bed, Ching, and check your messages in the morning.'

He turns to face the video screen. 'You too, Karl. Get some shuteye. We'll let you know what we decide.'

On the monitor, the man with the black tooth leans forward and reaches out his hand to a video control. 'Okey-dokey.' His image goes dark.

The first woman says, 'I told you using him was a mistake.' In a softer, more respectful voice she adds, 'What do you think, sir?'

The others turn to look at an elderly man sitting in the last row of the darkened room. The shiny plastic of his old-fashioned hearing aids appears strangely red in the neon glow from the nearby exit sign.

He says, in a gravelly voice, 'I think mistakes can be rectified.' Then he pauses for dramatic effect, learned over a lifetime of bending governmental bureaucrats to his will. 'We go to Plan B.'

SEVEN

The Stephens brownstone

Pippa is screening another of the blue strips with blocky black shapes when Gary rushes in.

'I know what that is!'

She looks at him, surprised. 'Something for Fisher-Price?'

Gary gives Army a dog treat and hurries over to his sister. 'It's a foreground plate.'

'Foreground? To what?'

Gary uses a brotherly bump with his tush to move her out of his chair.

'The moon.'

He rolls over to the main console and calls up the internet, entering *nasa.gov* and the drop-down window, *Missions*. Under *Apollo*, he goes to *Apollo Videos* and scrolls down to *Approaching the Moon*.

Gary hits *Play* and, simultaneously, a red button on the keyboard. Now the word *Download* appears over the 1969 image of the moon's surface looming up through the struts of the lunar module, the one he just saw in the bar.

Then he scrolls through the digital transfers he and his sister just made of Charlie's odds and ends. He finds a file and opens it: it's one of the black shapes at odd angles on blue. He clicks on another file, the out-of-focus moon surface. He screens one and another before choosing a third, one that starts with a stagehand's foot on the edge of the rubber, moon-like floor covering: Charlie's camera cranes above the surface, but it's all out of focus.

Pippa watches it playing over his shoulder.

'The whole thing's NG.'

Gary pauses the shot and turns to his sister.

'Not so fast.'

The words *Download Complete* appear on the big screen. More mouse clicks and now the NASA video is playing on the left side of a split screen. Then he starts the soft-focus moon strip playing on the right. He clicks on a pull-down window that says, *Bring to Front* and the blue image with the black shapes runs over it.

Gary returns to the NASA video on the left and pauses it near the beginning. On the right side, he pauses the composite he's made. Then he turns to Pippa.

'Ready?'

'For what?'

'This.'

Dramatically, he presses the *Play* button. The two split screens play side by side. And they're identical!

With the blue screen digitally dropped out, the black superimposed shapes are in the exact position of the Eagle's body and struts on the NASA footage at the left. The moon is out of focus, exactly as it is on the split screen across the way.

Pippa sputters, 'But, but . . .'

Her brother reaches out to the console and calls up the image of his dad in booties on the vast rubber floor mat.

Then, with a wave of his hand that includes the dog, he announces, 'Lady and gentleman, I give you Charlie Stephens, the first man on the moon!'

EIGHT

George C. Marshall Space Flight Center, Redstone Arsenal, Huntsville, Alabama

April 13, 1965

D r Wernher von Braun, Dr Franz Faber, and their team walk past huge Redstone rockets at the Army's Flight Center in Huntsville. Walt Disney, his brother Roy, and their executives are taking the tour as newsreel cameramen and print reporters capture the moment.

A newsman asks, 'What brings you to Alabama, Walt?'

Disney stops to respond. 'As many of you know, Doctor von Braun worked closely with me years ago on our *Man in Space* TV series. I'm here today to return the favor.'

A second reporter asks, 'Is that so, Doctor von Braun? Are you two planning a movie?'

Wernher Magnus Maximilian, Freiherr von Braun, still movie-star handsome in his early fifties, chuckles. 'We're a little busy for that right now, going to the moon and all.'

The news people share the scientist's jest.

Von Braun continues, with more gravity, 'But thanks to Mr Disney, anyone who saw those documentaries on TV or visited Tomorrowland with their family in California understands the importance of what we're doing.'

A TV reporter asks, 'You think the President gets it? Rumor has it his Great Society budget includes big cuts to your space program.'

Before von Braun can answer, Disney does.

'That's really why I'm here. Less than a month ago, a Russian cosmonaut actually walked in space. Working outside the capsule is a prerequisite for walking on the moon. So, make no mistake: the godless Communists right now are winning the space race. If I can help, through my TV shows and my appearance here today, to wake people up to the fact—' he whips off his glasses and gestures up to the heavens – 'Mr President, we've got to get there first!'

NINE

The Stephens brownstone

G ary and his sister are sharing Chinese take-out upstairs in the kitchen. They use chopsticks to pluck what they want from the half-dozen small white boxes, washing down the food with beers. The condolence book lies open next to a pad and pencil by Pippa's elbow.

'You're wrong, you know, bro.'

'You watched it with your own eyes!' he answers, his mouth full of kung pao chicken.

She expertly twirls a few sesame noodles between her wooden utensils. 'The Eagle underbelly and the moon elements you put together, how do you know Pop didn't "deconstruct" them from actual Apollo footage for some future simulation?'

Gary, having just picked up the box of steamed dumplings, slams it down on the table a little harder than he meant to. One of the dumplings goes flying.

'The dates on the film cans, for one thing. And the guy's foot. Are there stagehands in space?'

Army hurries over to eat the dumpling on the floor. Gary tries to stop him. 'No, Army, no!'

Pippa doesn't notice the dog coughing up the dumpling. 'Oh, the foot. Right.'

'Where's his water dish?'

'Outside, where it always is.' Pippa, closer to the back door, gets up. 'Here, Army.'

She lets the coughing dog out. He starts slurping up water from an unseen bowl as Pippa turns back to Gary. 'There must be another explanation. You think all those astronauts lied about going to the moon?'

Morosely, Gary wipes his mouth with a napkin. 'I don't know what to think.'

Absently he hovers over one little white box of food after another with his chopsticks before picking up a stir-fried shrimp, but stops before he eats it. An idea is forming. He gestures to the food in front of him.

'What, what if the Apollo missions were like these carry-out boxes, each one its own separate deal?'

He notices the shrimp and eats it. Then he uses the chopsticks to nudge one box away from the others. 'If there were different crews for each mission, maybe you could fake one without the others knowing.'

Pippa turns to her iPad and types *Apollo astronauts* in the Search box. She reads the results out loud.

'Armstrong/Collins/Aldrin. Conrad/Gordon/Bean. Lovell/Swigert/Haise. Shepard/Mitchell/Roosa. You're right, every flight had an entirely different crew.'

She picks up a shrimp with her chopsticks, unconvinced.

'Still, would Pop lie? And those tech guys in Houston, they *fixed* the most-watched event in human history? Really?'

'But Pop's footage . . .'

Pippa takes no notice. 'And your personal god, Neil Armstrong, he was in on it? You named your dog for a cheater?'

At the mention of the dog, Gary gets up to let Army back in. Pippa turns her attention to the condolence book, studying the names. When Gary returns with the dog, she asks, 'Any idea who Chet Predovic is?'

He looks over her shoulder at the book. 'Runs the PBS science unit, I think.'

Pippa moves her finger down the list of signatures. 'How about Chris Walsh?'

'No idea. I didn't meet him at the service. Address?'

'Just a phone number, three-two-one area code. Where's that?'

'Florida, I think. Didn't Pop call from a hotel down there on his last few NASA trips?'

She's looking at the book. 'The thing is, next to his number he wrote, *Call me. Vital.*'

Her brother picks up the landline and, looking at the condolence book for the number, punches in the digits. 'What would Miss Manners say about phoning in a thank-you?'

An older woman's voice on the phone answers, 'Yes?'

He presses the phone's Speaker button. 'Mr Walsh, please. Chris Walsh.'

The woman's voice with a hint of a foreign accent fills the kitchen. 'I'm Chris Walsh. Who's this?'

Gary gives his sister a 'who knew?' look. 'Sorry about that. You don't know me, ma'am; I'm Charlie Stephens's son.'

The voice on the speaker drops in volume. 'Gary! How are you? And Pippa?'

He's taken aback. 'Do we know you?'

'No, but I certainly know you two from Charlie. Wish I could have stayed after the service and introduced myself. Look, I need to call you back. Pippa got a phone?'

'You can call on this one. It's—'

'No, Pippa's. It's . . . better.'

He gives her Pippa's number.

'And no names when I call you back.'

The line goes dead.

He makes a 'she's crazy' gesture around his ear as he sits next to Pippa. Her cell rings. The Caller ID box says 'Call Restricted.'

She puts her phone on Speaker for Gary. 'Ms W—'

'I said no names. And it's "Mrs." I've been a widow a long time now.'

Brother and sister exchange quizzical looks as Pippa asks, 'And you knew Pop . . . how?'

'My husband was a NASA test pilot. An "almost astronaut." He was your dad's tech advisor on the project.'

Gary asks, 'What project was that?'

Mrs Walsh lowers her voice to a confidential tone. 'You know. The thing.'

'No, we don't know. What thing?'

'Uh . . . the moon thing.'

'You mean a simulation?' Pippa asks. 'For TV?'

The woman's laugh sounds even harsher coming from the phone's tiny speaker. 'That was one helluva "simulation."'

Gary says, 'Maybe you'd better explain.'

There's muttering on the Florida end of the line. 'Shit! Really? Shit!' What comes next is more decisive. 'I can't explain this over the phone. At least one of you better get your ass down here.'

Pippa lets frustration creep into her voice. 'Mrs, uh, W, we're not about to—'

The woman on the phone lowers her voice once again. 'I can't be sure, but I think they're starting to clean house.'

Pippa puts the phone down on the kitchen table so she can speak into it with her hands on her hips. 'Clean house?'

Gary leans in to add, 'Whose?'

'Well, yours, of course.' There's a sort of combined chuckle and smoker's cough before the woman continues. 'Look, we've been talking too long as it is; they keep phone logs. Get on the first plane out.'

'This is crazy,' Pippa barks. 'I have a husband coming home from Europe . . . kids . . . I—'

'Just your brother, then. I'll pick him up at the airport.'

Dubious, Gary says, 'I don't even know what city in—'

'Orlando. Delta has a seven from JFK. Take down this number: Two-nine-six.'

He gestures to Pippa to hand him the pad and pencil she was using for condolence thank-yous. 'Is that the flight?'

The voice on the phone says, 'Number of my taxi. I'm a cabbie, didn't I say?'

Pippa slaps the pencil and paper down on the table in front of her brother. The sound makes the dozing Army look up with a start.

'No, you didn't say! And what you did say doesn't make sense! How do we know this isn't some cock-and-bull—'

'They killed your dad.' Calmly, as if speaking to children, Chris Walsh says, 'And they'll kill you, too. So, hang up the phone and pack a bag. And get some burner phones like I did.'

On the paper in front of him Gary's written, *Delta, JFK/Orlando, 7 a.m.* He's adding the cab number when he stops.

'Killed? Pop drowned. He—'

The old woman's tone doesn't change. 'In the Harlem River on a calm night? Remember, two-nine-six. I'll be in the line outside.'

The cell phone goes dark, leaving them to look at one another.

TEN
Orlando International Airport

An agitated Gary Stephens trundles his suitcase behind him, inching toward the head of the airport's taxi line. Suddenly, even as the family ahead of him, bound for the Magic Kingdom, is still getting into their cab, a yellow taxi appears out of nowhere and opens its rear door. The number 296 is stenciled on the side.

As soon as Gary gets in, the cab tears away. From the back of the waiting line, a big man with bleached white hair elbows others aside to get the next one.

The eyes of the heavy-set, seventy-ish female driver are visible to Gary in the rear-view mirror. Speaking into that mirror, Chris Walsh says, 'Scrunch down, I think someone's following us. In fact, you better get all the way down.'

If he was agitated before, Gary's twice as agitated now. He lies down reluctantly, resting his head near the right-hand door and staring at the black leatherette of the taxi's front seat. 'Following us? Following me?'

From up in front, Mrs Walsh says, 'Old Boy Scout motto: "Be Prepared." Not that I was in the *Boy* Scouts.'

A couple of minutes later, Cab 296 makes a screeching left across three lanes of traffic. Centrifugal force slides Gary's head into the sharp plastic edge of the door handle.

'Ow! Why'd you do that?'

Ignoring him, she brakes to an abrupt stop, sending his suitcase crashing down from the seat to the floor, landing on his feet and wedging him in.

He gives out with another 'Ow!'

With the car now idling, she rolls down her window and speaks to someone outside. 'Hey, Ronnie. Let's go for the full detail, inside and out.'

Gary raises himself back up, stiffly, to a sitting position. They're parked in front of Big Al's Carwash on busy McCoy Road, where dozens of other Yellow Cab Company vehicles are getting ready to be hosed down in one of the three bays.

Standing by the open window, a skinny guy with scraggly chin hairs punches something into a phone. He shows her the result. 'See? You're not due for a wash till Friday. If I do you today, it's on you.'

'No prob.'

'It'll run ya, Chris. Forty even. And that's with the friend's discount.'

Mrs Walsh shrugs. 'My MasterCard still good?'

'Check.'

She drives forward and stops so workers can begin to attach chains for the carwash mechanism. Then she gets out and opens the rear door for her passenger. 'C'mon, my car's around the back.'

He's still wrestling his carry-on bag from where it was wedged when he feels a heavy grip on his arm.

'Leave it.'

Literally strong-armed around to the front of the cab and made to crouch down by the grille, Gary rebels with an expletive as he tries to stand up. 'What the fuck?'

Now she's crouching beside him, her heavy hand still on his shoulder. 'Stay low. There he is now.'

'Who?'

'Him.' She points over the top of the taxi's hood to yet another yellow cab that's driving slowly by on the far, west-bound side of the road. A man with bleached white hair is leaning out of the passenger window, scanning the carwash. Supported on two weight-lifter's arms and unconsciously grinning as he squints in the morning sun, the man's one black tooth makes him even scarier.

Chris Walsh says, 'Did you see him on the plane?'

Confused, Gary turns his head to look at this woman with the leathery skin and hair bleached by the sun. 'The plane?'

'He followed you down from New York.'

They watch the man in the cab move on up McCoy Road. She finally takes her hand off his shoulder. 'Let's go.'

Quickly retrieving his suitcase from the taxi, he follows this strange woman along the catwalk inside the carwash and out the back. She leads him over to an old blue Impala.

'Like I said, be prepared.'

She gets in behind the wheel and gestures to the back seat. 'Head down, same thing as before. It's a bit of a drive, and I'll tell you when you can get up.'

Shaken by the sight of the big man with the white hair, Gary does as she says. With his head lying uncomfortably on the suitcase jammed against the Impala's door, he's jolted twice by the double speed bumps at Big Al's rear exit.

What he can't see is worse: as they drive out the rear gate, Mr Bleach's cab passes them on the way in.

Chris Walsh murmurs to herself, 'Thought so.' Then she says, 'Stay down. If they got drones, they could see two heads.'

In more of a whine than he intended, Gary says, 'Drones? Phone logs? Who's after us, the NSA?'

The woman at the wheel says nothing and drives on. Now Gary's really worried.

Chris Walsh let Gary sit up once they left Orlando and were on Highway A1A. Now, an hour later, he's rolling his overnight bag behind her into a low-slung Cocoa Beach ranch house full of over-stuffed furniture and Afghan throws.

She walks by an upright piano with a dozen framed family photos on her way to the kitchen. 'Coffee? I got instant and I got drip.'

'Instant's fine,' he says, absently. 'With milk.'

He's studying the pictures. In the middle is a studio portrait of a handsome man in uniform. Her husband? Next to it are three smiling people: a younger Chris Walsh is flanked by the same man and Gary's own dad, Charlie, outside what looks like an aircraft hangar. There's one of a baby swaddled in a blanket. The woman holding the child has been cropped out except for her arms, but there's a line of yellow cabs visible in the background and part of a sign: *Arrivals*. An airport?

He picks up the photo beside it: just Mrs Walsh and Charlie, both a little older now, in bathing suits on a palm-studded beach, his arm draped over her shoulders. Gary's still studying it when she comes back with two mugs of coffee and an empty saucer.

She puts the saucer down and gestures with one of the mugs. 'That's right here in Cocoa. It really is a beach.'

He looks up from the photo, his mouth a straight line. Then he says, 'You and Pop were . . .'

'Yes. After Art died, and then your mother right after that.'

She hands him one of the mugs. He takes a drink.

'We had a lot in common already. And then we had the grief.'

'So, when he said he was calling from a hotel . . .'

She smiles. 'The Walsh. Best place on the strip.'

She puts a hand on his shoulder. He looks at it till she takes it away. Quietly, she says, 'Figured you should know how it was.'

He finally puts the picture down.

'I want to know how it *is*. You said Pop's death wasn't an accident, that they're cleaning house. First off, who's they?'

'Right. Come with me.'

She leads him into a 1960s-era kitchen with sunflower-yellow wallpaper and avocado cabinets. A set of four canisters with old-timey writing on them sits on the counter near the refrigerator, also in avocado. Reaching into the one marked *Flour*, Chris Walsh pulls out a pack of a dozen Polaroids held together with a couple of rubber bands.

Back in the dining room, they each take a seat as she spreads them out under the fake-Tiffany fixture. Then she picks up a nearby pack of Newports.

'Smoke?'

'No, thanks.'

She lights up and talks through the exhale, pointing with her cigarette at the Polaroids. 'OK, lemme tell you what these are. You needed security clearance just to get on the set, and they frisked everyone going in and coming out—'

'The set?'

The older woman sighs. 'The Hollywood set where they filmed the moon thing. May I continue?'

He gives a 'go on' wave of his hand. Things are starting to come together.

'Art, my Art in that picture there, flew recon over Korea. He'd signed the Secrets Oath; they knew he'd keep his trap shut. And he was good with cameras. So, they gave him the continuity job.'

'Like, movie continuity?'

'You use one, don't you?' She flicks some ash into the saucer she brought out earlier before pointing with her cigarette at his coffee cup. 'A girl who makes sure the cup is in the same hand from one scene to the next. Art's job was to Polaroid everything, avoid any screw-ups.' With that she gives a husky, smoker's laugh. 'Of course, they still screwed up.'

He puts his mug down. 'Go back. Pop worked for Cronkite, for NASA. How and where does a Hollywood movie come in?'

She stares at him, as if for the first time.

'You really don't know squat, do you? Apollo 1 burned down on the launch pad in '67. There *was* no NASA, at least till they figured out what went wrong. In real life it took twenty months. Hell, the Russians might've been camped on the moon by then. Add to that JFK's promise.'

'Huh?'

His hostess ruefully shakes her head. 'Schools these days. Kennedy, you know who *he* was? Well, he promised to land an American on the moon by the end of the sixties. No way Johnson was gonna come up short, even if he had to fake it.'

He picks up his coffee again and points to the Polaroids. 'OK, now tell me about these.'

She holds one out for Gary to look at. 'See the guy in the space suit?'

'That's Neil Armstrong!'

'Fuckin' A. The cover story was they were making a super-realistic space film using actual NASA hardware and Disney actors. Art got suspicious when the studio started frisking everybody. Then, when the real Apollo guys arrived . . . since when does NASA lend out a crew to make a movie?'

She hands the Polaroid with Armstrong in it across the table. 'So, he started taking two shots of everything and keeping one.'

Gary studies the image. 'You said there were searches. How did he get this out?'

'You don't wanna know.'

He looks at her. 'Try me.'

She looks right back. 'Two words: Body cavity.'

He drops the photo on to the table like a hot potato. 'Fuck!'

'Polaroids are washable.' She calmly runs her finger over the photo before picking it up and putting it back with the others. 'We did joke about Art having 'roids.'

He gets to his feet. 'Look, that picture isn't proof of anything. Armstrong could've just been visiting the set that day.'

'In a pressurized suit? And look at these others. They're—'

The overhead globe suddenly sizzles and dies with a pop.

'Crap! And I don't have a spare bulb.' Mrs Walsh stands up. 'Let's go out on the patio.'

She walks over to the sliding door leading to the backyard and, pulling it open, gestures for him to go first. He starts to head for a table with four cushioned chairs beside an avocado tree.

She holds him back, indicating side-by-side lounge chairs closer to the house. 'No, here, under the awning. Safer.'

They set their mugs on a little leaf-shaped table in between the seats.

'Meaning UV rays?' he asks.

'Meaning prying eyes. OK, you want hard proof? Here.'

She hands him the whole pack of Polaroids. Each image is a famous moment from the Apollo 11 mission, except with cameras and cameramen filming them on a huge soundstage. In one, a crane holds the 'Eagle' module five stories above the pockmarked surface his dad was standing on. A wind machine blows 'moon dust' on the lowered module, with sandwich wrappers and Coke bottles lying outside the lighted area where the crew left them.

The last shot is of Buzz Aldrin and Michael Collins laughing as a guy Windexes Armstrong's face shield. The 'earth' is partly reflected in the plastic. Gary turns the picture over. The back is stamped *07191969*.

She chuckles a little. 'It was a rush job. Charlie was scrambling to wrap it up, shooting insert stuff even after the so-called launch.'

Handing back the pack of pictures, he says, 'Let me think.'

He walks to the edge of the shade, looking out. He stoops to pick up a huge, fallen avocado and examines it, like Yorick's skull.

Noticing it, the woman says, 'Us locals call 'em alligator pears.'

He hefts it absently. 'This is some large pear you've got.'

She gets up and joins him, laughing. 'Your dad told me that once in another context.'

Gary drops the fruit the way he dropped the Polaroid earlier. 'Jesus, Mrs Walsh, don't say that stuff. He was my father.'

She runs a hand over his back. 'Will you forgive a crude ol' . . . it's just that you're so much like Charlie was. Like having him back.'

He's visibly angry now. 'Is that why I'm down here at the Hotel Walsh? On some wild goose chase so you can relive—'

A phone rings inside the house. She holds up a finger and goes to answer it. He follows her inside.

There's a cell phone in a cradle on the piano. She picks it up and listens. Then she says into the phone, 'Perfect timing, sweets! You OK?'

She listens some more before saying, 'Uh-huh, we just got in. I'm telling him now. But he's giving me—' she looks over at Gary, dubiously – 'the same stink eye you did.'

He mouths 'Who?' to her, which she ignores. Peeved, he eyes the pictures in the back of the grouping on the piano. There's one of a crew of astronauts in orange pressurized suits. Behind it is a touristy snap of a smiling couple in their twenties hugging each other under an oval seal reading, *Vice-President of the United States.*

Into the phone, Mrs Walsh says, 'How soon can you get here?' Then, 'Great, see you in ten.'

She blows a kiss and ends the call.

He asks, 'Boyfriend?'

She picks up the tourist photo and points to the girl in it. 'My daughter, Robin. She's got a few days off from work, so I asked her to join us. You like liverwurst?'

'Hi, Mom!'

Fifteen years older than her photo under the Vice-Presidential seal but still very attractive, with prominent cheekbones and hair the color of ripened wheat, Robin Walsh walks through the door with her dry cleaning and a brown bag from a deli. She doesn't look that much like her mother, which is a good thing. Doesn't sound much like her, either. She spots Gary and launches right in.

'What'll you have, Mr Stephens? Chicken salad? Turkey with Russian? Or the Big L?'

Her mother takes the deli bag from her and puts it down on the table. 'Please excuse my daughter. Rob can be a little abrupt.'

He gets up, moves over to the daughter and holds out his hand.

'Call me Gary. And you're . . .? "Rob" seems a little informal for someone I've just met.'

She shakes his hand strongly. 'You want formal? I'm Captain Walsh.'

She begins taking a Navy dress blouse out of the bag from the cleaner.

He watches her, fascinated. 'As in ships?'

She picks up a pair of silver Navy wings from a decorative dish on the sideboard and starts to attach them to the collars.

'Planes. Rockets, actually. I'm an astronaut.'

'Like her father.' Chris Walsh punctuates the fact by ripping open the deli bag.

'Careful, Mom,' Robin says. 'I got us all soup.'

A jumble of sandwiches, condiments, spoons, and napkins has spilled out on the table around three carry-out pints of soup. One has *CN* scrawled on the cardboard lid in marker. The other two have a *T* and a *B*. Chris picks up two of the containers and holds them out to Gary.

'Wanna start with soup? They're from Coastal Produce Market, all homemade. We didn't know what you'd like: Chicken noodle or tomato?'

'Nothing. Thanks.'

'Suit yourself.' She puts them back down and picks up the one marked *B*, twisting off the lid.

Forcing himself to make conversation with the mother and daughter, he asks, 'Bean?'

The older woman smiles and angles it toward him, revealing a purple liquid: 'Borscht. My favorite.' She holds it out to him. 'Tastes like they chopped up the beets ten minutes ago. You want?'

'Really, I'm not hungry.'

She shrugs and, picking up one of the plastic spoons, helps herself to the beet soup.

Robin is holding the blouse with the wings affixed. She says, 'Eat something. You must be hungry after your long flight.'

'You sound like my mother.'

She smiles. 'Actually, I sound like *my* mother.'

Gary looks at the two women and then the jumble of takeout on the table. He wants to get on with things. 'I'm fine.'

Robin puts down the blouse and takes one of the sandwiches for herself before handing another to her mom. She undoes the rubber band holding three pickles in butcher's paper.

'A pickle, then?'

He explodes. 'I didn't fly down from New York for a picnic! Did someone kill my dad?'

Suddenly, Robin is all business. 'We think so.'

'Do you know who? And why?'

She takes a bite from her pickle. 'I'm working on the who. We're pretty sure of the why. Sit.'

He's been standing all this time. Now he takes a chair.

'If Mom is right about those Polaroids, and we know she is, Apollo 11 never made it to the moon, and there is no flag in the Sea of Tranquility.'

Between bites of her ham sandwich, her mother adds, 'It was all a made-for-TV movie.'

Robin takes the chair next to Gary. 'More a week-long reality TV show. Your dad directed, my dad helped.' She gestures toward him with the pickle. 'You sure you won't have one? These kosher dills are good.'

'Thanks, but I'm a sour guy.'

The two women look at him strangely.

'A sour-pickle guy.'

'Now that we have that established.' Robin gives him a smile that seems to come from her eyes as much as her mouth. 'I know it sounds crazy, like some paranoid internet thing. But if the Commander-in-Chief ordered it, and classified it Top Secret—'

He feels compelled to channel Pippa and her doubts, a devil's advocate thing. 'Neil Armstrong and the others: they lied for all those years? Mission Control and all the support people?'

Picking up the rubber band from the pickles, Robin zings it off the burnt-out globe overhead so it comes back to her.

He's even more frustrated. 'You're not listening!'

Robin eyes him evenly. 'I heard you, and I just gave you your answer.'

'Wha—?'

She shows him the rubber band. 'Instead of receiving images from the Sea of Tranquility and then broadcasting them over the air, they did it the other way round. Produced the whole thing on earth and then bounced the show's signal off the moon, the way I just did with this thing. Signal Corps has been able to do it since 1946.'

'But—'

'Hear me out. Only a small group of very well-paid guys were in on it. The ones in Mission Control, most of them anyway, thought the signals they were getting were coming from space. And in a way, they were. As for the other astronauts on the later missions, well, good ol' NASA was back up and running by then. They'd redesigned the Apollo capsule to reduce the fire hazard by the time Apollo 12 was ready.'

Unsatisfied, Gary picks up the rubber band and tries Rob's rebound trick. Instead, he stings his fingers with it. 'But you're still saying Armstrong lied about going to the moon.'

Robin takes another pickle. 'Wouldn't you? I would, if the Commander-in-Chief told me I had to in order to keep an enemy like the Russians in the dark. And, hey, it worked.'

Gary, upset, walks as far from the two women as he can, landing on the living room sofa. 'But, if the other Apollos did make it to the moon, what's the problem? Why the house cleaning?'

Robin's mom gets up and joins him on the sofa. She rubs his back. 'The problem is, none of those other missions ever returned to the Sea of Tranquility. The Ocean of Storms, yes. The Fra Mauro, where Alan Shepard hit those golf balls, yes. But if the Chinese want to plant their flag next to ours, it won't be there. And our fraud will be exposed on worldwide TV.'

He slides away from her rubbing hand. 'That still doesn't explain why someone would kill Pop.'

Robin picks up her iPad from the sideboard. With her free hand she takes a chair, walks it over to the sofa and sits. 'Maybe this will.'

She taps the iPad's screen and turns it around. An image of Art Walsh with oxygen tubes in his nose fills the screen.

In a tremulous voice, he begins. 'My loving wife Christine, and my wonderful daughter Robin, today is February 6, 1997. I'm making this video as an extra, aside from my will, so the two people I love most in the world will know the whole truth and nothing but the truth: I played a role in faking' – on the video, Walsh suddenly spasms with a hacking cough and it takes an effort for him to continue in an even raspier voice – 'the first moon landing in 1969.'

Composing himself, he continues. 'Robin, sweetheart, your mother already knows most of this. But you're the one who chose to be a pilot like your old man, and now an astronaut too, something I never really managed, and, hold on.'

He reaches down for a clear plastic oxygen mask, and inhales deeply before turning back to the camera.

'Uh, maybe you're thinking these are just the ravings of a dying man. Or his regrets about not achieving what you have. Well, we achieved something too, me and Charlie. We bought time for Pete Conrad to become the first human to set foot on the moon.'

He begins to laugh, which turns into another hacking cough.

'Pete still doesn't know Apollo 12 made him the first. Funny.'

He holds up a small brass key, like the one Gary still has on his wrist. 'Chris, here's something you don't know: There's a safe deposit box; I'm leaving you the key.'

In his other hand he produces an old-fashioned bankbook. 'This book will be inside. They've been paying me all these years; Charlie, too. For our silence, I guess. The money stops coming when I die. Still, it's a lot.

'I want you to travel, Chris, to see the world instead of just this scrubby little strip of sand. I know Robin, my Navy flyer, will. Maybe not from the moon, the way she's always dreamed of. Well, anyway, promise me you'll get out of this company town.'

Art drops the bankbook and deeply inhales oxygen again before running a hand through his clumps of thinning hair.

'Besides Charlie and me, there were twenty-nine people who were in on the hoax. Twelve of them are already dead, including the President who ordered up the thing and the one who kept it going. In a few days or weeks, it'll be thirteen.

'A couple of those people, people I knew, couldn't keep the secret. One told a wife, the other a girlfriend. All four had accidents that weren't accidental. I don't know why, but someone still thinks what happened – what didn't happen – on the moon is worth killing for.

'This is our secret now, and Charlie's. So be careful. And remember, I love you.'

He reaches out and ends the video.

ELEVEN

The Stephens brownstone

Army is lying on Pippa's left foot as she digitizes film snippets from the last silver can. The phone on the edit console rings and she picks it up. 'Hello?'

A man's voice on the phone asks for Gary.

'He's not here right now.' The ringing of the phone has roused Army, who looks like he's getting ready for an ear-shattering howl. Pippa slips her right foot out of her shoe and, reaching one leg over the other, strokes the dog's head with her stockinged foot. 'May I take a message?'

In Orlando, across six lanes of traffic from Big Al's Car Wash, a muscular man with bleached hair sits on a bench at a bus stop. The bench is stenciled with the words *We Stop Foreclosures!* along with the name of a local law firm, Whitman/Rollins. The man speaks into his cell phone with a surprisingly cultured voice. 'It concerns some litigation.'

The anxiety in her voice is perfectly clear from a thousand miles away. 'Gary's being sued?'

The man on the bench has his field glasses in his other hand. He trains them on a washed and waxed taxicab, number 296, parked across the way at Big Al's.

'His late father, actually.'

The Florida sun is getting more intense, so Mr Bleached Hair puts the binoculars down on the bench and then reaches inside his windbreaker for a pair of sunglasses. The movement opens his jacket just enough to disclose the presence of a holstered Berretta, if anyone were close enough to see.

On the phone, Pippa is saying, 'I'm his sister. Give me your name and I'll pass on the message.'

'It's, uh . . .'

The man fumbles one-handed with the shades and drops them on the ground at his feet. He leans down to retrieve them and seems to notice something about the bench he's sitting on.

'Uh, it's Whit Rollins, ma'am. Whitman Rollins, to be formal about it. We've been defending your dad in a Florida suit brought by members of his film crew and their estates over what they allege is underpayment on a project from years ago. Decades ago. He said he would put seven cans of 35 mm film aside for me, proof that the suit is groundless. Have you come across them among his effects?'

In the Manhattan edit suite, she looks down at the stack of silver cans. 'Yes, I think so. What sort of project were these for?'

The man calling himself 'Rollins' finally has the sunglasses sitting snugly on his nose. He says, 'Something for NBC that never aired.'

Army rolls onto his back under Pippa's foot for a tummy rub. She starts one while saying into the phone, 'These cans are from the 1960s. Isn't there a statute of limitations or something?'

'Not, uh, for what's called "a pattern of fraud," not in Florida. So, can I have an associate from our New York office come by and—'

'You say Pop did the work for NBC?' Pippa stops stroking Army with her foot and reaches across the console for a pencil and paper.

'In early 1969, yes.'

An Orlando city bus grinds to a halt in front of the painted bench. The pneumatic doors in front and back open, but no one gets out. No one gets on, either. The driver glares at the man sitting at the bus stop, but Mr Bleach stares straight ahead behind his shades until the frustrated driver closes his doors and pulls away.

Meanwhile, she's written, *Pop, 1969, NBC?* on her pad.

The man on the phone says, 'If you need your brother's OK to release the films, let me know where he's staying down here and I'll be happy to go over it with him in person.'

Suddenly alarmed, Pippa slams down the phone. Then she picks it right back up again.

In Florida, Gary, Chris, and Robin are huddled over the Polaroids, discussing them, when his throwaway phone rings.

'Pips?'

'Gary, they know you're down there! I'm really worried!'

He holds a finger up to his lips, cutting off talk with the Walshes, and presses a button on his phone. 'I'm putting you on speaker. Now, slowly, what happened?'

Chris, Robin, and Gary lean forward to listen.

'Someone called about the moon films. Says he's Whit Rollins, Dad's Florida lawyer, and he needs to talk to you down there.'

Gary frowns. 'Did you tell him where I am?'

On the little phone's speaker, Pippa says, 'Of course not. I knew it was a lie when he said it was for NBC.'

The Walshes are looking at Gary, puzzled.

He explains. 'Pop and Reuven Frank had a big falling-out in 1965. He never went back to NBC.'

On the line, Pippa asks, 'Who are you talking to?'

'Chris and her daughter, Robin. I'll explain when I see you.'

'But—'

'Don't worry. I'm OK. Love you.' Gary ends the call.

Robin, concerned, turns to her mother. 'I think we need Uncle Hal.'

The older woman nods in agreement.

Gary asks, 'Who's Uncle Hal?'

Chris gets up and moves over to the piano. She picks up the picture of the young couple he was looking at before, the girl being Robin.

Her mother hands it to Gary, saying, 'Hal. Harold. The Vice-President. Robin was supposed to marry his nephew Brad.'

He looks at it again before handing it back. 'Supposed to?'

Chris says, shrugging, 'Brad is now Diana. Long story.'

Robin takes the picture and puts it back with the others. 'The important thing is, Uncle Hal stayed in touch,' she says. 'So, get your stuff. I'm flying us up to Andrews.'

TWELVE
Observatory Circle, Washington, DC

Gary and Robin, who's smartly dressed in her Navy flyer uniform, step away from a yellow cab in front of the official residence of the Vice-President of the United States. Built on the grounds of the US Naval Observatory, the home overlooks the Chinese Embassy on Wisconsin Avenue and the British one farther east on Massachusetts. The lights in the embassies are just starting to come on. The visitors don't stop to look at the view.

Two Secret Service guards, each with a curly-wired earpiece, guide them through the metal detectors just inside the door. On the far side of the machines, Gary is fumbling with the zipper of the laptop computer that holds Pippa's moon files when a fit-looking man of sixty emerges from a door across the way.

Under her breath, Robin asks Gary, 'Problem?'

With a yank, the zipper comes free as the Vice-President, all crinkling eyes and brilliant white teeth, comes up to them and wraps her in a hug. 'Robbie! So great to see you!'

When the man releases her, she indicates her companion. 'Mr Vice-President, may I introduce Gary Stephens?'

He turns his radiant smile on Gary. 'Good to meet you. Welcome. For the next hour or so, you're Gary and I'm Hal. OK?'

The Vice-President turns to lead them into a large conference room, so Gary replies to his broad back. 'Sure. Fine, uh, Hal.'

As the door closes, the Secret Service men slide into position outside the room. Inside, their host waves toward a sideboard set out with snacks. 'Coffee? Water? Filet mignon?' He grins some more.

'I'm good, thanks,' Robin tells him.

'Me too,' says Gary.

Lining the room are the portraits of every American Vice-President in chronological order, including 'Uncle Hal.' He takes a seat and gestures to the two across the table. Next to him, Buddha-like, sits someone who's easily eighty-five years old. The man has a hoary beard and is smoking a pipe.

'This is Otto Kurzweil, my adviser on . . . well, a bunch of stuff. Otto, meet Robin Walsh and Gary Stephens.'

Kurzweil cups his ear to hear Hal's words despite wearing antique transistor hearing aids. Now, without changing expression, he emits a cloud of smoke in silent greeting.

As Gary opens his laptop to play Pippa's moon materials, the VP checks his watch.

'Just so you know, I have a hard stop in fifty minutes; video briefing with the President who's traveling in Brazil.'

'Understood.' Gary turns the laptop on, angles it toward the two men, and hits Play.

Beyond the illuminated screen showing identical twin images of a lunar flyover, the Vice-President and his advisor put their heads together to better view the evidence. A cloud of smoke is slowly obscuring the painting of LBJ on the wall. When Gary's eyes trace the source of the cloud back to Kurzweil's pipe, the old man surprisingly gives him a great big toothy smile around the pipe stem, one that would have been perfect on the Cheshire Cat.

'This is crazy!'

The identical side-by-side moon sequences Pippa sent to Gary's laptop have just come to an end. The second-highest-ranking elected official in the country repeats himself, looking from one of his visitors to the other. 'This is crazy! And the craziest part is, I believe it.'

He turns to the man wreathed in pipe smoke beside him. 'Otto?'

'Perhaps it's the skeptic in me' – after an ostentatiously long suck on his pipe and another cloud of smoke, the advisor adds in a deep Germanic rumble – 'how do we know it's authentic?'

Gary is about to respond, hotly, when Robin does it for him, calmly ticking things off on her fingers.

'It's the actual Apollo crew on a film set, for one thing. When did that ever happen that we know of? And the images Gary edited, the way they conform inch for inch with NASA's own footage, for another. Plus, the labels on the film cans; the dates are all from the spring of 1969!'

Unperturbed, Kurzweil says, 'Labels can be faked.'

He looks at Gary, who's getting red in the face. 'Mr Stephens, you're a filmmaker. Isn't the technology today such that the heads, the faces of the actual crew from the actual footage, can be Photoshopped or whatever they call it on the bodies of three stand-ins?'

Without realizing what's he's doing, Gary gets to his feet, almost knocking his chair to the floor before Robin can steady it. 'You're saying I faked this? That I shot all this stuff and inserted Neil Armstrong's . . . it's preposterous!'

Unperturbed, the old man simply takes another pull on his pipe. He says, 'We have Wi-Fi here. I invite you to use that laptop to type in *Apollo 11 landing*. You'll find dozens, hundreds, of people saying the whole thing was faked and—'

Gary, sputtering, is about to say something he'll regret when Robin reaches over and, with a strong hand on his arm, pulls him back down into his seat.

The advisor keeps talking in the same lecturing way. 'And I wager you'll find more than a few movies on the subject. Perhaps this is simply—"

'It's simply the *truth*, Mr Kurzweil.' Gary is still hot. 'Besides—'

'Doctor.'

'I'm sorry, what?'

The old man smiles. 'I'm *Doctor* Kurzweil. Professor Kurzweil.'

Gary digests that and goes back to his point. 'Besides, *Dr Kurzweil*, you saw my father on that film set. Charlie died recently at eighty-one. He couldn't have been more than thirty or so when that was filmed.'

The man bangs his pipe on the ashtray by his elbow before saying, noncommittally, 'There's that.'

Leaning forward, the Vice-President injects himself into the conversation. 'Whatever doubts you have, Otto, I trust Robin here. If she's convinced the film is real, *I'm* convinced.'

The old man shrugs his shoulders before refilling his pipe from a pouch in his pocket. 'I'm just your advisor. But when you say the *film* is real, well, this isn't a film, it's a video *copy*. I'd find it much more convincing if these young people had brought the original, uh, celluloid material with them. And, as well, something more about the chain of custody over the past half-century. Something better than, "it was left in a boat locker."'

The man contrives to take ten seconds to relight his pipe before saying to Gary, 'These seven cans of film you speak of, do you have them with you?'

'No, sir, my sister has them in New York.'

'Can she fly them down here?'

'I'm not sure. She's got the kids; my brother-in-law is in Rome.'

'It's only an hour on the Shuttle. Or . . . tell you what . . . we can send a courier to her house to pick them up. Couldn't we, Mr Vice-President? If you give me her address, I'll—'

'We haven't got time for that, Otto.' The VP is looking at a schedule in a leather planner. 'The President is out of pocket for the next couple of days down there. She's gotta be told *now*.'

'Then I suppose you should read in POTUS on your conference call.'

'My thought exactly; better safe than sorry. Then, if you still feel strongly about it, we can courier the original films down afterwards.'

Otto smiles. 'Appears to be a plan.'

The Vice-President rises and turns his smile on his visitors, who also get to their feet. 'You two did the right thing.'

He lays a hand on the open laptop. 'Look, Gary, there's no time to download . . . may I hang on to this for show-and-tell in a couple of minutes?'

Gary steps back from the machine. 'Certainly, sir.'

'Gary, I can't call you "Gary" unless you call me "Hal," right?'

'Right . . . Hal.'

'Good. So, now, my driver will take you two to the W Hotel. On me.'

Gary's objection is waved away. 'We get a discount, or at least the taxpayer does. You can pick this up in the morning.'

Then 'Hal' shakes Gary's hand and gives Robin a hug.

She kisses him on the cheek. 'Thanks for seeing us, Uncle Hal.'

'No, thank *you*. Carmelo will pick you up at, say, eight thirty tomorrow.'

They start to leave, but the Vice-President lays a hand on Gary's shoulder. 'Oh, and you two . . .' He makes a 'zip up your lip' gesture. 'Mum's the word.'

They nod and walk out.

THIRTEEN
Kennedy Space Center, Cape Kennedy, Florida

April 5, 1967

A television reporter holding a microphone picks her way through blackened steel girders. She says, 'You're looking at all that remains of Launch Pad 34 here at the Kennedy Space Center.'

She continues even as she steps carefully over the twisted debris on the ground. 'This was the gantry where Apollo 1, with the astronauts Ed White, Roger Chaffee, and Virgil "Gus" Grissom, was to fire off into space. Instead, the fire took off on the ground. And the three men died in just a few harrowing moments here on the evening of January twenty-seventh.'

She walks away from the destroyed gantry and toward a table piled high with paper in neat folders. 'In the ten weeks since, a NASA Board of Inquiry has probed for the fire's cause. Today, they issued their report. Or, rather' – the reporter places her hand on the stack of papers – 'fourteen reports totaling three thousand pages. The Board's conclusion?'

She picks up the top report, opens the cover, and glances at the first page before looking back up.

'An electrical short ignited the pure, pressurized oxygen in the capsule and set fire to the flammable materials that surrounded the men. In addition, the dozen bolts holding the steel door in place made a quick exit impossible.'

She drops the report back down on the pile.

'For now, all future Apollo flights have been grounded.'

The unseen camera that's been filming her moves in for a close-up. 'But the Russians haven't called off their race to the moon. So, the question is, how long will it take to make Apollo safe? And, can we afford the wait?'

Incongruously, she gives the camera a slight smile. 'Candace Brooks from Cape Kennedy signing off.'

FOURTEEN
The W Hotel, Washington, DC

The rooftop terrace of the old Hotel Washington was a place where District residents and savvy tourists could have a drink and a bite and look down at the President's house, and maybe even the President, from their perch across 15th Street.

When Marriott took over the place, they gave the terrace and the entire hotel a jazzy makeover deluxe. Now called the POV Rooftop, the bar serves $17 cocktails and a $36 crab cake to patrons at tables jammed together at the windows. But the attraction is still the same: proximity to the residence of the most powerful person on the planet. Even if that person is momentarily out of the country in Brazil.

Robin, who changed out of her uniform when they got to the hotel and now wears a business-casual skirt and blouse, is finishing a story while Gary polishes off his steak salad.

'Then, a month ahead of our wedding, he invites me to dinner and sets our two gold bands on the table, before they were engraved.'

She mimes setting something down in front of Gary, who says 'Hmmm?' with his mouth full.

'Yeah. So, I ask, "What's the deal, Brad?" And he says, "Rob, call me Diana." Just like that. The strange part is, he – she – got married ten months later. To a guy. Even before he – she – had the surgery.

'And because I was happy that *she* was happy, I went! Big mistake. I can't think of anything worse than losing the love of your life to someone else before your life together has even started.'

Gary puts down his fork and looks at Robin a moment before speaking.

'I can. Losing the love of your life, the loves of your life, when you've known how good that life can be. Worse.'

In shock, Robin puts her hand to her mouth. 'Oh my God, your wife and daughter! Mom told me. How long has it been?'

Gary doesn't have to do the math. After a pause, he sighs and says, 'Four years, three months.'

'They ever catch the guy?'

'In New York, vehicular manslaughter is five years, three with good behavior. So, he's already out.' Then he takes a too-big swig of his drink.

She takes his hand in both of hers. 'Gary, can you ever forgive me?'

Before he can say anything, her phone rings. Reluctantly, she takes her hands from his and retrieves it from her purse. Reading the Caller ID, she says, 'It's Mom. Guess she wants to know how things went.'

Then she glances around at the nearby tables. They're occupied with a lot of Washington types, all close enough to overhear a conversation. To the phone she says, 'Hi, Mom. Hang on a moment.' To Gary she says, 'Sorry. I'll make this quick.'

Robin gets up and walks to the far side of the place where there's a quiet alcove leading to the restrooms. With her back to the room and the phone to her ear, she speaks with her mother.

Gary watches her from across the room. From this angle – with Robin leaning against the alcove wall – the dark skirt stretched a little across her hips betrays the woman's curves beneath the astronaut's veneer.

Gary still has his hand on the table where she left it. There's a pleasant something in the air having nothing to do with a steak salad. Her scent? He breathes it in. Barely there but nice.

And then she's back.

'Mom says hi. I told her we don't know what the brass are going to do with your video.'

Robin takes his hand again in both of hers. 'She's worried about you, Gary. Given what we believe happened to your dad, she thinks you're awfully exposed out here in public.'

She unconsciously rubs a thumb over the skin on the back of his hand. 'And there's that Whitman guy, the one you said called Pippa under false pretenses. If he's after the original films . . . Gary, *I'm* worried too. Maybe you should have Pippa ship the seven cans down to Mom's house. For safekeeping.'

He says, 'Gee, Robin, is there still any danger? I mean, now that Washington knows what we know?'

Looking him right in the eyes, she says, 'Here's what *I* know. You're a sweet guy and I don't want to lose you.'

It's been a long time, years, since he let himself feel this way about someone. And now, an attractive someone is telling him she feels the same way about him. He's out of practice, not knowing what to say. What he *does* know is he wants to stay right here, to prolong the pleasure of this woman's company.

So, he says, 'Dessert?'

She caresses his hand with both of hers. 'Will you think me terribly forward if I suggest we have it in my room?'

A smile begins on his face in the second before another, different buzzing sound comes from her handbag. She regretfully releases his hand and takes out her phone again.

'Someone's texted.'

Tapping into the app, she says, 'It's from Hal. They want us back, now! Carmelo's in the lobby.'

Gary has to fight back his disappointment by looking around for the waiter.

'Check!'

Carmelo meets Robin and Gary downstairs and escorts them outside into the official Lincoln with tiny Vice-Presidential flags mounted on the bumper. But he doesn't take them back to the Naval Observatory. Instead, the chauffeur drives a total of 150 yards across 15th Street and up to an entrance for official vehicles on the southeast side of the White House.

'Why the car?' Gary asks in surprise. 'We could have just walked over.'

Carmelo looks at him in the rear-view mirror. 'No, sir, you couldn't. Not on foot at this time of night, not without the paper-work. We're sort of pre-approved.'

As if on cue, the guards raise the barrier and Carmelo drives them up to the door to the Reception Room before heading back the way he came.

Inside, the foyer is not much larger than a child's bedroom. Or maybe the bulky metal detectors just make it seem that way. Robin's eyes are as wide as saucers. 'The White House! I've never even been on the tour.'

Once they're through the machines, an officious female aide with a clipboard hurries forward. 'Captain Walsh, Mr Stephens, this way. They're expecting you.'

She leads them along a corridor and down a flight of stairs to the John F. Kennedy Conference Room, colloquially known as the Situation Room. A black Marine guard manning the desk outside the door swivels a sign-in book toward Gary and holds out a pen.

'Visitors' book?'

The Marine briefly smiles. 'Secrecy Act.'

Gary signs and holds the pen out to Robin. The guard rises and takes the pen from Gary before ushering them inside. 'We got her years ago.'

The two are shown to seats at a long table lined with government officials and military people. The Vice-President rises. Beside him, Otto Kurzweil remains seated.

'Everyone, this is Gary Stephens, who figured this whole thing out. And Captain Robin Walsh, someone I know from, well, a previous engagement. Robin, you, uh, naturally, know your boss, NASA Operations Chief Lila Hensen.'

A fifty-ish woman with iron-gray hair cut fairly short doesn't get up. She's sitting in a motorized wheelchair and simply nods at the newcomers.

The VP continues, '*Her* boss is NASA Administrator Hahnfeldt.'

The man with auburn hair who's sitting on the other side of Hensen gets up a little reluctantly and gives Gary a tight smile.

'We'll skip the other introductions, except for the Commander-in-Chief.'

On a large monitor, the President, a woman of sixty-five or so with a short blond coif, sits in a room full of Brazilian flags. Her image on the screen speaks.

'So, you're the two troublemakers?' Then she chuckles. 'I thought faked moon landings were just an internet . . . thing.' She clears her throat. 'Before we go any further, Mr Stephens, I have to tell you: Everything we say here, everything you hear, is strictly on the QT. Mum's the word.'

Then she looks toward a black female official wearing a badge from the FBI with the name *Leah Davis*. 'You had him sign the book, right?'

'Signed, sealed, and delivered, Ms President. Now, may I ask, are you speaking from a secure location?'

The President looks behind herself and chuckles again. 'Oh, you mean the flags. Yes, very secure, Leah. So, Gary, Robin, I don't know if you've been given the heads up. But—'

Just then a sweaty, balding Under Secretary of State, Cy Talbott, hurries into the room with a stack of thin blue folders. 'Sorry, I just got these.'

On the monitor, the President sighs with comic exasperation. 'Cy, you stepped on my big line. Well, hurry up and hand them out.'

He gives everyone a folder, including Gary and Robin.

The President begins again. 'The white sheet you've been given summarizes the arguments my people have been having for the last couple of hours. But, sitting here all by my lonesome four thousand miles away, something's just occurred to me: why don't we simply train our most powerful telescope on the moon and see for ourselves whether the flag is up there or not? We can view all kinds of things billions of miles away; the moon is less than a quarter-million. Why not? Alf?'

She's looking at the man introduced as NASA's DC-based Administrator.

Alf Hanhfeldt looks around at his tech people before saying, 'Ms President, the things we can see through even our largest telescopes, whether from the US or Chile or anywhere – galaxies full of stars – are enormous. They're light years across. A flag on the moon, even though it's red, white, and blue and much, much closer, is, well, all of three by five *feet*. No lens on earth, especially given our atmosphere that's in the way, can see anything that small.'

Like the debater she was, the President continues. 'Don't we have a *space* telescope, the whatzit? The Hubble? Can't it tell us what we want to know?'

Hahnfeldt sighs under his breath this time. 'I wish it could. The Hubble's rapid orbit of the earth makes the moon appear to oscillate in the sky. It's really impossible for us to compensate and detect a flag.' His face brightens a little. 'We have a couple of science projects – satellites – orbiting the moon right now. If we adjusted the course of Artemis 1 so it passed over Tranquility, we could be sure. But . . .'

'But what, Alf?'

'That orbit change would be picked up by a lot of earth-based tracking stations, a couple of them in unfriendly countries.' He smiles that troubled smile of his again. 'I hate it that we don't have many options here.'

Now it's the President's turn to sigh. 'I get it. So, OK, getting back to my decision. Robin, Gary, suffice it to say we're not going to fess up to our little charade back in 1969.'

Gary blurts out, 'You're not?'

She continues as if he hadn't spoken. 'No one would believe us if we did. Certainly not China's leaders. Tell 'em, Otto.'

The elderly security advisor, who's had a sour expression on what is already a sour puss for most of the meeting, puts down the empty pipe he's had in his mouth and turns to the newcomers.

'It's 1941. June. Britain's broken the German Enigma codes and discovered Hitler is about to invade his ally, Russia. Churchill tells Stalin, but Uncle Joe doesn't believe him, thinks it's a British ploy to get Nazis and Reds fighting each other. Millions of dead Russians later . . .'

Talbott picks up the thread, running a hand through his all-but-extinct hair. 'They're not that crazy, but Beijing needs this moon shot to make a billion people forget how their economy is slowing to a walk.

'Plus, they got a real black eye when they lost control of the first space station they put up a couple of years ago, the so-called Heavenly Palace. Crashed into the Pacific. So, they'll see anything that gets in the way as an American trick. Off the record, we *have* pulled a few dirty tricks to make things worse over there. Nothing like what they've done to us, but still.'

Robin raises her hand to get the President's attention, as if the country's leader were sitting there and not 4,200 miles away.

'If you don't mind my asking, Ma'am, why are you telling us all this?'

'Oh, didn't I say?' The woman on the screen gives her head a brief little shake, as if to mock her own memory lapse. 'We want you to go to the moon and plant our flag for real before the Chinese get there.'

FIFTEEN

Apt. 1-D, West 88th Street, New York

Pippa Stephens opens the oven door in the garden apartment she shares on the Upper West Side with Roger and the twins, Ashley and Gracie. She checks on the chicken that was ready twenty minutes ago, basting it again with the juices that, even with the heat turned off, have been all but cooked away while waiting for her husband's delayed flight.

The once-roomy kitchen now accommodates the metal sleeping crate of their live-in guest, Armstrong the bulldog. Army sniffs at the chicken and then scratches at the back door and looks questioningly at Pippa. Then he scratches again.

She glances quickly at the wall clock: 7:50. 'It's late and you're hungry,' she tells him. 'I get it.'

Then she calls to the girls who are, possibly, doing homework in their room but are more likely texting their friends. 'Gracie, Ashley, come set the table! Your father's plane finally landed an hour ago. We're eating as soon as he walks in the door!'

As if on cue, the sound of the front door opening announces Roger's arrival. The tall, bearded lawyer sets his wheeled two-suiter down and walks into the kitchen. He drops his briefcase on the kitchen table and gives her a kiss. 'Remember me?'

She kisses him back. 'You're unforgettable. Now, get washed up, we have a dead chicken on our hands.'

He turns and picks up his briefcase. 'Roger that.'

He loves using his name in all its flyboy, walkie-talkie iterations: Roger That and Roger Wilco and Roger, Over and Out. Ignoring the eye roll Pippa's giving him for his lame-o wordplay, he heads down the hall, meeting the ten-year-old twins. Gracie and Ashley hug their dad and search his jacket pockets for the souvenirs he always brings home from a trip. Gracie gets a silver-plated trinket in the shape of the Colosseum for her charm bracelet while Ashley, the athlete, finds a slip of paper in her father's handwriting in the other pocket that reads, *Good for one Lazio T-shirt when I unpack my suitcase.*

They give him more hugs and kisses before heading for the silverware and the napkins respectively.

Retrieving Army's metal dish from under the kitchen table, Pippa fills it with fresh cold water. She takes a similar dish from its resting place under the sink and shakes dry dog food into it. Finally, she opens the back door, picks up the two bowls, and follows Army outside into the gloom of a Manhattan evening.

The lights from the apartment buildings that back onto their tiny patch of garden illuminate the patio just enough so Pippa can see where to place Army's twin dishes. When she straightens up again, she waves her arm over her head while looking at the light fixture over the back door. Under her breath she mutters, 'Damn.'

Back in the kitchen, Roger has removed his tie and is carving the chicken. Pippa tells him, 'Security light's out.'

'Oh?' Without looking up from his carving, he says, 'I'll get a bulb from the storage bin after dinner. Speaking of—' he lifts the platter full of chicken – 'who's hungry?'

Thirty-five minutes later, when the bird, the rice, the carrots, and a little green salad are history, it's Ash's turn to clear the table. Gracie opens the back door to let Army in.

No bulldog.

Gracie peers into the almost entirely black backyard. 'Army, here boy!'

Still no dog.

Her father joins her at the door. He adds his sternest 'Armstrong! Come here now!' to her voice. Then he turns to her. 'When you came home from school, did one of you girls leave the gate open again?'

Ashley has joined them in peering into the dark. 'No, Daddy, we walked through the lobby!'

'All right, I'm going to go get a bulb. Then we'll see what's what.'

With his thoughts still caught up in the Rome thing, he reaches the basement storage area having forgotten what he went down to get. Taking out his phone, he hits speed dial.

Pippa answers it upstairs. Without even waiting for the question, she says, 'Floodlight bulb.' This has happened before.

A couple of minutes later, Roger heads outside with a stepladder and the new floodlight. Pippa and the girls follow. The tall man only needs to mount a single step to reach the fixture. 'Hey!'

'What is it?' Pippa asks.

'There's no bulb here. If the light burned out, it oughta . . .' Rather than finish his thought, he screws the new bulb into the empty socket. Suddenly, the area around the door is bathed in light.

Ashley sees it first. 'Daddy, there's a light bulb on the table.'

Sure enough, the former bulb from the floodlight sits on the wrought-iron patio table. And, now that they can see the whole yard all the way to the closed gate at the far end, they know Armstrong is gone.

Roger, worried, speaks to his wife's back as she's bending down to pick up Army's empty bowls. 'Do you think he somehow burrowed under—'

'There's a note.'

She reaches into the food dish and holds up what looks like a ransom note, the kind they always use in the movies: its words were cut out of magazines and pasted on the eight-by-eleven sheet of paper. She reads it out loud.

'You took something of ours. So we took something of yours. Let's trade.'

SIXTEEN

The White House, Washington, DC

May 14, 1967

A husky Marine stands guard on the second floor of the White House outside the First Family's living quarters. In the bathroom off the master suite at the far end of the hallway, Lyndon Johnson sits on the toilet, his pants and briefs down around his ankles, and talks into the white wall phone he's had installed.

'Roy? Lyndon. How's it hangin'?'

After Roy says something on the other end, LBJ speaks again.

'Shit, I got a brother, too. If I lost Sam, don't know what. Still, it's been five months and life goes on. So, how's it comin'?'

This time, as the President listens, his face darkens.

'Don't give me your Disney World crap! That fuckin' orange grove'll still be settin' there next year. I got some real-world problems. I need this thing to happen now, before the damn election!'

The more he listens the madder Johnson gets. 'Is it money? If you need more, Roy, you little pissant, I got a war I'm losing. What do you got . . . union trouble? Hell, I gave you von Braun! Do I have to go out there and build that rocket myself? You call your-selves Walt Disney Productions. So fuckin' produce!'

He hears something that makes him calm down a bit.

'Ten months? That's cutting it close. But OK, Roy, I'm gonna hold you to that. No, don't involve Hubert. He can't . . . fuck, he wouldn't know how to pour piss out of a boot with the instructions printed on the heel!'

After a moment, LBJ looks at the receiver and smiles. 'Just so we're clear: We go April next year or it's your ass, Roy.'

The President happily hangs up and dials his next call.

SEVENTEEN

En route to Reagan National Airport, Washington, DC

It's a little after nine on a moonless night and Carmelo is again behind the wheel of the Vice-President's limo, hurrying Gary and Robin to the airport. As the speeding vehicle takes the curve onto the George Washington Memorial Highway, Robin is thrown to Gary's side of the back seat. Their bodies come together and her hand winds up covering his. When the car straightens out, she leaves it there. The Jefferson Memorial, sitting at the edge of the Tidal Basin, sends sparkles of light over the waves to their right.

Gary tries to ignore the signal her touch is sending to his brain. Instead, he says, 'Thanks for doing this, Carmelo.'

The man at the wheel pushes his phone's headset away from his ear and says, 'Sorry, sir. Didn't hear what you said.'

'I said, thanks for the VIP treatment.'

'Correction.' Carmelo chuckles. 'You're getting the *VP* treatment. Besides, if you had to wait for a cab to get through security back there, you would have missed your flight.'

Without taking his eyes off the road, the chauffeur reaches into his suit pocket and pulls out a ticket in an American Airlines folder. 'Better take this.' He hands it back to Gary. 'The eleven o'clock for LaGuardia. Check in as soon as you get in the terminal; it's the last one out.'

Gary looks at his ticket before turning to Robin. 'How long will you be in Houston, training for the . . . thing?'

Carmelo has his headset back on, but Gary's unsure of how much he should say.

Robin squeezes his hand. '*Too* long. If the Chinese are planning their moonwalk for the Fourth of July, we're going to need every second right up to the deadline to pull this thing off.'

He realizes she's been rubbing the back of his hand with her thumb the way she did in the restaurant. Her closeness is intoxicating. Taking her hand in his, he lifts it up and brushes her skin with his lips, saying, 'Can you at least come wait with me at my gate?'

'I wish I could. I'm hitching a ride to Andrews on Marine One, the President's helicopter.' With her free hand, she points out the window to their left. 'Leaves from Anacostia Joint Base, over there, right after yours. Sorry.'

He turns in his seat to face her, saying quietly, 'I don't want to lose you.'

She does the same. In a low voice she says, 'You won't.'

When Carmelo pulls up at Reagan just short of the entrance to the American check-in area, two men in suits who were just inside the waiting area rush out toward the car. The faster of the two, an athletic-looking guy with a blond mustache, is holding out some sort of badge to Carmelo, who looks at it and then unlocks the limo.

The other, heavy-set guy peers in the rear window at Gary and Robin before reaching for the door handle. Out of breath from the short sprint, he manages to say, 'Mr Stephens, change of plans.'

'Huh?' is all Gary can utter in his surprise.

The stout man opens the rear door and Gary starts to slide out.

But the man puts out a hold-it-right-there hand and, surprisingly, gets into the limo with them, squeezing Gary and Robin together. Meanwhile, Mustache Guy takes the passenger seat up front with Carmelo. He swivels in his seat to face them, holding his badge out. It's a flip-open thing with his photo and the words *FBI* and *Special Agent* printed above and an actual metal badge down below.

Gary reads his name out loud. 'Special Agent Eugene Corrigan.'

The man next to him also has his badge out. It reads, *Special Agent Melvin Bloom.*

Corrigan says, 'Sorry about this. There's news.'

Bloom holds out a cell phone to Gary and says, 'Your sister.'

'Pippa?'

Into the phone, Bloom says, 'Go ahead, Mrs Greenwald.'

His sister's voice over the speaker sounds strained. 'Gary, are you there?'

He gives the agents a look of concern even as he tries to keep it out of his voice. 'I'm here, Pips. What's going on?'

'Army is gone. Taken.'

Neither Bloom nor Corrigan registers surprise. They must know what this is about.

'Taken? I don't understand.'

Now his sister's crying can be heard clearly over the connection. 'I . . . we . . . you tell him, Roger.'

Her lawyer husband sounds only slightly more composed on the other end of the line when he says, 'Gary, it happened a couple of hours ago. I got home from my trip and Army wasn't in the back-yard. Instead, there was, well, I guess you'd call it a ransom note left in his bowl. "You took something of ours. So we took something of yours. Let's trade." Exact quote.'

'I don't understand. What did *we*, what did *I* take that could—'

'The seven cans of film!' Pippa says, between sobs. 'The ones Pop took and hid in that boat locker, the ones we edited together. What else could it be?'

Corrigan looks at Gary as if it should be obvious. 'Think. Why else would you be here?'

Gary tries to think, but his brain has turned to mud.

In an even shakier voice than before, Pippa asks, 'Where is *here*, Gary? Are you coming back to New York? Where are you, anyway?'

Bloom looks at Gary and shakes his head: No.

'I'm OK, Pippa. I'm just, uh, following up with some people.'

'Gary,' her voice on the phone wails, 'we're going out of our minds! First Mrs . . . uh, W. says don't use her name, don't use the phone, don't trust anyone. Then you fly down to see her and some Florida lawyer or something calls to say Pop is being sued and I know he's lying and then you don't answer my calls and, uh, you tell him, Roger.'

Her husband again picks up the thread. 'Pips and I went over to the police station on Eighty-second Street with the ransom . . . thing, and they said there's nothing they can do without more to go on. So we phoned that woman you flew down to see, who wouldn't tell us anything. Said you left with her daughter, that's all. None of this makes any sense! It's been a complete runaround up here. I mean, we just want Army back!'

Pippa adds, 'And I want *you* back!'

Roger continues, 'First they said there's nothing they can do. Then this group of Feds shows up and tells the cops we should go along with the bad guys when they call and to hand over Charlie's evidence. Is that right? Shouldn't we offer them money, instead? Those cans are all the leverage we have.'

Pippa, a little higher on the hysteria meter now, cuts in. 'And there's an FBI woman in the apartment right now! Says she'll be staying with us *for the duration*! The duration of *what*, Gary?'

Roger adds, 'We didn't want to do anything before talking with you.'

The man sitting next to Gary takes over. 'Look, Mr and Mrs Greenwald, this is Special Agent Bloom again. You've done everything right up to now. In fact, this probably helps, because—'

'How can stealing an innocent bulldog help *anything*?' Pippa shouts into her end of the phone.

'I'm sorry, Mrs Greenwald, I understand your concern and, yes, we're going to do whatever we can to get the animal home safely. It's just that, now that they've shown their hand—'

Corrigan reaches into the back seat and takes hold of Bloom's arm, stopping him.

'Mrs Greenwald,' he says, 'this is Agent Corrigan. May I call you Pippa? Gary's helping us with the film you two put together. It's, well, it's a national security thing now. And, frankly, the less you know till he's able to come back and tell you all about it the better. For everyone. So, please, listen to the agent up there with you and do what she says. We'll do everything in our power to keep you safe and return your dog. OK?'

'Keep *us* safe? I don't—'

Pippa is about to object some more when her husband cuts her off.

'We understand.'

When they've said their goodbyes, Bloom ends the call. The five of them sit there in the limo, looking at each other. Finally, Corrigan says, 'We don't think it's safe for you to go back to New York.'

Bloom adds, 'Not now, anyway. Not with what you know.'

'Then, when?' Gary asks.

'When we've caught whoever took your . . . whoever took Armstrong. Of course, they have to make contact first. Then we'll come up with a plan.'

Robin interjects, 'But, that could be days. Weeks.'

Corrigan shifts his gaze to her. 'This is a top priority effort, Captain. Everyone in the New York area, they're all on it. And, well, our orders in the meantime are to keep Mr Stephens here, and his sister in Manhattan, safe at all costs. Orders right from the top.'

Gary says, 'Well, if I can't fly back to New York, where will I—'

Bloom says, 'We have a safe house in Virginia. Less than an hour from here. You'll like it. There's a pool, a tennis court—'

'Tennis! I'm going out of my mind and you're talking about *tennis*?'

Robin reaches for the door handle on her side and says, 'Hang on. I have an idea.'

She gets out and closes the door. Through the window, Gary can see her take out her phone and punch in some numbers. As she waits for the call to be answered, Robin realizes she's standing on the traffic side of the limousine. So, she lets a couple of cabs go by and then hurries across the three lanes of the ramp to the walkway on the far side.

The four men watch her speak animatedly into her phone, listen for a bit, and speak some more. After a minute or more of conversation, she nods at something that was said before ending the call. Then, after several buses and car rental vans choose that moment to roll past her position, she recrosses the road and gets back into the car.

'We're all set.'

'Meaning?' Corrigan, who appears to be the agent in charge, has a skeptical look on his face.

Robin doesn't answer him. Instead, she takes Gary's hand in hers. 'I called my boss. It's perfect. You'll be flying down to Houston with me.'

Gary and Bloom, sitting beside him, say it in unison.

'Houston?'

EIGHTEEN

Johnson Space Center, Houston, Texas

Gary whispers to Robin, 'Tell me what's going on.' They landed twenty minutes ago on the flight from Washington and he's still playing mental catch-up. Physical catch-up, too.

It's morning, and they're hurrying to keep up with Chief Astronaut Kirk Casselmann, a humorless blond man in his mid-thirties who met them at the airport. He's affecting a pair of clichéd aviator sunglasses, so he isn't troubled by the glare from the Texas sun off a huge metal sign that says, *National Aeronautics & Space Admin/ Lyndon B. Johnson Space Center*.

Without turning around, their guide says, 'Walsh, Stephens, I hate to rush you, but the director isn't one to wait. The clock's ticking.'

The two recent arrivals, without shades, can't read the sign as they wheel their suitcases in Casselmann's wake, but they don't need to; the huge rocket on its gantry off to the left announces the fact loud and clear.

In the antiseptic lobby of the main building, where the décor is all brushed aluminum, Casselmann leads them past a tour group viewing a vintage training film of Mercury astronauts on a giant screen. He presses a button with vehemence for the Limited Area elevator.

As they wait, they watch the black-and-white video on the far wall along with the tourists. A title says, *1959: Stress Evaluation/Wright*

Air Force Base, Dayton, Ohio. It's a compilation of various grueling tests: men in centrifuges, their faces distorted by the G-forces; men tumbling in a weightless environment; men trying to remain upright on a special, gimballed chair that bucks like a bronco; and men in full uniform dumped into the water at high speed. No blacks, no women; everybody's male and white. With crew cuts.

The elevator door opens at last and the three get on.

They get off on six and Casselmann leads them to an office with a nameplate that reads, *Chief, Human Exploration and Operations Mission Directorate.* He knocks and then opens the door without waiting for a reply, saying, 'Director, I have Walsh and Stephens for you.'

Lila Hensen, the woman they met in Situation Room, is waiting for them in her wheelchair.

'Thank you, Kirk. Please have a seat next door, we'll be in shortly.'

Casselmann leaves, and Hensen does a sort of wheelie in the motorized chair, moving around her desk to shake their hands. She says, 'So, Robin, Gary, good flight?'

Robin salutes. 'A-OK, ma'am.'

'Gary, how are you doing?'

'I'd be lying if I said I knew what was going on.'

Saying 'Let's fix that,' she presses the intercom button on the phone and says, 'Renée?'

Her assistant comes to the door. 'Yes, ma'am?'

'Is the captain here?'

'In your conference room.'

'Thanks.'

With that she rolls out the door. They follow her next door into a room with a long, polished table where Casselmann and a man with weathered skin, his deeply tanned scalp showing through his barely-there buzz cut, are sitting. They get up when the Director enters with Gary and Robin.

'Folks, meet Captain Jack Maybin. Jack, this is Gary Stephens.'

The two men go to shake hands. Maybin's strong grip painfully crushes Gary's knuckles against his wedding band.

'Please be seated, everyone.'

In the middle of the table sits one of the ubiquitous three-legged conference phones that look like miniature lunar landers. Its light on top is lit.

Hensen says, 'Folks, we've asked Deputy Administrator Phil Beuerlein in Virginia and Leah Davis in DC to fill you in.'

Gary and Robin sit across from the astronauts. Hensen rolls forward and speaks into the gray plastic. 'Phil, Leah: Robin Walsh, Gary Stephens, Jack Maybin, and Chief Astronaut Casselmann are here on this end.'

The voice of the FBI's Leah Davis is strong and clear. 'Good morning, people. This isn't a briefing; that comes later. Lila, Phil, and I just want to welcome you and let you know what you're up against. Gary, you're here because, well, Robin was right to be concerned. We've ID'd the man who called himself Whit Rollins on the phone with your sister. Heavyset, bleached hair, a contract guy named Karl Rice. Has been known to work with, uh . . . foreign entities, shall we say. Not a nice man. We're looking for him, but in the meantime, we couldn't leave you out there alone. Not with what you know about Mission Dark Side.'

Lila Hensen smiles at the others. 'Moon mission appellation. Catchy, no?'

A man's voice on the phone continues, 'Beuerlein here. Mr Stephens, Gary, we understand you refused to accept the FBI's offer of protective custody here.'

Gary's about to contest the man's use of the word 'refused,' then thinks better of it.

'So, we've come up with something just as good, a hide-in-plain-sight sort of thing. You bike and rollerblade a bit to stay in shape, am I right?'

'I bike, mostly. Up and down the West Side Highway.' He shoots a puzzled look to the others in the room.

The Deputy on the speakerphone continues. 'Fitness will help sell the cover story of astronaut-in-training.'

Gary's mouth actually falls open. 'Me? I'm going to be forty! I direct TV commercials.'

The Director inches her wheelchair forward some more before speaking to him. 'Captain Maybin here is thirty-nine as well. He's already had a career flying jets for the Air Force. I've got a medical doctor from Colorado in his thirties who wants to get into space medicine. And there's a meteorologist in the training program who's forty-five. Says she wants to see beyond the clouds.'

Dubious, Gary says, 'If it's anything like the training I watched down in your lobby . . .'

The Director smiles, 'It's much tougher. But we think you'll survive. Jack, tell him what it's like.'

Now it's Maybin's turn to smile. 'Boring, mostly. Sweaty, too. And the food is . . . what's a different word for nourishing? Passable, I guess.'

Davis speaks. 'Right. My job's done. Over and out.'

The Deputy Administrator says, 'Me too. Ciao.'

The light on the conference phone goes out. The head of NASA eases her chair back to indicate the meeting is over.

'That's it for now. Casselmann, Walsh, Maybin, be back here at 1400 hours for your initial Dark Side briefing.'

Robin stands.

Hensen continues, 'Gary, you'll go to your new quarters with the Chief. We've got closed-circuit cameras all over the place for your safety. And all of you . . .' Gary stands next to Robin as Casselmann opens the conference room door. 'Mum's the word.'

'Funny,' Gary says. 'People keep telling us that.'

NINETEEN
Manchester, New Hampshire

March 12, 1968

A camera is trained on the building that houses New Hampshire's largest, most influential newspaper, *The Manchester Union-Leader*, as a light snow falls. An unseen television announcer intones, 'From NBC Election Central in New Hampshire, this is the news.'

The camera moves slightly right to discover the network's co-anchor, David Brinkley, holding a newspaper. He begins with his characteristic greeting.

'Good evening, Chet. Pundits said that if Minnesota Senator Eugene McCarthy got as much as thirty percent of the vote in the year's first Democratic primary against a sitting President, he could legitimately claim victory.'

He looks down at the paper he's holding.

'Well, here's what they're printing right now in that building behind me. It's the bulldog edition of the *Union-Leader*, and it says that, with ninety-six percent of the precincts in, the senator has forty-two percent of the vote to Lyndon Johnson's forty-nine percent, so far denying the President even a majority.'

Brinkley lowers the paper. 'Reliable sources tell us tonight's result, combined with the Viet Cong's surprise Tet offensive five weeks ago, opens the way for Senator Robert Kennedy to, finally, jump into the race as well.'

A voice with a Texas twang yells, 'Fuck! Fuck! Fuck! Bobby? Fuck!'

The news has been playing on a Magnavox color TV. Lady Bird Johnson reaches out and shuts it off, remonstrating with the man sitting on the couch beside her.

'Language, Lyndon!'

TWENTY
Cocoa Beach, Florida

After crossing the Banana River, the 7-Eleven fronting on East Cocoa Beach Causeway is to your right just before you bump into Alan Shepard Park. Drive any farther and you're in the Atlantic. Around the corner is the enormous Ron Jon Surf Shop. In other words, tourists wearing board shorts, flip-flops and cool shades don't stick out in the shops on the Causeway.

Karl Rice, in board shorts, flip-flops and cool shades, along with a windbreaker to hide the Berretta, takes a bottle of beer from the cooler at the rear of the store. Stepping back to avoid the camera aimed at the beer case, he pops the cap with the gun's trigger guard.

As he chugs, an incoming text appears on his phone. The screen reads: *You've been made. Lose the hair. Return NYC on alt ID. Call when back.*

He calmly finishes his beer and puts the empty back in the cooler.

Then he walks toward the front of the store, picking up a box of hair dye along the way. With the hair dye riding under his jacket next to the Berretta, he leaves without paying.

An hour later and a couple hundred yards west of the 7-Eleven, Cindy Kuester polishes her toenails with a foot up on the only chair in Room 107 of the Fawlty Towers Motel. Kuester, who's fifteen and looks it, is wearing just a bath towel, arranged so her intricate floral tramp stamp peeks out below the terrycloth. The dishwater blond is too young to know the motel owners named the place after a favorite TV show from the BBC. Too young, and too unaware, to know BBC has another meaning beyond porn.

The girl applies the Passion Pink color, careful to avoid touching the tissues that are keeping her toes apart and stares out the window at the rented SUV parked on the other side of the glass. She's thinking how cool it'll be to ride in that huge black car with what must be a great sound system all the way down to the Keys when the big man steps out of the bathroom. His brand-new brown hair is streaked with chemical highlights.

Rice throws the used box of dye at her. It just misses, landing on the bed.

She swivels in surprise. 'Hey!' And then she sees the hair. 'Wow, different.'

'That's the idea.'

Rice peels a couple of twenties off a wad and tosses them on the bed next to the box.

'What's this?'

'Out.'

'But you said—'

Rice grabs her things from the hook on the back of the door and throws them at her as well. They land beyond the bed on the floor. Hobbling with her wet nails, the girl scoops up the twenties before bending to pick up her clothes. With her ass still in the air, she looks back at her customer.

'Don't you want a third go at this?'

He moves in and rips off the towel. With the other hand, he grabs an ass cheek. Instead of foreplay, he uses it as a handle to lift her up and carry her, kicking and screaming, to the motel door. He throws her out before slamming it shut.

On her hands and scraped knees in the parking lot, the naked girl yells at the door. 'Hey, asshole, what about my bag?'

The motel door opens, and Rice flings a hippie-style shoulder bag in her general vicinity, sending lipsticks, contraceptives, and a cell phone in a bright pink case flying in a ten-foot arc. The naked girl crawls to retrieve her stuff as a family of four unloads their Chrysler Town and Country van outside Room 109. Their ten-year-old boy gawks in amazement.

TWENTY-ONE
Mission Ops/Bldg. 4-S, JSC

Gary Stephens is the only student sitting in a small classroom in one of the hundred buildings that make up the Johnson Space Center. Behind him, would-be astronauts hurry past the windows as the sky darkens and it begins to rain. But Gary's attention is on Director Hensen, who's rolled her chair next to the smartboard set up in front of him. Behind her, a couple of electronic devices sit on the brushed aluminum table that doubles as a teacher's desk.

'Gary, because the course for our next crop of people has already begun, and because need-to-know is such a critical factor here, I'm going to personally give you the orientation this morning and get you started on an accelerated training schedule.'

'Yes, ma'am.'

She smiles. 'Since it's just the two of us, in here you can call me Lila. OK, just so we're on the same page, our job for the next several days is to get you ready to mainstream with the other dozen candidates, men and women who've had a twelve-week head start on you. Clear?'

'Clear.'

'Good. About your dog, Army. I have nothing new on that front, but when I do, you'll know it first. OK?'

'Thanks.'

'Now, when you join the other candidates, you'll find Scuttlebutt

Topic A is always, "What did you do to get here?" Since you're not a flyer, and that's not something you can fake, you'll tell them this: You're a filmmaker, a pretty good one, who wants to see what's out there in space and capture it with your camera, so you can share it with millions of people around the world. And, since you *are* a filmmaker, it's plausible. OK?'

'Uh, Lila, may I ask you something?'

'Of course.'

'How long will I have to stay here?'

She smiles again. 'Not a question we usually get; all our trainees are such eager beavers. All right, the plan, such as it is, is this: We keep you here until the Dark Side mission wraps up.

'The Chinese still say they're on course to launch for the moon on July 1, a holiday over there that marks the founding day of their Communist Party a century ago. We're trying, off the record, to slow them down, but the calendar's working against us. A July 1 launch – which is really our June 30, thanks to the International Date Line – means they can plant their flag next to ours on July 4, our own Independence Day. Sort of a "screw you, America."

'They're moving heaven and earth – and, I guess, the moon – to make the symbolism of the two flags work. So, the Dark Side mission has to be in and out by July 3. If you want to take off after the hot dogs and fireworks, just say so and we'll wash you out. Like cutting you from the varsity.

'Besides, once the Chinese land and broadcast their PR thing, we think whoever's behind the danger you're in will realize the cover-up's been successful and they'll call off the dogs. Uh, sorry.'

Gary smiles tightly. 'There's another thing. How do I communicate from here? Is there a pay phone? I have – that is, Pippa and I have – a business to run. Quarterly taxes to file. And there's the Even Stephens to manage.'

'Even Stephens?'

Now it's his turn to smile. 'My Rotisserie baseball team. How will I replace the players on the DL? I need access to the Free Agent Pool.'

'I don't know a thing about baseball. Does DL mean the Down Low?'

'Disabled List.'

'Oh.' Hensen's eyebrows knit together briefly, then relax. 'I'll

stick with rocket science. Easier. In any event' – she picks up an
iPad from the desk behind her and hands it to him – 'for the next
six weeks you'll use this for everything. Calls and texts to the outside
world as well as note-taking during the training. And you'll sign
your messages with the new name we've given you.'

'I have a new name?'

Hensen picks up the remote behind her. Gary assumes she'll use
it to power up the whiteboard. Instead, she aims it at the windows
behind him and metal shades lower and click shut, blocking out the
world.

She responds to his surprised look. 'Like I said, need to know.'

Then she reaches out and powers up the board with a touch of
her finger. A document instantly appears, one that looks like a
contract. At the bottom, the place for the signature is blank, though
there's a name typed in beneath it: 'Robert Forrester.'

'I'm Robert Forrester?'

'Bob Forrester. Or Rob. Your choice.'

He squints at the small type above his new name. 'And this, this
contract or whatever it is?'

She waves a hand at the electronic board. 'Just a formality. It's
the standard agreement every candidate has to sign. That you're an
American citizen between sixty-two and seventy-five inches in
height; that your distant and near visual acuity is correctable to
twenty/twenty in each eye, and that your blood pressure does not
exceed one forty over ninety measured in a sitting position. Stuff
like that.'

She smiles an even bigger smile than she did before. 'Don't
worry, Bob Forrester has already qualified with flying colors. OK?'

'I guess.'

She indicates the iPad he's holding. 'Find the pull-down window
labeled *Documents* and click on *Applicant Agreement*.' She takes
something out of a pocket. 'Use this stylus to sign your name in
the space. Forrester with a double "r."'

As he writes, the signature appears on the whiteboard in the
proper place.

'Good.'

She takes back the stylus. 'In case we're hacked, we want your
Forrester signature on file. Now let's get started.'

TWENTY-TWO
Burbank, California

March 31, 1968

A young Latino TV reporter stands in front of a bulldozer pushing charred debris toward a dump truck. A big CBS eye all but covers the microphone it's affixed to.

'Vern, the war has come to Burbank. Or at least, the protests have.'

He swivels briefly to take in what's going on behind him before coming back. 'You're looking at what's left of a movie set here on the Disney lot.'

Now he shifts position and points to his left up the road.

'A luncheon yesterday at the Golden Mall, about two miles that way, for Vietnam-bound Marines was supposed to kick off "Burbank Night at Disneyland." The violence began after protesters carrying signs like this one' – he holds up a handmade sign that reads, *Our Boys Out of Nam* – began shouting, "Hell no, we won't go."

'Led by two drummers and a fife player in full Spirit of '76 regalia, they tried to stop buses taking the five hundred Marines to the evening's festivities. When they couldn't, authorities say, some continued on to Disneyland. Others then marched down Buena Vista here to protest Disney's backing for the war before scaling the fence behind me.'

He puts down the sign and picks up another. It's a printed square that reads, 'Closed Set. Authorized Persons Only.'

'They overran this movie set, lit a bonfire, and burned down most of the building that housed it, including a separate control room.'

He turns to look back at the bulldozer dumping blackened equipment into the dump truck. The camera moves in to see long tendrils of still-smoking 35 mm film falling into the truck.

'They even toppled a five-story crane holding aloft an ultra-realistic version of a NASA lunar module. The multi-million-dollar set and nearly all the film they shot is a total loss with, fortunately, only minor injuries.'

In the background, Roy Disney can be seen wading through the debris with another studio exec, unaware they're on camera. The reporter, realizing he has an opportunity for an exclusive, hurries toward the studio head.

From twenty feet away, the microphone picks up a visibly upset Disney's words. 'We're fucked . . . no time to reshoot. Tex will have to be told.'

The CBS reporter shoves his mic in front of the two execs. 'What about this film, Mr Disney? Will you still go ahead? Are you insured? And who's Tex?'

Angrily, Disney pushes the microphone away. 'Not now, dammit!'

Shrugging his shoulders, the reporter signs off. 'As you heard just now, Roy Disney is still unavailable for comment. In Burbank, this is Ronaldo Mendoza for CBS 2.'

TWENTY-THREE

Neutral Buoyancy Laboratory, Bldg. 29, JSC

I t's Friday afternoon, Gary's first as a 'mainstreamed' astronaut candidate. He's nervous as hell – which is strange, because he has no intention of riding into space, so what does any of it matter? Still, he wants to make a good impression, like a boy who's just moved into town on his first day of school.

Maybe a home-schooled kid is a better analogy, after four days of intensive one-on-ones in that classroom with the shades locked down. He doesn't know anyone and feels like they're all looking at him. And they are.

For another thing, he's standing with the other astronaut candidates – known colloquially as ASCANs – at the edge of an immense tank of water, twenty-five-feet deep and twice the size of the pools they hold the Olympics in. It's big enough to manage every one of the components of the International Space Station without a drop of its 6.2 million gallons spilling over the sides. Gary isn't sure he could swim a single, enormous lap without drowning.

There's a third reason to be nervous: the two instructors, Theo and Miriam, according to the names stitched on their black polo shirts under the words *Neutral Buoyancy Laboratory*, plus a squad of scuba divers in neoprene wetsuits, and finally the twelve other ASCANs in NASA-issue bathing suits, the ones who've been training hard for a couple of months, are all absurdly well-toned human beings. Well-toned and well-tanned, most of them.

The instructor named Theo, with a few gray hairs to show for his years on the job, has been looking at a clipboard. Now he looks up.

'Afternoon, folks. We've just got time before the weekend for another little dip in our pool. I'm sure you've noticed we've been joined today by a thirteenth victim, Robert Forrester from New York.' The man smiles at Gary. 'Do you prefer Bob or Rob? Or the full Robert?'

For some reason he answers, 'My friends call me Bert.'

Another smile. 'OK, Bert, welcome aboard.'

Most of the other candidates nod at him or smile. One guy, though, an intense sort with closely cropped hair, gives him a too-long, unfriendly stare.

Theo glances down again at the clipboard.

'Your write-up says you're a filmmaker, and that you'll be training people on our new zero-gravity cameras. That right?'

Gary thought he was ready for the question, but even so a flush of embarrassment starts at his cheeks and works its way down his neck. It used to do the same thing when he lied about something when he was a boy. And there's no pretending it isn't there with just the swimsuit on.

'Actually, sir, these cameras are so new, I'll need to train myself on them before I'm knowledgeable enough to help anyone else.'

Theo says, 'Fair enough. Then we'll figure things out as we go. Right now, we need everyone to head off to the changing station with your knowledgeable wardrobe person.' He says the last phrase looking at Miriam with a friendly twinkle in his eye.

She points toward the far end of the vast place. 'Into your diapers, everyone!'

The candidates head off around the pool toward the male and

female changing stations three-quarters of a football field away. Gary hurries to catch up and taps one of the guys on the shoulder.

'Excuse me, uh . . .'

The ASCAN stops and turns around. It's the man who was giving him the unfriendly stare. In a clipped tone he says, 'Name's Marty Bienstock. Got a question?'

'I do. Did she say diapers?'

'She did. Astronauts in training work here in the tank for up to six hours at a time. We can't have anyone piss in the water. Or worse.'

Gary tries another question. 'Is all this superstructure here just to train us for splashing down in the ocean?'

The guy has that judgmental look on his face again. 'We learned that one, too, a couple of months ago. But, seeing as how you're the new guy . . . OK, Bert – that's your name, right? – I'll answer your question if you'll answer mine: Who do you know that can enroll a numbskull into our program nine-plus weeks late?'

Gary fights down the urge to choke the guy. Instead, he gives the rehearsed reply. 'I was chosen to be part of this candidate class from the beginning, but by the time I was notified I was shooting a documentary about the fall-off in fishing in the Atlantic off Wellfleet. Lila thought the underwater experience was worth my joining late.'

'*Lila*? I see.' Bienstock gives him a smirk before walking away once more.

Gary hustles to catch up a second time and the trainee makes a big deal out of stopping again. He even throws in a sigh.

'OK, about the pool. On rare occasions, as part of an astronaut's pre-mission routine, they'll run through splashdown procedures here. But we practice our splashdowns in Clear Lake. It's half a mile away and deep as hell. No, this tank exists to simulate EVAs.' And then he turns on his heel and heads for the changing room.

Miriam, the instructor, was close enough to hear the last question and answer. She walks over to her new trainee.

'EVA: Extravehicular Activity. In laymen's terms, Bert, it means space walks. Anything you do outside your cocoon of a spacecraft – like, let's say, repairing a payload arm on the Space Station. Or, in your case, upgrading a camera on one of a dozen different kinds of geo-positional satellites. Either way you'll be working in zero gravity or microgravity conditions. For sustained environments like those, the closest we can get here on earth is this neutral-buoyancy tank.'

They've arrived at the changing stations, essentially a pair of high school locker rooms. Gary is about to follow the other guys into the male station when Miriam holds him back.

'Not so fast, pardner. We have to measure you first.'

At that, an older man with *Mel* stitched on his shirt approaches with a tape measure.

Gary says, 'I'm a forty-two regular. Right off the rack.'

Mel ignores him and runs the tape down the inside of Gary's left leg, starting with the crotch. Some of the scuba divers standing around are watching.

To ease the tension, Gary says, 'No cuffs. And I'd like just a little break in the trousers.'

A couple of the onlookers snicker in appreciation. But Theo, the other trainer who's come over to watch, isn't smiling.

'The thing is, Bert, we can simulate the weightlessness of space travel in the water, but only up to a point. Show him, Carrie.'

A young woman with a dark complexion and sun-streaked hair chopped short has just emerged from the female changing station all suited up. Now she gives the instructor the index finger-to-thumb 'OK' signal. Then she waits while two helpers lower a Lexan Apollo-type helmet over her head and turn some screws to tighten it to the neck rings on her suit.

After Carrie inhales a few times, causing a sucking sound to come from the oxygen-enriched tanks on her back, she gives another signal, all five fingers facing toward the water. A few scuba divers slide into the pool.

The crew working the cranes swings a cable, attached at the upper end to one of the ceiling girders, over to Carrie and hooks her up. Finally, they raise the hydraulic hoist with its human cargo and swing it out, slowly, over the water.

Meanwhile, Mel is entering Gary's measurements into a hand-held computer. His final reading is of Gary's right hand from thumb to pinkie with the fingers stretched out.

'Nine point six inches,' he says, entering the numbers. 'Not bad. We have twelve different glove sizes and you're a perfect Large.'

By this time, Carrie has given everyone a third hand sign of two fingers down, meaning 'lower me at medium speed.'

The safety divers wait beneath her in the water with open arms. The hoist is lowered until she's totally submerged. Then each helper takes one of her legs.

As Mel heads off, Theo continues. 'So, Bert, I'm sure you've noticed how you feel lighter when you go swimming. How your body tends to drift and float. That's the anti-gravity effect caused by water's buoyancy. But it simulates weightlessness just so far. There is no buoyancy in space, only less (or no) gravity to begin with: a third of earth's gravity on Mars, a sixth on the moon, none on the International Space Station.

'So, Terry and Connie are in there with Carrie to hold her down in her harness just enough to neutralize the buoyancy effect.'

'When do I go into the water?'

'Mel's getting your EMU together now.'

'Emu? Like the bird?'

'Funny. We call the suits Extravehicular Mobility Units. Better learn the jargon.'

'Right.'

'To continue, one disadvantage of neutral-buoyancy diving is the significant amount of drag created by the water. This makes it difficult to set an object in motion and keep it in motion. It also makes it easier to keep the object stationary. The vacuum of space is exactly the opposite: it's easy to set an object in motion but super tough to keep it still.'

Mel has returned. He says, 'Except for the gloves, you're a Medium in both upper and lower torsos. Ready to give it a go?'

Theo takes Gary by the elbow, holding him there.

He says, 'Learn from Carrie. She was our top ASCAN last marking period.'

'Marking? You mean, like school?'

He nods. 'Every ninety days.' Then he lets go of Gary's arm as he says, 'OK Mel, he's all yours.'

Inside the changing room, Mel leaves Gary standing halfway down a line of open dressing spaces while he collects articles of astronaut wear from a supply closet. Little plastic plaques above some of the cubicles bear the names 'Snyder,' 'Modugno,' and 'Maybin.' Other names are written in marker and taped to the wood. A fully-suited-up twenty-something guy with another NASA buzz cut sits in a nearby space, putting on thin cotton gloves. The name 'Lucci' is taped on the cubicle above his head.

The guy says, 'You're the newbie. Bert, that right? I'm Ralph.'

He holds out a hand and Gary shakes it. Ralph picks up a work glove with a metal cuff at the wrist and holds it out to Gary. 'I got a favor to ask, Bert. Would you help me on with my outer gloves? They're a bitch.'

'Sure.'

Gary takes one and Ralph forces his hand, already wearing the inner glove, through the too-small opening. They repeat the job with the other hand

Now that he's suited up, Ralph gives him a thank-you jab in the shoulder just as Mel returns with an armful of Gary's clothing. Mel's just in time to hear Ralph say, as he heads out to the pool, 'If the glove don't fit, you must acquit.'

Mel watches him go with an amused look. 'Ralph's our resident joker . . . unless you are.' He chuckles under his breath. 'No cuffs. Good one.' Then he points to a rack a little farther on that holds the separate halves of a space suit and says, like a gentleman's tailor, 'Your ensemble, sir.'

Gary moves toward it, but Mel, still in his tailor's voice, says, 'Undergarments first, sir. And if you have to hit the head, now's the time.'

Five minutes later, an embarrassed Gary is wearing a medium-sized Depends adult diaper under a top-and-bottom pair of cotton long johns 'to wick away any perspiration.' Mel hands him a liquid-cooled ventilation jumpsuit to put on next, saying, 'It's hot work in space. Even in the water.'

Then he shows Gary how to slip on the lower torso assembly and into the booties before squatting and twisting his body to slide up and under the rigid top half of the space suit. 'On an actual mission, you'll simply float into it.'

Next, he hands Gary a pair of gloves like the ones Ralph had, saying, 'There's a trade-off between comfort and dexterity with these things. That's why they're so snug.'

After the gloves are on, Mel picks up a soft fabric head covering. 'We call this our Snoopy cap. It's sort of a NASA trademark.'

Gary slips the brown communication cap on his head and Mel plugs the electrical prong hanging down from it into a socket on the suit. A microphone rides in front of Gary's mouth. Finally, he hands Gary a helmet.

'OK, let's see how it fits. If you're a fathead, I've got a slightly bigger one.'

Gary manages to slip his head into the plastic.

Mel says, 'Say something.'

Gary says, 'This is really cool!' Then he says, 'It's very echo-y in here.'

Mel nods. 'Don't worry. When the air supply is on, you won't notice it. Now, try walking around.'

Gary takes a few steps, more of a waddle than a walk.

Mel says, 'You'll get used to it.'

Gary gives him a thumbs-up sign. 'I guess.'

'Oh, I forgot to tell you. We don't use the thumbs-up thing in the suit; it's too close to the one finger raised for "lift me up slowly." Instead, we use the circled thumb and index finger to signal "OK." Like civilians do.'

Gary does it and says, 'OK.'

'Right. There's a chart with all the hand signals on the wall under the Training Center sign. Why not study it while you wait your turn?'

Gary smiles at him from inside the helmet. 'Will hand signals be on the test?'

They start to walk out to the water. Mel says, seriously, 'Everything's on the test.'

TWENTY-FOUR
The Gilruth Center, Houston

About the time Gary is walking out to the neutral buoyancy tank, Lila Hensen is maneuvering her chair a little closer to the console at the front of the room. She's getting ready to address the two dozen men and women gathered in a small amphitheater upstairs in the Robert R. Gilruth Center, a conference facility named for the first director of the Johnson Space Center that's located at the northeast edge of the vast campus just off Space Center Boulevard.

Sitting shoulder to shoulder among those waiting for the first vendor briefing to begin are astronauts Walsh, Casselmann, Maybin, and a fourth member of the upcoming mission, backup Cesar Modugno, a Cuban-American and former record-setting triathlete.

Hensen clears her throat. 'Good afternoon, folks.' She looks at a clock on the wall over the door. 'If we go a little long I want to apologize in advance. We set this up to accommodate everyone's schedules, including the out-of-towners. I promise you I won't keep you here past your East Coast bedtime.'

A few people chuckle politely.

'We're getting started even later than we planned thanks to the traffic jam at the card reader we set up in the hallway. If you haven't had the barcode on your badge read by the machine, please get up and do it now.'

She looks around, but no one stands up.

'Fine. In case you're wondering, we're here, instead of the Mission Briefing Center, for a couple of reasons. One is the sensitive nature of what we'll be discussing, so we don't want tour groups wandering anywhere in the vicinity while we have the maps up.'

With this she gestures over her shoulder to the three large video screens, all of them blank for the moment, behind her on the wall.

'The second reason we're up here this evening is that our video conference capability is temporarily on the fritz. Fortunately, our tech people have come up with a work-around. Renée?'

With that, her assistant gets up and opens the door to the hall as Hensen adds, 'Please have patience; these folks can't move any faster than four miles an hour.'

There's a pause in the room for several moments until a buzzing noise is heard in the hall. Then the first of nine VGo Telepresence robots slowly rolls into the room. Designed for doctors to bring their expertise to distant operating theaters and students who want to learn across borders, they look like Segway scooters with iPad screens mounted on top.

The VGos arrange themselves on the side of the room, jostling each other like so many teenagers fighting for space at a sold-out concert. The fact that each mounted iPad shows a different person's live image just adds to the strange realism.

Director Hensen says, 'Settle down, everyone. Dark Side is going to be – going to *have* to be – an all-hands-on-deck effort. To that end, I've invited our vendors, who are in some cases our competitors, to join us for this first mission-wide briefing.'

Mention of their competitors in the private sector causes an unmistakable groan to escape the lips of many of the NASA employees sitting in the room. The Director continues as if she hasn't heard.

'We're joined tonight by representatives from Boeing as well as the SpaceX rocketry group. Because this mission is "off the books" so to speak, we've decided to use the previously announced testing program of the new, privately built crew capsules – Boeing's CST Starliner and the Crew Dragon from SpaceX – as a cover for Dark Side. And because Crew Dragon flew to the Space Station in April, it's the Starliner's turn at bat.

'The good news is, these rival organizations have agreed to set aside their differences and work with our launch group. Barney, Marilyn, please stand with your teams so we can give you a round of appreciation for your patriotism.'

Seven people rise to their feet and accept the heartfelt applause before sitting down again.

Hensen continues. 'Carnegie Mellon's Astrobotic Technologies people are here; they'll work with our guidance system team. And Moon Express will provide our team's ground transportation to Tranquility. Rise and be recognized.'

There's more applause.

'Our colleagues at NASA headquarters in Washington, the White House, the FBI, and a couple of other agencies who ask not to be named are here playing catch-up as well. To be briefed on Dark Side and, to put our cards on the table, to begin their surveillance of each of the project participants in this room.'

She turns to the VGos and asks, 'Isn't that so, folks?'

The men and women on several of the iPad screens, each image broadcast from a different government office more than 1,400 miles away, nod in agreement. One gives Hensen the thumbs-up sign. She gives it right back.

'In case you're wondering, each person pictured on the screens to my left is connected by Skype via his or her own individual video-conference call. It'll just be for tonight's briefing. An app allows them to direct their own robot's mobility, and the camera on their computer shows us to them with a clarity equal to the images you're seeing on those screens. So, watch your step. The Watchers are watching.'

A few people chuckle, hesitantly this time.

She clears her throat. 'All right, down to cases.'

Pressing a button on the console in front of her causes the three screens in back to come to life. The left-hand one shows a Mercator projection of the surface of the moon at a scale of one millimeter to ten kilometers. The map is festooned with the Latin names of all the prominent features, mountains and craters, hundreds of them. The Sea of Tranquility sits about where Louisville would be in a map of the United States.

The right-hand screen is also a map of the moon we see in the sky, but this one is topographic. The whole thing is done in shades of blue, with the highest elevations and the deepest craters shown in the darkest color. Tranquility is the largest area of pale blue on the entire surface.

For the moment, the middle screen simply says, *Mission Dark Side*.

Hensen picks up a remote from the console and aims it at the middle screen. Under the title it now reads, *Deliver payload to Tranquility Base, distribute materials, lift back off by July 3*.

She clicks again. The heading of the next slide is, *Payload*. Beneath it is a long list, four columns of twenty-six items each, beginning with *LFA (Lunar Flag Assembly), consisting of nylon American flag, sun-bleached, on telescoping one-inch anodized aluminum tube*.

The woman in the wheelchair looks back at the list and then out at the group.

'Each of you has been briefed individually during the vetting process as to the purpose of this mission, which was authorized directly by the Commander-in-Chief. So, I won't dwell on any of the items listed behind me except to say they are all artifacts that will be deployed at Tranquility Base by astronauts Casselmann, Walsh, and Maybin, here with us today along with Captain Modugno.'

Just then a loud buzzing noise comes from the hall as before. It's followed by the sound of something heavy bumping into the closed door at the back of the room.

Hensen looks at her assistant. 'Renée, would you please get up and see what's making that noise?'

The young woman looks briefly at the iPad she's carrying. 'A latecomer; confirmation just came through, ma'am.' She goes over to the door and opens it, nodding to the guard outside. He steps aside as a tenth VGo robot, one showing a man with *café au lait*-colored skin on its iPad screen, bangs again, this time into the door jamb, like a Roomba stymied by a furniture leg. Renée pulls it clear and the robot slowly works its way into the room.

Annoyed by the delay, Hensen asks, 'And you are?'

The face of the man on the far end of the connection reddens visibly. 'Taye Griggs, ma'am. Full name: Tayshaun Griggs.'

'From?'

'The FBI, ma'am. Right now I'm, physically, at Quantico. They just pulled me in an hour ago as part of the surveillance team.' His face reddens even more. 'They showed me how to use this wheelie thing, but I'm afraid I'm still not that good a driver. Sorry.'

'One last question, Mr Griggs: Who, exactly, are you supposed to surveille?'

'Why, uh, you, ma'am.'

Taken aback momentarily, the Director says, 'All right, Mr Griggs.' Then she gestures toward the other nine robots along the wall. 'Would you please find a spot as best you can?'

'Yes, ma'am.'

'Now, where was I? Oh yes. For the benefit of those who haven't taken courses in astrophysics, or even astronomy,' she says this glancing over to the VGos, 'here's my quick Solar System for Dummies speech, and I emphasize quick.'

She rolls her chair back so she's sitting under the left-hand image of the moon on the wall. 'OK, the earth revolves around the sun, and the moon around the earth. We, in turn, drag it with us on our 365-day orbit. Meanwhile, the earth rotates on its axis every twenty-four hours . . . hence, our days and nights.

'The moon rotates as well, but much more slowly: a little less than once every thirty days. That's almost exactly the length of time it takes to make one circuit around us. Which is why we always see the same side of the thing. Now, I'm sure even the liberal arts majors with us today have seen the moon in its various phases in the night sky, depending on its position relative to the light from the sun. Long before telescopes, man could see and plot these changes. Trivia tidbit: Henry Hudson sailed past Manhattan up the river named for him in 1609 in a ship called the *Half Moon*.'

She reaches for a glass of water and takes a sip. Then, with a click of the remote, the familiar image of a full moon in the night sky takes the place of the previous moon map on the left-hand screen. A tiny American flag appears superimposed on the Sea of Tranquility, precisely where Neil Armstrong and Buzz Aldrin appeared to have planted it.

'Watch carefully.'

She clicks again, and a shadow slowly moves across and covers the moon's surface from right to left, creating all the phases from Full (a completely lit-up disk) to New (complete shadow) before continuing from New back to Full.

'We'll save phases like waxing gibbous and waning crescent for the advanced class. Now, the phases you just saw represent a real challenge for the Chinese. It would be virtually impossible, for reasons of payload weight, for their crew to bring the kind of Hollywood lighting required to televise the planting of their flag next to ours in the dark. They need full sunlight. They need it for their solar batteries as well. So, watch again, and this time, I'll add a little extra touch.'

When she again clicks the remote, the shadow begins its slow trip as before while a digital calendar rapidly counts the days from June 27 to July 26, full moon to full moon.

With her demonstration at an end, Hensen places the remote back on the desk and swivels her chair toward the wall of faces on the Telepresence robots.

'OK, visitors, who wants to ace Solar System for Dummies? Tell me what you saw just now on that screen that dictates how Mission Dark Side should go?'

A woman on the fifth iPad from the left has her hand raised near her face, but the NASA director gives her a little shake of her head.

'Not you, Doreen, you're our DC liaison. I want a civilian to give it a shot. Anyone?'

Griggs, the latecomer at the far end of the line of robots, speaks up. 'May I, Madame Director?'

Hensen makes eye contact. 'A simple "Director" will do, Mr Griggs. All right, you're my, uh, personal observer. So, what did you *observe* when I ran the moon thing just now?'

'Well, I tried to watch the shadow overtaking that little American flag while also watching the counter spinning through the days. I can't be sure, but it seems tricky.'

He pauses.

'What makes you say that, Taye . . . if I may call you that?'

'Certainly, ma'am. I'm no scientist, and I don't really know what Beijing is planning, but if this is as big a deal for them as it would be for us, their people will be filming . . . recording . . . the moon every inch of the way, starting with their launch on the first of July.'

'Go on.'

'Well, ma'am, unless we want our folks to be the reality stars of Chinese television that first week of July, they better approach the Sea of Tranquility from the eastern . . . the, uh, shady side, so to speak. And then drive a golf cart or something past a bunch of craters until they're ready to scatter all that stuff you showed on your slide just now. And, if I'm right, that'll be the easy part, because—'

Just then an ear-piercing siren goes off in the hall outside. Instantly, the video screens behind the NASA Director go blank. An equally loud klaxon starts clanging inside the small auditorium, and the room's lights begin to flash on and off and on at half-second intervals. Hensen wheels herself with surprising speed over to a telephone on the wall and lifts the receiver. As soon as she does, all the sirens cease and the lights stop flashing.

The Director listens to someone at the other end of the line. Then she hangs up the phone. Wheeling herself more slowly back to the console, she announces, 'This briefing will have to be postponed. Someone is here under false pretenses.'

TWENTY-FIVE

North Michigan Avenue, Chicago

March 31, 1968

A small knot of passersby has formed outside Lake Shore TV/ Radio, an appliance store that's closed for the night. More than a dozen television sets of various sizes, each with a little white card listing the maker, model and price, are all showing the same thing: President Lyndon Johnson's address to the nation from the White House.

'Good evening, my fellow Americans. Tonight, I want to speak to you of peace in Vietnam. No other question so preoccupies our people.'

If anyone were still inside the darkened store, they'd see the cluster of office workers, shoppers, and students pausing on their way home to watch the President, who speaks from the Oval Office flanked by flags behind his desk.

'A strong, confident and vigilant America stands ready tonight to seek an honorable peace.'

The President's voice sounds particularly raspy and shrill coming from the one set with the audio turned up, a small black-and-white portable that's on sale.

'Whatever the price, whatever the burden, whatever the sacrifice that duty may require.'

A bus stops in front of the store. Several passengers get out, pause, and join the little crowd. The lights from inside the bus momentarily reflect the onlookers' faces back to themselves in the shop's glass: An old white man sports a weathered Bears cap with a block C; a black teenager wears a long-sleeve White Sox T-shirt over a sweatshirt.

'So, I would ask all Americans to guard against divisiveness and all its ugly consequences. The ultimate strength of our country and our cause will lie not in powerful weapons, but in the unity of our people.'

There's a pneumatic whoosh as the driver closes the bus doors and pulls away from the curb, eliminating the reflections over Johnson's face on the screens.

'Believing this as I do, I do not believe that I should devote an hour or a day of my time to any personal partisan causes or to any duties other than the awesome duties of this office, the Presidency of your country.'

The largest color TV, a twenty-five-inch Sylvania encased in a wood cabinet with record player and radio for $499, reveals the worry lines in LBJ's face.

'Accordingly, I shall not seek, and I will not accept, the nomination of my party for another term as your President.'

The little crowd, shocked, is quiet for a moment. Then, as the realization dawns, they break out in surprised cheers. So do people watching TV in their apartments across the avenue.

'Yeah? Wow!' Passersby up and down the block and across the way join in. 'Really! He *did?* All riiight!'

Drivers listening to the speech in their cars begin honking their horns. Four people start to whoop it up and dance in the street. It's New Year's Eve in Chicago, and it isn't even April.

TWENTY-SIX
The Gilruth Center

The folks who dubbed the small, upper-level amphitheater 'Inspiration' probably had in mind an event like the one they hold here every Tuesday from 4:30 to 5:30 p.m. It's called 'Relax, Receive, Restore: Introduction to Meditation, Yoga, and Reiki for Space Center Employees and their Families.' Relaxed? Restored? This isn't that. This is pandemonium.

Forty minutes ago, an entire roomful of people was told they're on lockdown, and with every minute they sit here they like it less and less. Normally a sober, subdued group, the NASA people are either barking at each other or hurling questions at the Director.

'False pretenses?' 'What?' 'Who?'

Several of the people on the robotic Skype connections are calling out to her as well: 'Who was on the other end of the phone?' 'What's this all about?' 'Is this the end of the briefing?' 'Is this the end of the mission?' With the place in an uproar, Captain Robin Walsh, sitting with her Dark Side crew on the end of the row of seats nearest the wall, just happens to glance to her right in time to see a drama suddenly unfold on one of the VGo monitors. The image of a mousy, middle-aged female with graying hair and glasses sitting at a standard government-issue desk starts going in and out of focus. Then the wheels of the woman's 'pogo stick' begin to shake and twitch.

At first the movements are little more than small shudders; soon they involve quickening starts and wrenching stops forward and back, which bang the monitor on top once or twice hard against the wall. It's as if the machine itself is stricken with St Vitus' Dance.

It gets worse. On the VGo's iPad, the camera on the faraway woman's computer transmits an unseen man's hands reaching for her, attempting to pull her out of her seat. She tries to resist with one hand while keeping the other on the keyboard controls in front of her. But every time her hands come up to ward off the man, the VGo lurches violently.

The assailant goes for her face and knocks her eyeglasses off her head. With a wrenching effort she pulls free momentarily and leans forward toward her monitor, about to yell or cry for help. Before she can, a big hand reaches out and covers the woman's mouth and nose. The man's other hand then grabs her hair and yanks it back.

Now the rest of the group in the Texas meeting room has locked on to what Robin's been watching: a deadly brawl playing out on a TV screen, like a Hitchcock movie or one of those Wild Kingdom programs showing a lion attacking a gazelle. Lila Hensen is instantly on the wall phone again, speaking urgently to an unknown someone as the knockdown, drag-out fight continues to her left.

Different, larger hands join the fray. A second man tries pulling her chair away from her desk. She grips the edge of the workstation with both hands, preventing him. The remote computer is knocked awry; its camera briefly shows a hairy arm and a few inches of stubbled jaw.

The melee causes her VGo in the Texas briefing room to shift from lurching back and forth to left and right, in wider and wider arcs, on its wheels. Commander Maybin, on the aisle a row away, hurriedly gets out of his seat to keep the thing upright. But it spins away and knocks over the one next to it, the eighth one in line.

The surveillance man on that screen, suddenly viewing the room at a 90° angle, adds his voice to the mix. 'Hey, what the—?'

Back to the woman and her desperate fight with the two assailants. The man with the bigger hands finally is able to clap one mitt over her mouth and keep it there. She tries to pull it away but he's too strong. Instead, she manages to bite down on two of the fingers. Hard. The still-unseen man pulls his injured hand away with a whelp of pain and an expletive.

'Bitch!'

Breathlessly, the woman, so composed just moments before, manages a single cry into her computer's microphone.

'*Pomogite!*'

Maybin asks, 'What the hell was that?'

Without taking her eyes off the action, Robin says, 'It's Russian for "help."'

Surprised, Maybin says, 'You know Russian?'

'Just enough to be dangerous. I spent a month with them on the International Space Station.'

Maybin grins. 'Lots of cries for help up there?'

There's no letup in the drama on the iPad screen. When the man who wasn't bitten re-enters the frame with a hypodermic needle, he jabs the syringe filled with amber fluid all the way into the woman's neck.

She screams something unintelligible and almost immediately goes limp.

The man with the stubbled jaw leans into the picture. Oddly, though he's hoarse and out of breath, he smiles.

Then he says, 'It's OK, Director. We got her.'

The second, bigger man can be seen sucking on his bitten hand. He adds, 'We'll have to check the hard drive. Can't be sure if she had time to tell them anything.'

TWENTY-SEVEN

The Vietnam Memorial, Washington, DC

It's raining. Two men stand side by side, facing the polished black granite wall. The much younger and taller of the two, a black man with a shaved head, holds a golf umbrella over them both and speaks facing forward.

'My shoes are getting wet. These fuckers are handmade and they aren't waterproof.'

Instead of responding, the older man reaches out and runs a finger over one of the 58,318 names inscribed on the wall. The water that was caught in the last name's initial letter C drips down and finds the name immediately below it to run into.

Shaved Head shakes first one foot and then the other, trying to get the water off. Then he tries a different tactic, stamping his foot hard on the pavement. All it does is splash water into the cuffs of his Paul Smith trousers, making his ankles even wetter. He breaks protocol and turns to face the man nearly half a century his senior.

'Why the hell did you drag us out here anyway, Professor? We could have covered this back there in the theater.'

The old man looks at him for the first time. 'Did you say something, Raheem?' The low rumble of his voice could be mistaken for the rolling thunder that accompanies the rain. 'That's the trouble with these hearing aids. The sound of the raindrops drowns out—'

'Goddamn right I said something! Look around! This place is built on an angle, a couple of them actually, and all the water in the entire District of Columbia is running right over my shoes. Cost me twelve hundred dollars!'

The tall man pronounces 'dollars' as 'dolluhs,' the Carolina twang creeping back into his voice the way it always does when he's irritated or angry. He points to the combination souvenir shop-cum-rest station on the other side of the pathway from the Memorial, and then he all but pulls the older man with him in that direction.

'Let's get the fuck out of this!'

Inside the place, the man called Raheem ducks into the men's room to grab a bunch of paper towels and returns to pat down his soaked footwear. The two of them sit on a peeling olive-green iron bench in the deserted shop as the rain beats vigorously on the roof. The manager must be on break.

Even so, Raheem speaks in a semi-whisper. 'I won't even ask you why I had to sacrifice my John Lobbs.'

The other man looks down at the dabbing of the shoes. When he speaks, his voice betrays his Germanic origin. 'Sacrifice is the operative word, Raheem. George Whitney Carpenter back there sacrificed his life more than fifty years ago.'

Raheem pauses and looks over. 'They all did, didn't they?'

'I suppose you're right. But George is the only one I taught at Yale. Freshman seminar. American History.'

Raheem has untied his shoelaces and removed his shoes and stockings. Very deliberately, he wrings out his black socks with the little red diamonds, creating a puddle on the gift shop floor. He says, 'There must be a moral in there somewhere, Professor.'

Now it's the older man's turn to look directly at his companion.

'The moral is, when we're called to sacrifice for the flag, the best of us do it with no questions asked.'

'And that's what we're doing now?'

'It's what we've *been* doing for the last fifty years.'

The black man is trying his best to pull his still-damp socks over his size 13 feet.

'OK, but why does everything you say always sound like a pronouncement from the fucking Oracle of Delphi? I'll ask you again: Why'd you drag me out here in all this weather? For a pep talk about sacrificing for the flag?'

The professor reaches into his left jacket pocket and removes a pipe. He pulls a small pouch of tobacco from his other pocket and expertly crooks a forefinger around just enough of the stuff to fill the bowl. Then he snaps a stainless-steel Zippo lighter open and lights up before replying, sucking air in until the cherry-flavored tobacco catches. 'Precisely.'

Raheem stops what he's doing, his left sock halfway on. 'Huh?'

'Ever play *Call of Duty: Black Ops*, Raheem?'

'Not that specific one. Others. Your point?'

'I bought that game for my grandchildren. Did a little research: All the online war games involve teamwork in reaching a specific goal or series of goals. One of the *Call of Duty* scenarios is called "Capture the Flag." You know what that is?'

'We played it in summer camp. You have to grab the other team's banner and bring it back to your home base.'

Another cloud of aromatic smoke. 'Somehow, Raheem, I don't see you as a camper.'

'I'm not. It was a YMCA camp for kids from the wrong side of Charlotte. Ship us out of the ghetto for two weeks of boredom in the country.'

'Well, I – we . . . a few of us – have been playing a kind of Capture the Flag. Longitudinally.'

'Can you put that in English?'

'Over the last half-century. And we're on the verge of winning.'

The black man finally has both socks back on. He's trying to slip his feet back into his shoes.

'Look, Prof, if you don't come right out and tell me what I'm doing here, I'm taking my marbles and going home.'

The older man sticks the pipe back in his mouth and keeps it there as he talks.

'All right. How much do you know about the Outer Space Treaty of the United Nations?'

'That's easy. Nothing.'

'LBJ, you know who he was, right? He signed that piece of paper in the Oval Office. It forbids countries from "taking celestial bodies as their own" through "claim of sovereignty, by means of occupation, or by any other means." He signed it the exact same day, just a couple of hours after, Gus Grissom and the crew of Apollo 1 burned up on the launch pad in Florida.'

'Sorry to hear it. So?'

'So, he only signed a treaty banning military force in space because he thought NASA was down for the count and the Russians would get there first. Keep them from putting an armed base up there. A month earlier, their Luna 13 spacecraft made a soft landing in the Ocean of Storms and began sending pictures back to earth. Johnson thought they were on the verge of a manned moon landing two years before Apollo.'

Raheem is nearly done retying his laces when the old man adds, 'Now, the shoe is on the other foot.'

For a nanosecond, the younger man, concerned, looks down at his feet. Then he stands up and takes a squishy trial step. Staring down at the man puffing on his pipe, he says, 'LBJ. Apollo 11. Ancient history, man.'

The 'Prof' takes a deep, satisfying pull on his tobacco. 'I taught Ancient History, Raheem. Ancient at least as far as our country is concerned.'

The man with the shaved head walks his still-soaked John Lobbs over to the umbrella stand, creating a squelching noise with each step. He stops and says, 'You're telling me we're doing all this over a scrap of paper and some colored fabric on a stick?'

'That colored fabric on a stick, as you call it, was employed for centuries by European colonial powers to claim a newly discovered territory for themselves. Explorers from England or Spain would plant their flag in the ground and thus signal a particular land and its peoples were theirs. Columbus appropriated the whole of the New World for Spain that way. Balboa laid claim, absurdly, to the entire Pacific Ocean merely by driving *his* sharpened stick with a piece of colored cloth into a Panamanian hill.'

Raheem retrieves his golf umbrella from the stand. The remaining water drips from it on to the floor.

'So, you're saying we own the moon because Neil Armstrong and Buzz Aldrin planted the Stars and Stripes in it?'

The old man takes his pipe out of his mouth and clucks his tongue.

'Haven't you been listening? When we signed that treaty, we agreed, despite Apollo 11 and the flag, that we *don't* own it. However, and here's the beauty part, Raheem.'

The professor uses a couple of fingers to make his point.

'One: Armstrong and Aldrin never left the earth. There *is* no flag in the Sea of Tranquility. Never was. And two: the last Administration pulled us out of that Outer Space treaty, thanks in part to my advice.

'With the treaty null and void, we've been waiting, hoping actually, that some country – any country – would get it into their heads to go to the moon. The Russians, the Chinese, the Mexicans, *any*body. Only then could we *leak* the old footage the Disney people shot, give the White House proof that Apollo was a fake. Force them to stop pissing the space budget away and go for . . .'

He coughs, and looks at his pipe, questioningly, before continuing.

'The problem was, we didn't *have* that proof. The Apollo director, a brilliant young comer back then, thought he was doing the patriotic thing by getting his hands on a few key reels and stashing them away. Keep any one country from militarizing space.'

The black man gives his umbrella a couple of half-openings and closings to shake out the remaining water. 'And that's where I come in?'

'That where you *came* in. I believe you made his acquaintance right at the end of his life.'

The old man knocks the bowl of his pipe into his other palm and then relights it, taking a healthy draw to try getting it started.

'Thanks to you, my boy, the original footage has come to light. So, if we can obtain it and, *meanwhile*, beat the Chinese to the moon, we can prove we just planted Old Glory up there five minutes ago. Then, you and I and 350 million Americans will own the whole damn thing. Military base, American colony, precious minerals to dig up from under the surface. The whole shebang.'

Raheem has been doing a slow burn. Now, he puts down the umbrella and balls up the wet paper towels he's been holding. Vehemently, he says 'Let's get one thing straight, Professor' – he aims for the nearby wastebasket, and throws the soggy mess in with real venom – 'I may work for you, but I'm not your *boy*.'

The old man looks down at his not-working pipe. Then he gets up as well, going over to the wastebasket and tapping the extinguished tobacco on top of the paper towels. He says, 'I'm sorry, Raheem. Turn of phrase.'

'Well, turn off that turn of phrase when you speak to me. I—'

A loud flushing sound comes from the Ladies Room in the far corner of the store. In three quick strides, Raheem makes it to the door just as it opens. A balding man, the manager in a Parks Service uniform, comes out with a mop and pail.

The man says, 'Oh, sorry, I didn't know anybody was here. Rain on the tin roof, I guess.'

He leaves the mop in the pail and moves toward the glass case of the souvenir counter. 'You gentlemen customers? We've got flags of every description. Badges, too, from all the services.'

Raheem looks at his older companion with a should-I-wring-his-neck look.

The Professor says, calmly, 'No thanks, we just wanted to dry off a little.'

He takes a small plastic pouch from his jacket pocket, unbuttons it, and extracts a plastic rain hat. Putting it on his head, he says in that Germanic rumble of his, 'And now we are.'

Raheem picks up his damp golf umbrella and they walk toward the door of the souvenir stand. It's still raining. The black man steps outside and touches the umbrella's mechanism one more time, snapping it all the way open. Then he holds the door for his companion.

'Thank you, Raheem.'

They stand under the overhang.

Agitated, the man with the shaved head says, 'Think he heard anything?'

'How would I know? I'm the one wearing the hearing aids.' Then the Professor carefully pockets his empty pipe before saying, 'No, I don't.'

The younger man is still agitated. 'OK, I gotta ask: What's the point of kidnapping a dog only to exchange it for a bunch of film they've already made copies of? I don't get it.'

The Professor smiles. '*Digital* copies, my . . . good man. I've already planted the idea that the whole "faked moon" thing is just so much digital trickery.'

'But, arguing they're fake means there's been a *real* flag up there this whole time. Isn't that just the opposite?'

The old man sighs audibly, despite the rain tattooing the overhang. 'You know how guns work, Raheem, right? I know committees.' He puts a hand on the taller man's shoulder. 'Every committee needs a Devil's Advocate, someone to punch holes in what the majority wants to do. I'm the local Devil's Advocate, licensed to practice here in Washington since Nixon brought me down from New Haven.'

He grins that Cheshire grin. 'I give them something to debate, a point of view they will then work hard to refute. Make them feel they've exhausted all the options. And then, when it suits me, I give in. Gracefully.'

He pats the black man's shoulder. 'In any case, Dark Side *has* to go, because we're going to hitchhike on it.'

'But . . . help me out here . . . what do I do about the animal? He bit one of the kids, nearly broke the skin. And we're almost out of dog food.'

'The dog? Make the exchange. Give it back.'

'Christ, why didn't you say that in the first place?'

Before going their separate ways, the Professor gestures toward the Vietnam Memorial. 'You know what was here years ago, long before George and the others were killed?'

'No. What?'

'The old Navy Department building. A maze of corridors, thrown up in a rush during the Second World War. You never knew if you were coming or going.'

Raheem takes the man's hand and shakes it firmly. 'I do. I'm going. Got a train to catch.'

He begins to walk away and then stops. He has to yell over the rain to be heard.

'I didn't need to play *Black Ops*. I *am* Black Ops.'

The old man has cupped his hand around his ear. Now he drops it to his side and nods before walking off toward Constitution

Avenue. Under his breath, Dr Otto Kurzweil chuckles and says, 'That's why I chose you, Raheem.'

That night, the local TV stations run film of a District police spokesperson announcing a 'vigorous investigation' into the murder of a Parks Service employee who was strangled in the men's room of his own gift shop.

TWENTY-EIGHT
China Central Television HQ, East Third Ring Road, Beijing

P en in hand, Ying Lianbo angrily stabs at the back-up script on the desk in front of her in the moments before the camera's red light goes on. A quick glance at her TelePrompTer has shown the anchorperson yet another mangled English-language idiom in the story she's about to read. Looking up at the TelePrompTer technician, the woman snaps, 'Scroll down to paragraph two.'

'We can't.' He points to the big clock on the newsroom wall. 'Only twelve seconds to air.'

'Do it or it's your ass, chucklehead!' *How's that for an English-language idiom?*

The simpleton just stands there and asks in Chinese, 'What's a chucklehead?'

Li allows herself a deep sigh. As usual, she'll have to correct the copy on the fly. The news – especially in the case of major breaking stories when speed is of the essence – is written by Chinese speakers on the twentieth floor and then hurriedly translated into English, French, Spanish, Russian, Korean, and Arabic, the six different tongues that correspond to CCTV's six foreign-language channels. So, idioms like 'high, *thick*, and handsome' to describe the Long March rocket's vapor trail still find their way on to the screen of the English-language TelePrompTer, her goddamn PrompTer, here on thirty-one.

Li knows, because her English and American friends have kidded her about it, that it makes her sound like an uneducated *xiāngbālǎo* from the countryside. Worse, the two ninnies who share Chinese-to-English translation duties must both be real ass-kissers. Or some big shot's relations. So, her complaints about them always fall on deaf ears.

Three. Two. One. Red light on. Another deep prolonged sigh, this time on-air.

'The China National Space Administration announced today the successful launch of a Long March 4 rocket and separation of its *Queqiao* satellite, a relay module expected to arrive in lunar orbit two days from now.

'As you can see from this footage, the Long March – latest in the family of rockets named for the glorious people's uprising led by Chairman Mao in the 1940s – created a high, wide, and handsome vapor trail as it disappeared into the skies above the Xichang Satellite Launch Center in Sichuan province.

'The *Queqiao*, or "Moon Bridge," is an advanced 400-kilogram satellite that will "park" itself one hundred kilometers above the surface of the moon, so as to improve communications between Beijing and our intrepid adventurers once they arrive in the Sea of Tranquility in a few weeks' time.'

Now, liftoff footage is replaced by animation. A silver-colored ball on screen starts sending and receiving transmissions – depicted by a series of tiny arrows streaming to and from it – toward both the nearby moon and the distant earth. Reading ahead, Li spots a typo coming up on the screen. She mentally changes 'shipping' to 'shopping.'

'The American astronomer Neil DeGrasse Tyson has described parking a satellite in this way as trying to keep "a barely balanced shopping cart atop a steep hill." Even so, the benefits outweigh the problems, because the Moon Bridge all but eliminates the outages caused by lunar hills and craters, as last year's unmanned mission to the far side proved. And it will provide sufficient bandwidth for the high-definition video our brave crew will be transmitting back to us from Tranquility.'

With that, two little animated flags, one the Chinese Five-Star Red Flag and the other the American Stars and Stripes, appear side by side on the lunar surface.

Of the dozen or so people watching the international feed in a darkened room halfway around the globe, one gives voice – in a Carolina drawl – to what the others are thinking.

'Suckuhs!'

TWENTY-NINE

Ellington Field Joint Reserve Base, Houston

t's dead quiet in the early-morning shuttle taking Gary and the dozen other candidates on the ten-minute ride from the Space Center north along Route 3 to the airstrip at Ellington Field. Whatever Ralph, Cassie, and the others are thinking, they're keeping it to themselves. Or maybe they're still asleep, dreaming of flying like birds.

Yesterday was definitely for the birds. And if it was a dream, the session in the Altitude Chamber was a bad one. A trainer named Barb – thank God for her – led him into a room that reminded Gary of a recording studio, the kind they have back in New York for TV commercial post-production work. She had him sit on a bench and fitted him with a space helmet hooked up to air-intake hoses. Then she sat down next to him.

'Bert,' she said, speaking into her own mic so he could hear her over the sound of the air coming and going from his helmet, 'we can simulate several different things in this hyperbaric lab. But don't worry, today is just about the oxygen.'

She then gave a hand signal, and the staff on the other side of a glass window – they call themselves 'mixologists,' like high-end bartenders – began reducing the oxygen in his helmet little by little, as if he were flying a plane into the upper reaches of the atmosphere.

Gary found himself getting lightheaded in a hurry. He compensated by taking in more air with faster gulps, but the dizziness just got worse. Barb leaned in closer and put a calming hand on his thigh. Her soothing voice in his earpiece said, 'When humans are confronted with certain stressful situations, there's a tendency to breathe too rapidly, to hyperventilate.

'I can see you're feeling it now. So, Bert, the thing is, breathe slower, not faster. It's counter-intuitive, I know, but shallow, slowed-down breathing reduces your need for oxygen. Try it.'

He did. Although the lowered oxygen level was affecting his brain and his thinking, he knew he was going to do anything Barb told him to in order to survive the morning. And then, a little over forty minutes later, the training was over, the helmet off, and the oxygen plentiful. And that's merely the test you have to pass to make it on to this van.

The driver pulls up at a blue and white Boeing 727 with a huge *ZERO-G* logo painted on the side. Parked nearby is one of those luggage vans the airlines use on the tarmac, its doors lifted open on both sides. Gary can see blue jumpsuits hanging on a bar inside. A strip of blue carpeting leads from the van to the plane. The pilot and her crew are waiting at the foot of the plane's portable stairway.

The pilot says, 'Good morning, folks, and welcome back. For most of you, this will be a refresher trip, so let's make it a fun one.'

Then she looks directly at Gary.

'And, speaking for the entire Zero-G Corporation . . . welcome to my world, Mr Forrester. May I call you Bert?'

'Yes, Bert's fine.'

'And I'm Helaine Swarbrick, Lainie to you, your captain and tour guide.'

She touches her cap in a kind of salute.

'OK, everybody, grab yourself a jumpsuit and slip it on over what you're wearing. We don't want any loose buckles or what-have-you screwing up your joyride. Then you know the drill . . . take the plastic pack of blue Zero-G booties out of the hip pocket of the suit and put them on, leaving your shoes in our van. Once you're all dressed for the occasion, follow the blue carpet and join me upstairs.' She indicates the plane's door at the top of the portable steps.

Gary can feel new, bigger butterflies flitting around the pit of his stomach, joining the ones still hanging around from yesterday's low-oxygen prep day. He didn't volunteer for this roller coaster ride in the ionosphere; he didn't volunteer for any of this. Wearing the blue size medium jumpsuit with the Zero-G logo over the pocket and trying to look like he belongs, Gary follows the candidates across the carpet and up the plane's stairs, pausing at the top to take his first look inside the converted passenger jet.

Built a lot like the Delta that flew him down to the Walshes in Florida, its insides have been stripped to the bone. The overhead panels that usually hold air vents, call buttons, and the like have been removed along with all but a few rows of the standard seats. What's left is a completely padded fuselage – not a window anywhere – with Floating Zones marked off by silver, blue, and gold tape, designed to allow free movement for up to a dozen individuals each. Grab lines run along the fuselage walls on both sides of the Floating Zones. An oversized video screen is built into the bulkhead behind the cockpit.

'Don't worry, it's all washable,' Lainie says at his elbow, grinning.

Once Gary is strapped in with the others, Lainie introduces her three crew members: there's co-pilot Max, a steward named Stewart, and a nurse named Melanie. Stewart and Melanie begin handing out wrist sensors that fasten with Velcro straps. Melanie tells Gary, 'The mini-GPS in the wristband registers your body position throughout each of the fifteen parabolas.'

He raises a Velcro-covered wrist to catch Lainie's attention. 'I don't . . . that is, parabolas?'

She gives him a sly grin. 'The good news, Bert, is that this is a movie flight.' Then she uses a remote to switch on the video monitor recessed into the forward cabin wall. 'The rest of you, at ease, unless you like reruns.'

An image of Lainie Swarbrick herself comes on the screen, like one of those Fasten Seatbelt tutorials they play on United or American. Her video self says, 'You're watching me in a state-of-the-art, weightlessness-generating machine, G-Force One.

'From the very beginning in the 1950s, NASA knew its test pilots would have to conquer weightlessness if they were to conquer space. So, for the next half-century, they simulated a zero-gravity environment by taking would-be astronauts up in high-altitude planes' – her image is replaced by that of a cartoon airplane taking off from the ground and flying in an up-and-down series of parabolic arcs – 'and dropping the plane, and its human cargo again and again before returning to earth.'

The video Lainie returns to the screen.

'NASA terminated its in-house Zero Gravity Research Program a few years ago, licensing Zero-G instead to conduct all astronaut training in the Boeing aircraft you're sitting in.

'Now, at the start of each maneuver, you'll feel G-forces equal to 1.8 times earth's gravity. In other words, if you're lying down in one of the Floating Zones, you'll be pinned to the floor by your extra weight. Then, nearing the top of the parabola and over the hump, there'll be about twenty-five seconds of weightlessness – including the dive down from 32,000 to 24,000 feet – for every minute or so of flight. Thank you for your kind attention.'

The on-screen version of their pilot turns as if to go, and then turns back. 'I almost forgot: the nickname . . . you're sitting in the Vomit Comet. Would you cover that for me please, Lainie?'

The flesh-and-blood Lainie Swarbrick salutes her on-screen avatar, who salutes back before the video comes to an end.

The pilot, standing next to the screen, says rhetorically, 'Why does that woman always dump this on me?' Then she turns to face Gary.

'OK. Bert, extensive studies done by NASA show that anxiety contributes most to passengers' airsickness, whether they're aboard my plane or a commercial aircraft. For some people, about a third of the population, the stress on their bodies – or rather, the removal of gravitational stress – creates a sense of panic and causes them to become violently ill, another third feel queasy, and a final third will experience no adverse effects at all.'

Gary says, 'And by "ill," you mean puking.'

'Hence the name. But don't worry. We've deliberately scheduled this training session before breakfast. And Melanie has an ample supply of Scopolamine if you do feel discomfort. Tell me, do you ever get seasick on a boat?'

'Not that I recall. My dad was a good sailor. Maybe I get it from him.'

'Let's hope so. It's a lot more fun without the upchuck. Now, any other questions before we take off?'

'None that I can think of.'

'Then,' she says, giving the passengers her brightest smile, 'it's up, up, and away time.'

Lainie and Max disappear inside the cockpit to take the controls. With everyone strapped in, the plane revs its engines and Lainie's voice comes on over the intercom.

'All right, everyone, this will be your last training flight for a while, so do whatever takes your fancy up there. Stewart will be available to take videos and stills for your memory book, and for your instructors to scrutinize.'

The plane begins to lift off the runway. As though she were reading his mind, she adds, 'And, Bert, you know how they say the real test comes when "the rubber meets the road?" They're wrong. It's when the rubber leaves the road, like it just did!'

Soon, at the point when commercial pilots turn off the Fasten Seat Belt sign, she comes back on. 'Hi, everyone. We're still climbing to 24,000 feet before leveling off for a bit, so keep your belts on a little longer. While you wait, Zero-G has supplied us with a new, ninety-second piece featuring our commercial clients. Maybe you'll recognize someone.'

With that, the monitor begins playing a video with a soundtrack supplied by the 5th Dimension singing, predictably, 'Up, Up and Away.'

The presentation begins with someone Gary doesn't recognize. According to the crawl along the bottom of the screen, he's Keith Urban, a country singer and Nicole Kidman's husband. He does a forward roll in the blue section, with the chyron at the bottom quoting him as saying, 'When you're floating in the air, and you can do somersaults and back flips, it's a pretty wild experience.' Apparently, he made the flight to promote a record album called, *Defying Gravity*.

Urban gives way to Martha Stewart, of all people, followed by a pro skateboarder and, incredibly, Apollo 11's Buzz Aldrin. The big finale shows the late physicist Stephen Hawking, released at last from his wheelchair, zooming around the gold section. The quote beneath his vignette reads, 'It was amazing. The zero-G part was wonderful, and the high-G part was no problem. I could have gone on and on.'

Well, if Stephen Hawking could do it.

THIRTY
Manhattan's Upper West Side

Roger Greenwald knows he should be thinking about the important stuff, Armstrong the dog and how to get him back. Not the great parking spot he just vacated on 88th Street. But he can't help it, he's a New Yorker. The old Volvo wagon could have stayed there till Thursday before he'd have to move it. Why do they even have alternate-side-of-the-street parking, anyway? They sure as hell don't do any alternate-side-of-the-street cleaning.

He thinks, 'C'mon, Roger, focus.' Yeah, but a spot like that, right across from the house? Gold, that's what it is.

Twenty-five minutes of his life lost crossing and recrossing the Upper West Side. Dammit! And then he sees a cream-colored hatchback pulling out of a space on the left just before Riverside goes two-way at 125th Street. Roger steps on the gas and neatly beats out a VW driver with the same idea. Ta da!

After two or three forward and reverse moves to wedge the wagon, barely, into the parking place, the lawyer exits the car. He moves around to the back and lifts the Volvo's tailgate just enough to slide out the shopping cart, the one the film cans arrived in. He sets it on its wheels and locks the handle in place. Then, careful not to make his chronic bad back any worse, he takes the large silver cans out of the canvas sack one at a time and drops them into the wire cart. Finally, he places the sack on top of the stack of cans, adjusts the Mets cap so it's neatly covering his bald spot, and closes the hatch.

Roger trundles the cart behind him for a block and a half on the Hudson River side of the Drive before he finds the cement pathway into the park, right where the instructions said he would. You don't want to be caught in Riverside Park at night, not if you're wearing a Rolex. It crosses his mind that he should have left it in the car. But, anyway, it's not that bad; there's still light out at eight thirty in early June. So, the thieves won't be up and about yet. Dognappers? Another story.

Less than a minute of pulling the cart along the path brings him to a stretch of cobblestones in front of the entrance to Grant's Tomb. Or more formally, the General Grant National Monument, as it says on the plaque from the National Register of Historic Places, sitting here on a pedestal.

Roger's mind refuses to stay fixed on the task at hand. Instead, it wanders off to the trick question those third-graders, the wise guys, used to ask at school: 'Who's buried in Grant's Tomb?' Aha, question answered. The helpful people at the National Register say the correct answer is Grant *and* Mrs Grant. Now, if only he could go back to Meadowlawn Elementary and shove that answer right down Jeffrey Grabel's throat, the little know-it-all.

Roger has focus pills back at the house. He's thinking he should have taken one. Or two. He's thinking, 'Pippa's depending on me. So are the girls.'

He can see the closest waste receptacles, two of them side by side, are right where they're supposed to be, over there at the edge of the cobbled area under the trees. But the uneven cobblestones make schlepping the cart over to the cans a major production.

Thirty seconds later he's standing by the cans. They're identical, except one is green and the other's blue. Neither one has that white triangle decal thingy with the arrows. So, which is the recycling one?

He says it out loud. 'Hey, guys, which is the recycling one?'

The voice that comes back from the tiny microphone/speaker under the collar of his shirt says, 'Blue. Blue is for recycling.'

Roger looks skyward. 'Thanks, guys.'

The voice in his shirt says, 'And you're wearing the cap the wrong way. They said backwards.'

He looks up again. 'Roger that.'

He twists the cap around so the bill and the logo are in back, the way the kids wear them. Another glance up. 'Like this?'

The disembodied voice, slightly exasperated, says, 'And stop looking up! We don't want them tipped off to the drone.'

Roger lifts the lid of the blue receptacle and lets it hang off the back. Then he takes the canvas bag out of the shopping cart and spreads it open before dropping it into the mostly empty bin. Lifting each silver can out of the cart, careful once more to use his knees and not his back, he gently lets it fall into the bag. When all seven are in the recycling bin, he flips the blue plastic cover back up. Then he folds up the cart and, carrying it under his arm, walks back the way he came.

As soon as he steps out of the park, Roger's cell phone rings. He puts down the shopping cart and looks at the screen. Caller ID blocked. He presses the green phone icon and says, 'This is Roger Greenwald.'

A muffled voice, a man's, says, 'Cross Riverside.'

Roger says, 'And what do I do after that?'

The voice on the phone says, 'Head downtown. We're watching you. We'll call you back when we're sure no one is following.'

'No one is. I promise.'

'So you say.' The caller clicks off.

Now his shirt collar speaks up. 'We heard that. Just do what they say.'

'Roger wilco,' he tells his shirt.

The lawyer waits for a couple of cars to pass before crossing to the east side of Riverside just above 123rd. He looks down at the empty cart he's holding and wonders if he should have dropped it off the two blocks uptown at the car. No, better do exactly what they said.

He heads south, crossing West 123rd.There are wooded parks on both sides of Riverside Drive right here, and the overhanging trees on this, the eastern side, are filtering out most of what's left of the twilight. Can the drone even see him? His phone rings again.

The voice says, 'OK. Continue the way you're headed. You're almost there.'

This time, the caller doesn't disconnect. Which is a problem, because Roger's phone starts vibrating with another incoming call. A client, maybe?

The call-waiting screen says, 'R. Forrester.' Someone working on the Rome deal?

Into the phone, Roger says, 'I have another call.'

The voice says, 'What?'

Roger says, 'It may be important.'

The dognapper says, 'No, moron, *this* is important.'

'I'm putting you on hold; I'll be right back.'

The voice, angry now, says, 'If you put me on hold, fuckuh, you'll never see your goddamn pooch again!'

'But—'

Roger's shirt collar butts in. 'Stay with the call, you idiot!'

The man on the phone says, 'Hey, is there someone there with you? We said to come alone!'

Rattled, Roger has stopped walking a few steps short of West 123rd. Across the street sits the massive stone edifice of Riverside Church, its Gothic Revival rear entrances deep in shadow.

'No, there's no one here with me. Not actually.'

The man on the phone says, 'Not *actually*? What the hell does that mean? Don't fuck with me, fuckah!' There's that Carolina twang again. 'Are you alone, numb-nuts, or aren't you?'

Roger stands there, unable to walk or talk. Then the Call Waiting message on his phone's screen goes dark. Shit.

The phone voice waits another moment or two and then he says, 'Fuck it! Life's too short for this kind of . . . Look, your fuckin' dog's tied to the knob of the back door of the church across the street! Have a nice day, motherfuckah!'

THIRTY-ONE

Planetary Analog Test Site, Johnson Space Center

Next morning, half a mile southwest of the Gilruth Center on the vast Space Center grounds, Gary is stumbling around the 'Rock Yard' training course. He's still alive. In fact, not only didn't he embarrass himself during yesterday's fifteen barrel rolls, he got a huge kick out of them.

During the last few parabolas, he let himself go for a change, doing all manner of back flips and crazy moves. He even got Stewart to take a video of him seemingly standing on his head in the Vomit Comet for Pippa's benefit. Even better, no vomit. None.

Today's challenge takes place on the ground in the section of the Space Center officially designated JSC Area 268a. Its square mile of terrain has been manufactured to mimic that of the moon in one quadrant of the field and Mars in another. With artificial hills and craters covered in a thick, heavy dust, the site is used for testing vehicle and spacesuit design. It's also the place where the Dark Side team will train to navigate the lunar surface without any light to guide them, thanks to specially designed virtual reality headsets.

The astronaut candidates are all wearing them right now. Unlike night-vision lenses that amplify the available light, these VR goggles allow the wearer to scan the landscape while reducing even the strongest daylight in increments: by a half, three-quarters, or all the way on down to near-total darkness, the level they're set on now.

Incorporating over-the-ear headphones, the headset also blocks out the other dozen candidates, men and women, who are groping their way over the 'lunar' surface as they chart their own course around the man-made obstacles. Worse, the goggles are programmed to mask the actual surface by adding digital rises and dips to the land as it appears on their screens. Gary has just stubbed his toe on an unseen rock when the call comes over his earphones.

'Robert Forrester, you have a priority call. Remove your headgear and return to base.'

Gary continues to work his way around a particularly imposing crater when the intercom crackles again. 'Bert Forrester, priority call. Return to base now.'

That 'Bert' reminds Gary Stephens that he's Robert Forrester. He unsnaps the VR helmet, revealing the crazy, sunlit environment he's been struggling to negotiate. Nearby, two of his fellow wanderers have made it to the top of the crater wall and are heading down the other side. A hundred yards away, a woman is waving to him from the shed that serves as the Rock Yard's lunar base. Her voice speaks to him over the helmet headphone in his hand.

'This way, Mr Forrester. You have an urgent call.'

When he approaches the shed, the NASA official, a thirty-something redhead whose sewn-on nametag reads *Chabot*, reaches out for the plastic name card attached to Gary's breast pocket and flips it around so she can read it.

'"Forrester." Check. Come with me.'

She hustles him into an all-terrain vehicle for the half-mile ride back to Command Headquarters. As she floors it, Chabot says, 'Maybe I'm like the fortieth person to ask but, if your name is Robert, why not Robbie or something cute?'

'I don't know. My friends started calling me Bert in school and I guess it stuck.'

'OK, Bert,' she shouts over the whine of the ATV's engine. 'At least one of your friends must be pretty high up. Nobody's ever been pulled off the Rock Yard for a phone call.'

When the elevator doors open on Level 6 of the Space Center Command, Gary and his escort Chabot head for the Director's office. They walk past a knot of people milling around in the executive conference room, waiting for a meeting to start. The venetian blinds are up along the glass wall that faces the elevators and Gary can see Robin's in there, pouring herself a fresh coffee from the silver urn in the far corner.

Through Hensen's open door, Gary spots the young FBI agent with the blond mustache, the one at Reagan Airport who sat in on the phone call from Pippa and Roger. Corrigan, he said he was. And there's a light-skinned black man sitting next to him, writing something down in a lined yellow pad. Gary doesn't recognize him from the back of his head.

'Bert, I'm glad Renée found you!' Hensen calls out from her desk. 'Would you join us, please? And Renée, if you don't mind, please tell them we'll be in there in a couple of secs.'

Chabot peels off toward the conference room, leaving Gary to walk into Hensen's office as 'Bert.' The charade lasts only until the door automatically closes behind him.

'Gentlemen, this is Gary Stephens, the man who started all of this. Gary, you've already met Agent Corrigan. And this is his colleague, Special Agent Tayshaun Griggs. I asked him to join us. He just flew in from Quantico.'

Even as handshakes are being exchanged, the Director points to the chair between the two men. 'Have a seat. Gene and Taye here have good news, sort of. And a couple of questions.'

Gary pulls out the empty chair and sits down.

Corrigan says, 'You'll be happy to know Armstrong's been found. He's safe and sound.'

An intense wave of relief washes over Gary. 'Wow, that *is* good news!'

Lila Hensen adds, 'He's already back with Pippa and Roger.'

Gary tells her, 'I guess I've been more worried than I realized. Army's been through the wars with our family.'

Griggs turns to him and says, 'That's what we need to talk to you about, your family. Specifically, this Roger Greenwald.'

Surprised, Gary says, 'What's to know? Roger's my brother-in-law, the father of my nieces Ashley and Gracie.'

'He's a lawyer, isn't he?' Corrigan asks.

'Wait, is there a problem? Is Roger OK?'

'He's fine,' Griggs says. 'It's your dad's movies. They were the ransom.'

'I don't understand.' Gary slides his chair back a few feet so he doesn't have to keep looking between the two men like someone at a tennis match. 'Did something go wrong?'

Hensen uses the moment to wheel her chair toward the door. She says, 'Why don't I give you some space while I gather the troops together next door? Gene, Taye, join me in the conference room when you're through here.'

She rolls out of the room. The office door closes behind her.

'So,' Gary asks, 'what's the deal with Roger?'

Griggs ignores the question. 'He recently flew to Rome. Any idea why?'

'Business, I guess. Roger's firm has clients all over the place.'

Now it's Corrigan's turn. 'Any of those clients have Russian or Ukrainian ties?'

'I don't, I wouldn't know.' So much for the relief Gary was feeling just moments before. 'What does Roger's work have to do with anything?'

'Nothing, maybe,' Corrigan says.

Gary looks over at the pad Griggs is taking notes in. It's covered with shorthand symbols.

Gary says, 'Wait, what's going on? Are you writing down what I'm saying?'

Griggs puts the pad and pencil down on Hensen's desk. 'Just notes to myself; my memory's awful.'

Corrigan inches in his seat toward Gary. 'Here's the thing: your brother-in-law exchanged the seven cans of film for the dog, left them in a recycling bin the kidnappers, um, dognappers, specified. We had a couple guys on the ground, agents, watching. Plus, an eye-in-the-sky overhead drone. The moment Roger found Army, they took out our agents.'

In his shock, Gary says, 'Took out? You mean killed?'

'Took out, as in chloroformed from behind.' Griggs looks grim when he adds, 'Didn't see a thing.'

Corrigan continues, 'There's a bunch of ways to disable a drone. First and foremost: Shoot it down. The hard part is the getaway when it's a populated area like Riverside Park. Or, you can drop a net on it from another drone. But, too many trees for the net.'

With a hint of professional jealousy, Griggs says, 'The high-tech ways include blinding it with a laser, one of those pens, and jamming its programming with your own programming. We know these guys are pros because, well, they did *both*. And, poof! Seven cans of film disappear into thin air.'

'So, you're saying Roger's to blame?'

'We think he tipped them off to the drone, possibly by mistake. And he stopped right in the middle of the handoff when his phone rang with a call. From you.'

Gary looks from one agent to the other. Is he supposed to say something?

'Yes, I called Pippa while we were eating downstairs, from the iPad they gave me. I wanted to know if they were having any luck finding Army. You know, how the two of them were holding up. And, to be honest, to tell her about my ride on the Vomit Comet. Rub it in a little. She told me Roger was out trying to get Army back. So, I called his cell, but he didn't pick up.'

The FBI agents exchange looks, and Griggs grabs up his pad and pencil to make another note. He says, 'You spell Vomit with an "I?"'

Alarmed, Gary says, 'Look, Roger can be kind of wifty at times. His mind wanders, that sort of thing. But he takes medication for it and he's OK. So, you think, what?'

Corrigan says, 'To be honest with you, Gary, we don't know how any of this adds up. Yet. Look at it our way: A guy discovers a really big secret, the government goes all Code Blue, and then a person or persons unknown steals *your dog* to get the whatever-you-found back in their possession. And they do it, no problem, with the FBI watching. Grabbed the film from us in broad, um, twilight. Film you already made copies of. Does that make sense to you?'

'None of it does.'

The office door opens and Casselmann sticks his head in.

'Are you done with him, fellas? Boss wants you guys next door.'

They all get to their feet.

Casselmann says to Gary, "Not you, ASCAN. Why not sit your butt back down while the grownups talk?"

As they head out of the room, Griggs says to Corrigan, 'One thing's for sure about this business with Army. They got us chasing our tails.'

THIRTY-TWO
The White House South Entrance, Washington, DC

January 20, 1969

A little before noon on a cold, clear winter morning, Senate Minority Leader Everett Dirksen of Illinois emerges from the White House in his official capacity as Congressional escort to the outgoing President and the President-Elect for the short drive up Pennsylvania Avenue to the Inauguration. Lyndon Johnson and Richard Nixon, two former senators, probably could find the Capitol on their own, but tradition must be served.

With the elderly Dirksen, ten years older than he was when he sat on NASA's oversight committee, wedged between the two presidents in the back of the stretch Lincoln Continental – and with a pair of motorcycle riders and eight Secret Service outriders standing in the open doors of two trailing escort vehicles just behind them – Johnson and Nixon have no more than eight minutes to converse before they will emerge from the car to face Dan Rather of CBS, David Broder of *The Washington Post*, and the entire press corps assembled at the foot of the Capitol steps.

Nixon begins. 'Funny how things work out, isn't it, Lyndon? I lose the closest election in history to you and Jack, and yet here I am.'

LBJ leans across the aged Dirksen to say, amiably, 'I lost to Jack as well, at the convention in Los Angeles. And yet here I am.'

Dirksen, still quick-witted at seventy-three, grins and says, 'I've won every one of my elections since 1930. And I'm the only one here who isn't President.'

Johnson puts an affable paw on Dirksen's leg. 'And yet, here you are, Ev. So, I'm gonna include you in a little President-to-President thing.'

At this point Johnson presses a button on the armrest that raises the privacy glass separating the three politicians in back from the Secret Service driver and bodyguard up front. Before the glass is all the way up, the driver hears LBJ say, 'Dick, you're gonna get a call from Roy Disney, and I think you better take it.'

Driving home from the ceremony to Heart's Desire, their ranch-style home in Virginia's horse country, the Dirksens listen to news of Nixon's inauguration on the car's radio. At the wheel, Everett is quiet, as usual. And then, without warning, he switches off the radio.

'Lou, I think something's going on.'

Louella, his wife of more than fifty years, doesn't pick up on the concern in his voice. 'Of course it is. We have a Republican in the White House again. Imagine that!'

After a moment, and with a sigh under his breath, Dirksen turns the radio back on.

THIRTY-THREE
The Director's Conference Room

'Mea culpa, mea culpa, mea maxima culpa. Welcome to the Dark Side mission briefing, part deux, as they say in the movies.'

Lila Hensen is speaking to her assembled troops around the large conference table while gesturing 'come on in' to the FBI agents. They take a couple of seats across from Robin.

Hensen continues, 'It was my idea to go "high tech" over at the Gilruth Center, thinking I could keep this mission undercover without making the folks in the DC area fly in and maybe attract too much attention. Instead, that hacker you saw rode in on one of those pogo sticks.

'We were led to believe she was a top-level security wonk sitting at a desk in Langley, but it was only when that actual person called in to say her feed had gone dark, and when the IT people there confirmed the hack, that a trace was initiated.

'We don't know if she's connected to the people who just grabbed the seven cans of film that were shot in Hollywood. They're working on it. The good news, if there is any, is that our technical people in Virginia are good. Very good. I believe you may have noticed the woman being apprehended by our, uh, support staff.'

Jack Maybin asks, 'And the bad news, as if we need any more?'

Hensen is immediately serious. 'The bad news is that, now, a few of the wrong guys know what we're doing, when we're doing it, and why. If we weren't locked in to the launch window we've got, of course we'd postpone. But we can't. So, I've asked FBI agents Gene Corrigan and Tayshaun Griggs – you'll remember him as the *smart* pogo-stick guy – to join us in person for the briefing.'

The two men nod to the others.

She gestures around the table with a wave of her hand. 'With us tonight, without going through another round of introductions, are Deputy Beuerlein, reps from each of our civilian space partners, and Leah Davis from FBI HQ.'

The black woman from the White House Situation Room is sitting between Robin and Maybin. She gives the others a tight, professional smile.

Davis says, 'The President wants a filmed image of the flag in place up there, one we can backdate fifty years and leak to the press if we have to. Just in case the bad guys who stole the original sound-stage footage in New York try to use it against us.'

The Director takes another sip of water before picking up the thread. 'And now, for a little more bad news. All NASA leaves are cancelled until our expected splashdown back on earth on July 7. All vacations too. We're applying a full-court press starting right now until we hit the button that says Mission Accomplished. Got it?'

The crestfallen looks around the table tell her everything Hensen needs to know. Kirk Casselmann takes it upon himself to speak for the room.

'Got it, ma'am.'

The small, dark-skinned man with a pile of loose-leaf folders in front of him, the one whose image appeared on one of the VGo robots in the Gilruth Center and was introduced as Dr Sheth, coughs to get her attention. When she nods to the man, he speaks with a British accent.

'From my company's point of view, Director, we believe yours is, well, an overly optimistic schedule.' He pronounces it 'shedule.'

Hensen pulls on the middle finger of her right hand with her left, cracking the knuckle. 'What makes you say that, Deepak?'

He slides the top folder over to her and places the others in the middle of the table. Everybody takes one. The logo of a company called Moon Express is embossed on the cover that Gary picks up.

Deepak says, 'The top summary page is our timetable for the rover's delivery. The items in green have been signed off by your people. Those in red, not as yet.'

A woman wearing a NASA badge three places along from Gary says, defensively, 'There's no delay coming from our side, Dr Sheth.'

'I didn't say there was, Ms Dorneles.'

He smiles and briefly pulls on his earlobe. 'The column to the right summarizes the days we estimate remain for each module to pass through our final safety testing. That last item, the polymer lithium battery that powers our rover, is still—'

Robin looks up from reading ahead. 'Thirty-nine days away? Sir, how can that be?'

Unruffled, the man continues. 'Both alkaline and lithium-ion batteries degrade in extreme heat and cold. As I'm sure you know, Captain, when the sun goes down the surface of the moon can drop as low as 173° below zero on the centigrade scale, colder by far than any reading ever recorded on earth. More to the point where Dark Side is concerned, it can reach 127° Celsius in sunlight. Of course, *we* have an atmosphere and our moon does not.'

Something about the man's calm demeanor is maddening. Hensen says, 'And the batteries, Deepak?'

He tugs on his earlobe again but his voice betrays no stress. 'Quite. You chose Moon Express *because* of our battery. And because Dark Side proposes' – here he turns to Robin – 'that, after landing, you traverse the surface for four-plus hours at the rover's top speed of just under ten kilometers an hour in order to rendezvous at Tranquility, spend an hour there, and then drive another four-plus hours back to liftoff. That makes at least ten hours on a single charge. No other battery in production anywhere in the world can provide that kind of vehicular power in that kind of environment on one charge.'

He places his palms flat on the table. 'Quite frankly, neither can ours. Yet. We've achieved eight hours and a fraction in our limited-gravity room, but—'

'You promised us twelve, Deepak.'

He turns to face Hensen. 'True, Director. What did you say at the beginning of this briefing? "Mea culpa, mea maxima culpa." But, we have a suggestion.'

'Yes?'

'If your esteemed crew will land closer to Tranquility, say thirty-five kilometers away rather than the site you currently propose that's over fifty, we could deliver the rover and its battery next week. Fully tested and with nearly a two-hour margin of safety.'

Another NASA department head, a man with an obvious comb-over whose badge reads *Goldfarb*, says, 'Every location three or even four hours from rendezvous is either in a crater with steep walls or on an exposed highland. They'll spot us with their cameras if we land on level ground any closer than where we currently put down.'

Sheth turns both palms face up on the table, 'Understood, Lew. I was just putting it out there.'

'And I'm putting *this* out there,' Hensen says, curtly. 'I'm not having my people sit on the moon in harm's way. How long will it take you to deliver at least a ten-hour battery, Deepak? I'm talking balls to the wall.'

For the first time, the man seems embarrassed. 'Our best estimate, keeping in mind your colorful phrase, is a schedule push-back of at least two weeks.'

'Two weeks!' Casselmann bangs the table with his fist to under-score his point, spilling coffee from the cup of the woman sitting next to him.

Hensen smiles grimly. 'Thank you, Kirk. We all appreciate your eagerness to get going.'

To Deepak, she says, 'Two weeks? I'm gonna hold you to that.' She starts to gather up her things. 'I have to go up the chain with this unwelcome news. The briefing is adjourned. Again!'

With that, she drops the briefing documents in her lap and rolls her chair toward the door. Over her shoulder she says, 'Renée, call downstairs and have the van take our visitors back to their hotels.'

THIRTY-FOUR

Federal Detention Center, D Street SE, Washington, DC

There are worse places to be jailed, Anya thinks to herself, not for the first time. The food is all right, and it comes three times a day. She looks down at the remains of the supper finished hours ago but not yet taken away. The printed sheet called it 'gumbo.' She uses her spoon to push through what's left of the rice. Those tiny pieces, the only ones that taste like anything, must be shrimp. Or crab. Or . . . what else do the Americans add to gumbo? Sausage? The only drawback is that whatever it is gets caught between your teeth.

She laughs to herself. Nothing in the prison food back in Chelyabinsk could ever get caught in your teeth. What wasn't water looked and tasted like water. At best, it was potato water.

Of course, there are always drawbacks in any situation. Isolation from the other prisoners here means the only exercise you get is when you walk from the mattress to the toilet to the door with the bars in it and back to the mattress. Seventeen steps if you make them little ones.

The other, more important, thing about solitary is you can't be sure that what you got by hacking into the briefing was enough for your contacts to act on. Or that it went where it's supposed to go.

They could use the screen shots she managed to send off of the people in the room, run it through some facial recognition software, maybe, and deduce all the players that way. Still, that's always the field agent's lot, the not knowing. Even if the 'field' is just a desk and a chair.

She feels a quick pang of something. Regret? Yes, regret, calling for help the way she did. Now, to the four walls she yells, '*Pomogite!*'

Nothing. Nobody running to the rescue. There's no 'help' to be had in solitary. Not in English-speaking America.

Was that a bird that just flew by the window? Something did, but now the view out of it, set so high in the wall you can't see down, is just black, unending American sky. How long has it been since she's seen anything other than clouds? There was the Anacostia River she glimpsed through the steel mesh of the van's window, the van that brought her here six days ago. And the cemetery for Washington big shots the driver pointed out a couple of blocks to the south.

He said someone named J. Edgar Hoover is buried there, the Director of the FBI. But, wasn't Hoover President during their Depression? And isn't there a different cemetery for Presidents? Anya's remaining memories from that one year of Soviet-style American History are now so much mental porridge.

Porridge. Which brings her back to food. And the particles of it lodged between her teeth for the last couple of hours. She walks over to the sink hanging from the wall (six small steps) and picks up the little – what did he call it? – 'personal hygiene kit' with the toothbrush and toothpaste and floss inside. Floss for a political prisoner!

The man, in spite of his looks, had been kind. Big, black, with a shaved head. And nice shoes. Said the kits were from some prisoners' aid thing they call the Fortune Society. A better name would be 'Bad Fortune Society.' Literally.

Bedtime. She picks up the toothbrush, squeezes some paste on it from the little tube of Colgate, and gives her teeth a vigorous workout. Back home, the dentistry is so bad you better do everything you can to keep your teeth. So, Anya makes extra sure the shrimp and crab and sausage don't hang around.

When she's through, she rinses off the toothbrush, dries it with several flicks of her wrist, and returns it to the little kit.

Of course, she has no way of knowing that the toothbrush is a special one. With bristles made to wear away just enough in a week of brushing to expose the Polonium-210 inside them. Anya's strenuous efforts have just done the job a little bit faster. In a few minutes she will start to sicken. In a few hours she'll be dead.

They'll find her body in the morning. And no one will know how she was poisoned. Or why.

THIRTY-FIVE
Level Six, JSC

When Hensen rolled out of the room and into the elevator, Sheth and the other civilian vendors followed. So did the NASA department people. Next door, Gary can hear a few of them discussing things while waiting for the elevator. As he gets up to join them, the Director's office door swings open. Robin is standing there.

'Come with me. There's something I've been meaning to give you.'

'Oh?'

She walks back into the conference room and Gary follows.

Beyond the glass wall, a dozen of the participants, including the Director, are packed in the elevator as the doors start to close. The rest of them, all men, are following Casselmann, Modugno, and Maybin down the six flights of stairs in a show of brotherhood. Or eagerness to get to bed.

Robin says, 'I was going to share it with you at the hotel in DC.' She moves over to the cords that control the now empty room's venetian blinds. 'But then we got interrupted.'

With the vestibule area now deserted, Robin lowers the blinds. Then she walks up to Gary and plants a long and loving kiss on his mouth.

When they come up for air, she says, 'Actually, I've been wanting to do that since you snapped that rubber band back on your fingers at Mom's house. You looked . . . crushed.'

'I was.' He wraps his arms around her, pulling her back into an embrace. 'I am.'

She gives him a sly smile and says, 'I've got the remedy for that.' And then she kisses him again.

For a moment he just stands there. Then he begins to run his fingers slowly, tenderly, through her silky blond hair, inhaling the magical mixture of the scent coming from the woman's body and NASA's brand of shampoo.

'You smell delicious. I'm thinking we have a special chemistry.'

'I *know* we do. And I was a Chem major in college.'

He kisses her hair, then her neck where it joins her shoulders, murmuring, 'I haven't felt this way in years.'

She takes a deep breath. 'Neither have I.'

With his hands on her shoulders – an astronaut with soft skin! – he leans back a little to take all of her in. He says, 'This is the point in the evening when the guys asks, "Your place or mine?"'

She puts her hands on her hips, like she's considering it. 'And what's the girl supposed to say?'

He grins at her. 'Either answer is fine by me.'

'Then,' she grins right back, a little mischievously, 'my answer is, your place or mine would capture us both, together, on the closed circuit TV in the living quarters. Fraternization with the astronaut candidates is, uh, definitely frowned upon.'

Seeing the crestfallen look on his face, she says, 'So, ask me again.'

Hesitantly, he asks, 'Uh, your place or mine?'

She moves in close once more. Then she stretches out a hand and runs it along the smooth surface of the conference table.

'What's wrong with right here?'

THIRTY-SIX

A foreign capital in the Middle East

The mentor and his protégé sit in front of their side-by-side Kray supercomputer workstations. Inside the underground bunker built of hardened concrete and steel and buried several stories below the country's Defense HQ, the air hums with the electronic whir coming from the cooling fans in the server farm down the hall.

While the officials working in the building upstairs speak the local language, Osofsky and the younger man, Khinshin, talk to each other, when they need to, in their mother tongue: Russian. But they hardly ever need to. Or want to.

Right now, Osofsky is wolfing down the morning's second *ponchiki* – a kind of fried donut hole filled with farmer cheese and dusted with powdered sugar – while stirring his refill of strong, hot tea and clinking the glass, deliberately to Khinshin's way of thinking, with his steel spoon. So, Khinshin is doing what he always does in return: he's chewing two sticks of imported Orbit wintergreen sugarless gum at the same time as loudly as possible.

Osofsky sees the update first on the terminal in front of him. '*Poslushay, my poluchili udar!*'

Khinshin searches his own screen. 'We got a hit? Where?'

The older man leans around his own terminal to run a bony finger down Khinshin's screen, which shows a long list of digital rocket components sitting in the Chinese National Space Administration's main computer hub in central Beijing.

'There, eighth or ninth one down, the satellite's stabilizer. It's at sixty-two percent shutdown. I knew all that programming would pay off!'

Khinshin should be happy, but the greasy trail of powdered sugar down his computer screen from the old man's finger just makes him more irritated.

'Why not one hundred percent?'

Now it's Osofsky's turn to be irritated. 'How should I know? These subassemblies are made up of smaller subassemblies. Perhaps they already had a patch for one or more of those. Does it matter? All the client wants is a two-week delay; sixty-two percent will more than do the trick.'

Khinshin wets his own finger and runs it over the line of powdered sugar. Then he licks it off his finger and uses his pocket handkerchief to wipe the screen. 'So, why's it called "*Queqiao*" anyway? Doesn't exactly roll off the tongue.'

Osofsky gives his junior partner a sour look. 'It might help if you cracked open a briefing book every now and then. What's the point of all your programming smarts if you don't know why you're doing anything?'

'Hey, old man, I know why I'm doing what I'm doing. For the paycheck. Happy clients mean fat stacks.'

Osofsky gives out with an extra-long sigh. 'OK, Mr Breaking Bad, Mr Pinkman. For your information, the Chinese translate

Queqiao as "Moon Bridge" when they talk to Westerners, but it really means "Bridge of Magpies."'

'Magpies? Like the birds?'

'Like the birds. It's from an old Chinese folktale. On the seventh night of the seventh month of the lunar calendar, magpies form a bridge with their wings to enable Zhi Nu, the seventh daughter of the Goddess of Heaven, to cross and meet her beloved husband, separated from her by the Milky Way.'

Khinshin takes his used-up gum out of his mouth and drops it into the wastebasket at his feet before saying, 'Man, can you believe the crap some people are into?'

'As a matter of fact, I can.'

Osofsky is back to staring at his own screen for more proof that the Stuxnet worm, the improved version of the one they used a decade ago to disable all those Iranian centrifuges, has found its many targets half a world away.

'And don't be so high and mighty about other people's belief systems,' he goes on. 'What about yours?'

'Mine? I believe in math, physics. Real world stuff.'

'Oh? What about the angel of death flying over the Egyptians' homes, taking their first-born sons?'

'I didn't mean—'

'Or lamps with just enough oil to last a day, lamps that go on burning for more than a week? Or the walls of an armed city that come tumbling down when one particular bugler plays a solo on his horn? Don't bullshit me, Alexei. We Jews believe in myths just as weird as any those Chi— oh, look, another hit! *Fantastika*!'

Khinshin pushes his desk chair back and gets up. 'You keep watching, I gotta go and practice my baloney beliefs upstairs for an hour or two. It's Shabbos.'

Osofsky turns in his chair. 'So, which place is it this week?'

'The HaGra on Zakai Street. Do you know it?' Khinshin points up, as if they can see the street from where they're sitting through multiple stories of concrete. 'It's over that way, just a block or two from the Jerusalem Medical Center. I met this girl who goes to the early service there. A real stunner.'

Osofsky, his joints already stiff from sitting for forty minutes, gets up as well. 'Mind if I join you? I—'

And then he notices yet another update on his screen. This one shows the latest hit has been entirely wiped out by the target's antivirus package. Worse, the sixty-two percent effectiveness of their efforts on the *Queqiao*'s stabilizer system has been downgraded to nineteen percent. Not nearly good enough.

'Shite!'

'What?'

Osofsky points to the flashing message on his terminal. 'Wouldn't you know it, they must have hacked the NSA, grabbed the Stuxnet program, and built a defense. It's patching itself automatically as soon as we get in.'

Even before he finishes speaking, the *19* on the screen changes to a *3*. 'See? Shite!'

'Must you be so fucking British with your swearing?'

'You're right. Sorry.' He leans over and puts his mouth to Khinshin's ear. 'Shit, shit, shit! That better?' Then, more to himself than to his co-worker, he says, 'What's the good of malware if you can't use it on anybody?'

He slugs down the last of his tea before adding, 'I blame this on the Americans. I'll bet one of their so-called free enterprise billionaires turned around and sold Stuxnet to the Chinks.'

Khinshin calmly presses Control+S on his keyboard, putting his terminal to sleep. 'Don't be such a Socialist. Besides, this isn't on the Americans.'

'No?'

'No. Act of God, pure and simple. I'm gonna go upstairs and pray He changes His mind so we can get paid all those lovely dead Presidents. But, I'm guessing you've got a call to make.'

At the door that leads to the lift, he adds, 'DC area code is two-oh-two.'

THIRTY-SEVEN
ABC Broadcast Centre, Sydney

July 21, 1969

B ob Conrad puts down the phone. It's too early in the morning to deal with hysterical Sheilas babbling about Coke bottles. Why they ever put the call through to the control room while he was directing the biggest event in Australian television history he'll never know.

The woman was right, of course. Conrad saw it too.

A Coca-Cola bottle *did* roll right through a corner of the image. Or seemed to. But unlike Mrs Ronald, he's pretty sure they don't have Coke on the moon.

The TV director reaches into his pocket and shakes a Rothmans out of the pack. He sticks it in his mouth without lighting it – smoking in the control room is verboten – and considers the possibilities, coming up with two: one complicated and one not.

Complicated first. Thanks to the curvature of the Earth, when NASA planned the moon shoot they commissioned tracking stations be built around the world so Apollo 11 would be always within line of sight of one of them. Hours ago, before the moon dropped below the horizon at the Fresnedillas facility west of Madrid, the techs there had a three-hour window to 'hand off' the job to the Goldstone Observatory in California's Mojave Desert, where the moon was just coming up. Then, two hours ago, with the moon setting in California, it was rising above the western edge of the Pacific here in Australia.

Conrad checks his watch. Twenty minutes ago, Goldstone signed off and the broadcast switched over seamlessly to the Land Down Under and NASA's twenty-six-meter installation at Honeysuckle Creek near Canberra. At least, that was the original idea.

But Conrad, trained as an engineer, knows there's an unintended kink in the system, thanks to Australia's National Science Agency and its own larger, sixty-four-meter receiver at Parkes. Lovingly known to the locals as 'The Dish,' the Parkes Radio Telescope, located on the other side of Strahorn State Forest from the village of Trangie, wasn't intended for spacecraft tracking, so it can't tilt as low to the horizon as Honeysuckle's or come online as early. But its pictures are clearer and less susceptible to the drop-off in quality created by the country's out-of-date collection of coaxial hookups. For the last twenty minutes, Parkes has given Conrad a choice of images for his own national network before sending the signal on to Houston and the world.

Second kink: the so-called national Australian network is really an assembly of a dozen regional sub-networks, each with an on–off switch here in the control room. Maybe, when his assistant Kevin Boyle flipped the first switch – the one for the nearly unpopulated 200-square-mile area of New South Wales Central that includes Trangie – over to the clearer Parkes picture, he picked up a Coca-Cola advert in progress, somehow creating a double image on the screen for that small group of viewers.

The cigarette is getting soggy in his mouth, so Conrad chucks it into the bin. The uncomplicated explanation hits closer to home: someone downstairs in Continuity missed their cue and started running a Coke commercial while the live space feed was still on the air. Conrad promises himself he'll personally kick the butt of the joker responsible when he gets off duty.

In any case, it's a good thing there's a seven-second delay built into the international feed. With that and all that damn lunar dust, Kevin was able to wipe it before anyone else saw it.

On the monitor in front of him, Neil Armstrong is starting his descent. Conrad allows himself a deep sigh. Thank God the fuck-ups were down here and not up there.

THIRTY-EIGHT
Astral Lounge, Building B11, JSC

Long after the steam tables in the cafeteria next door have shut down for the night, the Astral Lounge, the name given by an earlier astronaut class to this combination of student union and G-rated juke joint, is still going strong. If drinking Diet Cokes and playing ping-pong is going strong.

Having survived his third EVA in the training tank this morning, 'Bert' Forrester sits with two of the more accomplished swimmers: Carrie Hasegawa, the one they dropped in the water for his benefit on Day One, and Ralph Lucci, the glove man. They're watching a couple of ASCANs shoot pool at the table ten feet away. Their topic now, though, is the Space Center's food.

Carrie says, 'I think that was swordfish steak, but I can't be sure. The sauce was so overwhelming, it could have been pork.'

Ralph clinks her can of soda pop with his. 'I'll drink to that.' He turns to Gary. 'We're nineteen weeks in, and my taste buds are shot. Everything they give you in space is low sodium, something to do with preventing the osteoporosis in zero gravity. They're gearing us up – though *down* is more like it – to deal with it on an actual mission.'

Gary says, 'I had the chicken, I think, with a giblet gravy. But that could have been pork as well. Pretty bland.'

Carrie clinks Gary's half-finished cup of coffee with her glass. 'Mystery meat! Join the club, Bert. If you're looking for a well-seasoned steak, abandon hope all ye who enter here.'

'Speaking of . . .' Gary takes a sip of his rapidly cooling coffee before asking, 'what made you enter here?'

Carrie smiles. 'Me? I grew up in Montana. Lots of dust, lots of rocks, lots of Jurassic bones in the hills. I was going to be a dinosaur hunter.' She lifts an index finger to the heavens. 'When I found out Mars has dust and rocks and, just maybe, Martian bones, guess I got sidetracked.'

She turns to Ralph. 'How about you, big guy? I never asked what brought you here.'

'Greyhound bus.'

Ralph takes a final swig of his drink. 'But seriously, there was a bumper sticker the guy next door had on this insane car of his, a chopped '39 Chevy Coupe, when I was a kid growing up in New Jersey. "Aim High." Air Force slogan. When I went to college, I needed help paying for my tuition, so I joined Air Force ROTC. I owed them four years anyway, so I became a flyer. I aimed high. And then, that qualified me for this.'

Gary asks, 'See any combat?'

'Nah. By the time I had my hours in and got certified, we'd already pulled back in the two theaters. If you want to know about flying combat, you'll have to ask Jack Maybin.'

'I met him. What's his story?'

Carrie says, 'He's the Air Force John McCain. Shot down over Afghanistan. Shot up as well. Maybin was the Taliban's prisoner for a couple of years. Torture, the whole nine yards.'

Ralph leans in a little and, lowering his voice, says, 'When I said, "ask him about combat," it was, you know, rhetorical. He won't talk about it. Real closed-mouth fucker. Can't blame him, though.'

Carrie says, 'The guy's a real enigma. Which, of course, is catnip to every girl on the base. Including her.'

Carrie is pointing to the three full-fledged astronauts who've just walked in: Maybin, Kirk Casselmann, and Robin Walsh. Gary watches as they grab sodas from a cooler full of ice. Maybin must have said something funny, because Robin turns to him and laughs, putting her hand on his muscled arm and giving it a squeeze.

Ralph says, 'He's worked his way through practically every girl on the base.'

To which, in the voice of a Betty or a Veronica from the *Archie* comics, Carrie adds, 'We all think he's *dreamy*!'

With that, she and Ralph crack up in hysterics. Their sudden burst of laughter causes one of the pool players, Marty Bienstock – the guy who gave Gary such a hard time at the buoyancy tank that first day – to completely mess up his break shot. He looks over at the laughing trio and decides Gary's the one to blame.

He says, 'Wouldn't you know? The mystery man, fucking Forrester,' with an edge to his voice.

Carrie picks up on the thought. 'NASA's just full of mysteries
. . . the meat, the men.' She breaks into a grin. 'He's right, you
know: you're Bert Forrester, our Man of Mystery. You never told
us; what's the deal with the late arrival? Or is it classified?'

'Yeah, man.' From the pool table ten feet away, Marty's voice
has a confrontational edge to it. 'I'd loved to have skipped the
pushups and the miles of roadwork these last couple of months.
Who'd you brown-nose to get here?'

Gary takes a gulp from what's left of his cold coffee, trying to
come up with a response, trying to think. But, something about the
way Robin is looking at Jack across the room, the way she's touching
him, is messing with him. What the fuck?

He's still trying to deal with the bile that jerk Marty brought up
while searching for a way to mold the fishing-off-Wellfleet story
into something he can say a second time when the three astronauts
head for the door to the Limited Area Elevators. Robin looks this
way and, noticing Gary, says something to her companions before
walking over.

'Hey, Carrie, Ralph,' she smiles, 'introduce me to your friend. I
don't think I've seen him around before.'

Ralph says, 'Robin Walsh, this is Bert Forrester, our newest
ASCAN. Bert, this is Captain Walsh, our role model.'

She smiles at Ralph and says, 'Watch out, Carrie. This guy . . .'

Then she holds out her hand to Gary. 'Nice to meet you, Curt.'

He rises from his seat. They make eye contact ever so briefly.
He says, 'It's Bert.'

'Sorry, it's so noisy in here. "Bert." Got it.'

Then she turns on her heel to rejoin Jack and Kirk, leaving Gary
in a half-sitting, half-standing position.

Marty has overheard the introduction. Now he says, 'Curt
Forrester. Yeah. Think I'll call you that from now on.' As if to
punctuate the point, he reaches up with his cue stick and viciously
slides all the scoring counters on the overhead string to his side of
the table.

Carrie continues to find the humor in the situation. 'Well, Curt,
what do they say in those Head & Shoulders commercials? "You
never get a second chance to make a first impression."'

Ralph says, 'Yeah. Good luck with that. And her.'

THIRTY-NINE

Approaching Qinglan Harbor, Hainan, China

Half a nautical mile from Hainan island, where the South China Sea mixes with the outflow from Gaolong Bay, the water is supposed to change color from midnight blue to turquoise. At least, that's what the Ops doc says. But now, practically midnight on a moonless evening, it could be hot pink for all Rocco Pulise knows down here in the hold.

'Join the Navy and see the world.' Really? Pulise, one of a dozen Seal Team One members crammed into the Stiletto with only a week's training for the mission, can't see a blessed thing. Can't hear a thing, either. The sides of the Navy's newest Special Operations craft see to that, the way they wrap up and over their heads like the Batmobile.

And, adding to the bat look, the special M-hull that sends the boat over the water, not through it, cuts down on the acoustic signature the old MAKO boats generated when they slapped through the waves at merely moderate speeds. So, even though they're making sixty knots in this chop, the only way he'd see or hear the other squad out there in the sister Stiletto is if he were watching it on one of the Command Center screens.

But he's not. He's the Language Tech, so he's down here with the dead guy.

Pulise feels the boat slow down. Must be approaching the shore. Boy, what will those Chinese guys think when they see twenty-four Navy Seals in Stilettos heading right at their Wenchang base? Think? Hell, they'll run for their lives. What was that song Hanlon made up? Oh yeah, *Everybody Wenchang Tonight*. Funny. He starts humming it to himself when the red light over his head goes on. Right. He slips the black surgical mask over his face.

The three Seals assigned to the stiff do the same. And then they unzip the body bag and slide him into position. Ugh, the smell. Formaldehyde. The mask helps a little, but still. The second red light comes on. He takes the gun off safety.

Up and at 'em.

Chen Xu dips his piece of cold boiled chicken into the mixture of chopped ginger and salt. And then he sighs. If it's Wednesday, it's Wenchang chicken, a dish developed right here in town long ago. He sighs again. There's no getting away from Wenchang chicken on Wednesday. Unless he were to wait another half hour. Then it'd be Thursday. But that would just make this plate of leftovers half an hour older. And colder.

Of course, he *could* be back in the mountains at Xichang, launching his satellites and his moon probes and enjoying the wonderfully piquant Sichuan food he grew up with. But no, when the manned program became a reality and the payloads got heavier, Chen Xu had to open his big yap and explain the physics to Chairman Xi Jinping and the others. And so he wound up here, at Wenchang Spacecraft Launch Site on Hainan, eating chicken the island people think is spicy and still at his desk three hours late because of another damn computer breach. Good thing Hong is such a whiz with the server patches.

He smiles as he recalls his somewhat younger, eager-beaver self the day he explained to that room full of laymen, though *very* powerful laymen, that the earth rotates faster at the equator than it does at the poles. The old guys couldn't get it, not until he'd used the crack-the-whip analogy. They'd all played it as kids back in the poverty-stricken, make-your-own-fun days of the Great Leap Forward. How the child who started it could just turn in place while the urchin at the far end of the line had to run as fast as he could just to hold on. Until he couldn't.

So, the closer you get to the equator – already moving at 1,670 kilometers per hour relative to space like the kid holding hands on the outside of the line – the more snap, the more thrust the earth gives to a rocket taking off. Hainan Island, the southernmost place in China, is only 19° from the equator, so they had to build the new launch center here . . . despite the food being bland and the site uncomfortably close to Hanoi, Hong Kong, and the Americans over there in the Philippines.

Suddenly the night sky over the island is lit up like it's the middle of the day. Are those fireworks? Is it a holiday? He can't think of one that starts at midnight. Then, from his top-floor perch, he looks down and sees armed men with blackened faces swarming over and past the perimeter fencing. He races to press the alarm on the control panel, but it's already going off.

His security team is being overwhelmed. Looking down he can see two or three of the invaders have reached the building. Now they're inside! He can hear one of them running up the stairs. No, thank goodness, it's Hong Yun-Choi, his assistant, with the gun from the cabinet next door. She tosses it to him, but it drops from his clumsy fingers and falls to the floor.

And then three men burst into the room, assault weapons pointed straight at the two of them. The men's faces are distorted. No, they're wearing some kind of surgical masks, like people in Beijing when the air gets bad. Only, black instead of white, like cowboy villains.

The first man through the door barks at them in foreign-accented Mandarin. 'Either of you speak Korean?'

In a shaky voice Hong says, 'I'm from Korea.'

Switching to a Pyonyang dialect, the invader says, 'Then, hands in the air. Move away from the board, both of you.'

He waves the gun at Chen and Hong to back up his words. When his assistant takes a couple of steps to the side, Chen Xu puts his own hands in the air and whispers to her with alarm, 'What did he say?'

Before she can answer the three men open fire, sending at least fifty rounds into the control board and nicking Chen in the left forearm – maybe deliberately, maybe not. Then they turn and run from the room the way they came, leaving the horrified assistant to go find the first aid kit so she can bind up his wound.

Getting out is harder than getting in. Extraction often is. For one thing, the element of surprise is gone. Wenchang's civilians have been roused from their beds and are streaming toward the base and the harbor, a couple of them firing at the retreating vessel with pistols. Though they haven't a prayer of hitting anything.

For another thing, the Stilettos are running at only half speed. A full-throttle getaway, at a speed no Chinese or Korean boat can attain, would give the game away as an American operation. As would the boats' silhouette, the Batmobile thing, especially with the harbor patrol firing off flares the way they're doing now. So, the tarps draping the craft will have to stay in place until they rendezvous with the C-5 Galaxy transport plane.

Despite the mission's success, two wounded, neither one life-threatening, Rocco Pulise isn't feeling all that well. Sure, he destroyed months of Chinese ingenuity and effort when the three of them fired their Russian-made AK-47s into the control room's setup. So, check that box. But he hit the rocket boss with a stray. That's what you get sending a language specialist out into the world with an unfamiliar gun.

The other thing is the lingering smell. The dead Korean guy, the one they dropped into the edge of the surf, was kept fresh as a daisy in the body bag. But that formaldehyde; the bag was only open for maybe twenty seconds, but it was enough. Pulise is going be the first guy topside when they take the tarp off the hatch, that's for sure.

At least he didn't have to dress the corpse in the Russian underwear.

FORTY
China Central Television HQ, Beijing

Ying Lianbo knows someone, or more likely a sub-committee of someones, from the Central Committee of the Chinese Communist Party has written the lead story on her TelePrompTer tonight, replacing the bozos on the twentieth floor. What's more, she knows it's been through so many hands and been written and rewritten so many times that the latest version made it on to her PrompTer just two minutes ago. Thus, with so many important eyes on her, Li had better read it word for word, even though down near the bottom she can see there's another one of those mistranslations into English. *Damn!*

'Police and military investigators have confirmed this evening that the intruders who two nights ago temporarily disabled the rocket launch center on Hainan Island, the very place where our intrepid moonwalk adventurers were to have blasted off from on Founding Day, were political dissidents from Pyongyang. And that the body of the invader killed by our glorious island defense team has been identified by State Security as Park Chung-soo, a twenty-four-year-old student who had spent several months studying Russian at Valdivostok University. The North Korean government has disavowed any knowledge of, or support for, the intrusion inside our launch site's defensive perimeter. A spokesman for the Ministry of State Security had this to say . . .'

The clip lasts forty-eight seconds. Li has to wait because the video of the news conference here in Beijing has its own English subtitles. She titters to herself, just a little, at the sight of the spokesman holding up a pair of black Russian men's briefs. Now it's her turn again.

'Dr Chen Xu, Director of our space program, was shot in the Korean attack. Fortunately, his wound was a minor one, allowing the China National Space Administration to decide, after consultation with the government and the Director, that the launch to the moon will proceed with only a short delay.

'The satellite center in Xichang, once the home of all intergalactic launch activities and most recently the departure point of the *Queqiao*, or Moon Bridge, communications satellite, will be retrofitted to enable a Long March 4 takeoff on the eighteenth of next month.

'By working around the clock, our heroic scientists and technicians expect to be able to meet the new deadline, a timetable that mandates we plant our flag on the moon on July 21, exactly half a century to the day after Apollo 11 initially accomplished the feat.'

Crap, here it comes. Li braces herself.

'The spokesman for the Ministry of State Security announced today that the effort to determine exactly which foreign elements attacked us, and why, will continue. He pledged to keep at it "until we get to the basement of all this." Stay tuned for further updates as developments warrant.'

With the newscast over, Li decides she'll go to the rice wine bar across the street and get drunk.

FORTY-ONE
Planetary Analog Test Site, JSC

On their fourth circuit around the Rock Yard, Robin is back behind the wheel of the Space Exploration Vehicle, the Moon Express lunar rover. Unlike either the modified golf carts the later Apollo missions drove or the RV with wings flown by the hero in Mel Brooks's movie *Spaceballs*, it's based on an actual automobile – a Mercedes Smart car – with a one-of-a-kind electric motor dropped in and that controversial polymer lithium battery supplying the juice.

The SEV can seat two comfortably, three uncomfortably, and four crushed together. Fully collapsible, it's stored on its own bracket in the Boeing Starliner. The rover is a cinch to start, with the ignition switch on a key-fob remote, but a bitch to drive, with most of the weight in the back thanks to dozens of extra aluminum rods connected to the chassis. The rods can be assembled on the spot in five minutes, locked together in such a way as to provide more cargo capability in back and overhead than any SUV on earth.

In the rear as well, attached to the bumper, is a six-by-three-foot steel-mesh mat – the kind baseball teams use to smooth their infields. It can be raised while driving and, because there wasn't a rover on Apollo 11, lowered to erase their tire treads all the way back to the Starliner.

The South Texas sun is beating down but, except for the sweat, you'd never know it inside the VR goggles, reset this go-round to five percent available light.

Is it heat sweat or flop sweat that's produced the sheen on Robin's skin? The fear of not running a clean circuit the way Casselmann just did on his go-round? Of course, he ran the course with the setting at ten percent. Big difference – twice as much light. Still, he didn't run aground on the rocky lip of a crater, the way she did in her first run in this SEV thing.

'Rob, two o'clock!'

It's Jack's voice from the rover's back seat. Sure enough, she didn't notice the rise in elevation coming up on them.

She barely has time to breathe, 'Got it!' before steering away from the trouble. Thank God for Maybin!

'Walsh, crank it down a minute, will you?'

Even with her helmet set to zero percent light, she'd still know it was Casselmann sitting beside her. Only Casselmann still calls her just 'Walsh.' She uses the palm-sized remote to bring the rover to a stop.

Now he says, 'Goggles up.'

Robin lifts hers off, and the noonday sun is even more blinding than it usually is. When she can focus, the look on Casselmann's face tells her it's lecture time. God, she hates lecture time.

'Lunar gravity is one-sixth of ours,' he says. 'So that hard left you just pulled would have sent us over on our kiesters. Dark Side kaput, know what I mean?'

'Yes Kirk, I know what you mean. I didn't want to ram us into a hill, either.'

From the back, Maybin butts in. 'Hey man, it's Driver's Ed. This is a five percent run, let the captain make her mistakes so she can learn from them, like I did. And, by the way, like you did.'

Casselmann turns in his seat to face his crewmate. 'If I make a mistake you can point it out to me. *If.*'

And then he puts the combined goggles and headset back on, saying, 'OK Walsh, take us around.'

End of lecture time, so Robin puts her own helmet back on and returns the Rock Yard inside her VR environment to near-total darkness. She's just pressed the rover's Start button when she feels a tap on her shoulder. It's Maybin again.

'Rob, cut the engine. The Boss.'

The astronauts in the front seat take off their headgear to discover Director Hensen heading their way in her specially designed golf cart. Modugno sits beside her in the passenger seat as it pulls up alongside.

'So, team, how's it going?'

Casselmann speaks for the crew, the way he always does. 'Fine, Boss. Just ironing out the kinks.'

'Good. Cesar and I have got a little good news for a change. The brass bought us another couple weeks. New liftoff is on the fifteenth'

– she leans over and raps on the rover's door in a knock-on-wood gesture – 'if Dr Sheth comes through with the ten-hour battery for this baby the way he promises.'

Maybin, a glass-half-empty guy if ever there was one, says, 'Five hours to Tranquility and five back means there's no safety margin.'

She looks at him and shakes her head familiarly. 'For every silver lining there's a thundercloud, right Jack? As it happens, we're trying to shave just a little mileage off the trip, see if we can make it nine hours, give or take.

'Anyway, I know how much you, Kirk, and Robin like my little intrusions, so I'm clearing out for a couple of days. Flying over to Canaveral for a walk-through with the Starliner. Anything you want me to drop off with your mom in Cocoa Beach, Robin? It's right next door.'

'No, thank you, Director. We're good.'

'All right, then. I'll leave you to it.'

She revs her golf cart's engine.

'And give Cesar a turn behind the wheel, won't you?'

Her passenger gets out and joins the others. The Director backs her golf cart up and drives off through the dusty surface, leaving a plume behind her as she steers a path parallel to the public fence along Space Center Boulevard on her way back to her office.

The grit is still hanging in the air forty-five feet below the top of the ladder that's telescoped up from the StarTex Power bucket truck parked on the far side of the Boulevard. The thickly built man standing in the bucket has his cell phone out and he's playing back the conversation he just recorded on the hidden microphone their helper on the inside affixed to the base of the golf cart's steering column in the JSC parking lot earlier in the morning.

Even without headphones, Hensen's voice and the others come through loud and clear. And that's in spite of Houston's traffic, mostly pickups, flashing past the truck on the four lanes below his feet.

After fast-forwarding to the end, he sends the numerical 'eraser' text based on his birthday, 120689, to the SIM card sitting in the tiny Q-Bug. With the SIM wiped of its call history, he's just cut the cord between himself and the people he's been eavesdropping on.

When he climbs down, he'll take out his laptop and go through the photo array of astronauts on NASA's website, confirming the

backgrounds of the 'Dark Side' crew, as they're calling it. It won't
be hard: Hensen clearly said the names Kirk, Jack, and Robin, as
well as 'Cesar.' Must be the same guy they had him tail on Sunday;
how many Cesars can there be? Up with the sun for a jog, breakfast,
a couple of hours at that church two blocks from here, and then the
rest of the day on the base. Boring!

Of course, boring guys make the job easy. This one? Like candy
from a baby. Maybe he'll treat himself, for a job very well done,
with a little feminine companionship before he heads back. Young
feminine companionship.

The thought of it makes the big man up there on the ladder smile.
Dark tooth and all.

FORTY-TWO
Ulitsa Optikov, Saint Petersburg, Russia

T he Internet Research Agency is the sole tenant occupying
the anonymous eighties-era office block that sits near the
eastern end of Optikov Street. Far from the high-rise towers
where the Westerners live and work, the IRA has scrap yards and
car repair shops for neighbors. The term 'wrong side of the tracks'
doesn't do the place justice; road repair crews haven't bothered to
fill any of the yawning potholes left over from the winter. And the
winter before that. Which means the buses must halt and disgorge
their passengers well before the end of the line just to keep their
axles in one piece.

So, at ten minutes to ten this morning in a light rain, Andrei
Balkin is part of a cadre of Russian- and English-language bloggers,
commenters, and sharers walking the two long city blocks from
where the bus turns around. Still, how else in Russia can someone
without a university education earn 95,000 rubles a month? It's
payday, so Andrei and his companions smoke their cigarettes and
compare their tattoos in especially good humor this morning as they
make their way across the parking lot, inside the main doors, and
up the stairs.

Andrei's busload will join the hundreds of other IRA workers already sitting at their identical dark brown desks in front of their identical all-black computers for their twelve-hour shift. And they'll get right to work; you can't comment on eighty different posts and share those posts on twenty different social platforms if your fingers aren't flying on those keyboards from morning till night. Or, for the other half of the workforce, from night until morning.

He stubs out his Prima cigarette in the old-fashioned receptacle filled with sand that stands at the top of the stairs, and uses his hip to bump himself through the turnstile. Then he heads straight to the break room and pours himself a cup of coffee, his third of the morning. Andrei carries it back to his desk, saucer on top of cup to keep it warm. He passes the small, windowless room on the fourth floor, number 414, unaware of the strange meeting going on behind the locked door.

But when he sits down at his workstation and finally takes that wonderful hit of caffeine, he can see his manager, Vitaly, sitting up straight in the glass-walled office up front with his Bluetooth headset on. Most mornings just before starting time he's stalking the aisles, looking for slackers. Something must be up.

Nobody is inside Room 414. But the meeting is already well underway. Six large computer screens sit on desks facing each other so as to form a hexagon. Six Russian faces are visible on those screens, Russians sitting in Moscow, New York, Washington, and three right here in Saint Petersburg. In fact, one of them, English-language Unit Manager Vitaly Sorkin, is right down the hall. This way, no one will be curious as to the comings and goings in Room 414, because there aren't any.

As usual, the man they call Putin's Chef chairs the session. Yevgeny Prigozhin earned his nickname selling hot dogs from carts on the streets of Moscow before falling into a happy, and lucrative, association with one of his customers, Vladimir Putin.

'I'm authorizing another four million rubles on the Russian-speaking side and six English. Let's use three additional platforms. Gimme, uh, Snapchat, Buzzfeed, and Yandex over here. Main thread: The US celebrates their own patriotic Independence Day in two weeks; why not Crimea? These days, when people rise up against their oppressors and win their fight for independence, just as the US colonies did, Washington calls it subversion. Ninety-seven percent of Crimeans voted for integration with Russia. Fair is fair.'

'Let's have thirty or so new identities pick up the theme, and put a bunch of our re-Tweeters on it, too. I need it to be trending, a couple million page views by Tuesday. Got it?'

Five faces on five screens say, 'Got it' within milliseconds of each other.

'*Khorosho*! Good! Now, new business: this one's exciting. Alexei, fill us in.'

Alexei Morozov, in Washington, reads from a newspaper in front of him. 'This is from yesterday's *Post*: "The former President again called for the US to create a Space Force to join the Air Force and the other arms of the American military. Giving his most articulated pitch to date for a new, space-focused military service, he said China has created a military space organization to disrupt communications, blind satellites, and jam transmissions that threaten our battlefield operations."'

Alexei continues reading. '"The man who was once Commander-in-Chief said, 'I've seen things that you don't even want to see, what our enemies are doing, and how advanced they are in weaponizing space. We'll be catching them very shortly . . . If we get to work, we can be so far ahead of them in a very short period of time, it'll make your head spin.' He went on to say, 'If we lose GPS, we lose banking in the United States of America. There's no milk in the grocery store in a matter of three days.'"'

'Wow!' Prigozhin exclaims.

'Hold on, Chief, there's more. The story winds up this way: "The ex-President, who led America in walking away from the United Nations Treaty that banned military bases on the moon and in space, ended by criticizing calls for its re-ratification by Congress."'

One of the men on the Russian-language side in Saint Petersburg says, 'I don't believe you, Alexei. It's too good to be true. You're making it up!'

Morozov holds the paper with the *Washington Post* masthead up to his computer's camera. 'See for yourself.'

The woman sitting in New York says, 'We have to get on this, Yevgeny.'

The Hot Dog King is already nodding. 'My thoughts exactly. What do they say about gift horses and mouths? OK, everybody who isn't doing Ukraine, get on this.'

The English-language manager down the hall, Vitaly Sorkin, speaks up. 'All my assets are on Crimea.'

Prigozhin looks and sounds irritated. 'You have how many trolls now, seven hundred, eight hundred? There must be someone who can play a concerned citizen raising the alarm. A what-do-they-call-them, a "soccer mom," or a born-again whatever. Use your imagination, such as it is.'

'Yes, Chief.'

Putin's Chef is already moving on. 'How soon can we get a video that looks like Chinese soldiers loading weapons on a rocket? Go through the archive and Photoshop something of ours. And everybody, I'm told we have something huge in the works, a real game-changer, so we need to have this "Space is Ours" meme trending on every American platform. I don't care if it's a dating site for poofters or an app that rates plumbers and electricians, if it's on the web or a phone, I want us on it.'

He gives the thumb-up sign, his customary sign-off. Five other people on five other screens do the same.

Which is how, that afternoon, Andrei Balkin became a mother of three in Idaho worried about there being enough milk in the store for her baby.

FORTY-THREE
4230 Lenore Lane NW, Washington, DC

D r Otto Kurzweil eases into his desk chair and turns on the computer Marianne bought him for Christmas, the HP Envy 34. Aptly named, considering the covetous looks his friends gave its new owner when he finally fought his way past the gift wrap and pulled the forty-pound monster out of the shipping box. Not bad for an old guy.

So, does he need a terabyte of hard-drive memory just to hold a videoconference? Probably not. But the four front-mounted speakers really do make it easier for the hearing aids to make out what people are saying. And the curved screen that's nearly three-feet wide? He can line up all their picture-in-pictures along the bottom and keep tabs on whether they look like they're listening to what he says.

He takes a satisfying draw on his pipe and a quick look out at his backyard nature preserve, so close to the levers of global power but hidden out here in the foliage of northwest Washington. A bright red cardinal is pecking away at the string of suet and sunflower seeds he hung out there a week ago. All's right with the world.

'People, thanks for being prompt. This won't take more than five minutes or so; just so you understand the question I'm putting to you.'

'And that question is?'

Raheem, impatient as always.

'I've been thinking long and hard about the flag business, and I've come to the conclusion that we can't just GoPro the planting. We need a second astronaut to independently get proof – video proof – that it happened the way we say it did, the way it will. So he/she can testify to the fact back here on earth.

'One isn't enough; we need two people to work it. So, given that the astronaut corps is all over the place – some are right now in residence at the Johnson Space Center in Texas, others at Kennedy Space in Florida, and that's not counting the four Americans up in the International Space Station – how do we incapacitate enough of the thirty-nine to get our second guy to move up the wait list and onto the Dark Side ride?'

'Food poisoning?'

Always quick when it comes to nasty stuff, but not a deep thinker is our Karl.

'As I said, NASA has them spread out all over the place, including the two on a PR thing on the West Coast. Coordination would be too tricky. We need them all in one place.'

'Maybe we could—'

'No, Chang, let's not brainstorm it on the phone. I have to get over to the Observatory, and I want your best thinking, not your fastest.'

'Before you go, Otto, I need something confirmed.'

'Yes, Madelyn?'

'Is this backup, Modugno, a Catholic?'

That's what he likes about Madelyn Connors, one of his protégées over at Defense. Always a different angle from everyone else.

'He's from Cuba, so I suppose he is.'

'I have to be sure, Otto. Can someone research him and let me know?'

'I've got it right here.' Larry Wilbur over at IRS is holding a sheet of paper in the right-hand picture at the bottom of the screen. 'Karl put in for lunch money last Sunday while waiting for the guy to get out of Mass.'

'Thanks, Larry,' Kurzweil intones. 'Now, think the problem through, each of you, and get back to me. All right?'

Nods of the head from all seven pictures-in-picture.

'I told you it would be a five-minute call. Bye.'

He disconnects, and the screensaver of Old Glory, whipping in the video breeze, is back in place as if nothing had happened. And the cardinal out on the feeder has been joined by Mrs Cardinal.

Idyllic.

FORTY-FOUR
The USS *Hornet* in the South Pacific

July 24, 1969

It's 8:55 in the morning, Hawaii Standard Time. As the Navy Band plays 'Hail to the Chief,' President Richard M. Nixon walks along a red carpet laid on the hangar deck of the Essex Class aircraft carrier *Hornet*. Grinning all the way, he passes a gaggle of dignitaries gathered under a huge banner reading *Hornet + Three* and continues toward the Apollo 11 Mobile Quarantine Facility, a converted Airstream trailer.

The President was already aboard the ship when, a few hours ago, it deployed a helicopter to pluck Neil Armstrong, Edwin 'Buzz' Aldrin, and Michael Collins – and the Columbia Command Module they were supposed to have traveled half a million miles in – out of the Pacific Ocean. Where they had been deposited by the trawler half an hour earlier.

Almost immediately, the three were told to put on biological containment uniforms, in case any of the lunar dust they came back with contains unknown moon critters. (Although how many moon critters there actually are on a Burbank movie set remains unanswered.) It will be three weeks before the trio of explorers is allowed to emerge from quarantine, so this ceremony is taking place hundreds of miles due south of Honolulu and a little north of the equator at 169°W longitude, the line on the map that runs through the least land and most water in the world.

The honor guard accompanying the Commander-in-Chief, including the *Hornet*'s captain and its chaplain, hangs back as Nixon approaches the small, chest-high window of the quarantine cell. Tan curtains, probably leftovers from its life as a civilian trailer, part and the men of Apollo 11 appear at the window. They scrunch down together to peer out at the President beneath another *Hornet + Three* sign, this one homemade.

The leader of the free world clears his throat and begins.

'Neil, Buzz, and Mike, I want you to know that I think I am the luckiest man in the world because I have the privilege of speaking for so many in welcoming you back to earth.

'Over one hundred foreign governments, emperors, presidents, prime ministers, and kings have sent congratulatory messages. They represent over two billion people on this earth, all of them who have had the opportunity, through television, to see what you have done.'

The astronauts look on as President Nixon tells them he has invited their wives Jan, Joan, and Pat – 'three of the most courageous ladies in the whole world today' – to a state dinner in Los Angeles when the men get out of quarantine.

'All I want to know is: Will you come? We want to honor you then.'

Neil Armstrong responds for his crew. 'We will do anything you say, Mr President, any time.'

With his invitation accepted, the President tries to initiate a little small talk. 'Have you been able to follow some of the things that happened since you have been gone? Did you know about the All-Star Game?'

Armstrong answers, 'We're sorry you missed that.'

Nixon says, 'You know about the game?'

'Yes, we heard about the rain.'

Soon, the President winds up the conversation and calls for the chaplain to offer a prayer of thanksgiving. Then the C-in-C gives the space travelers one final rousing salute before retracing his steps along the red carpet, accompanied by 'Ruffles and Flourishes' and the playing, once more, of 'Hail to the Chief.'

The rest of the ship's officers and a clutch of White House and NASA brass follow behind in an untidy crowd. The men in suits and ties pass an open microphone that's positioned to amplify the sound of the band's woodwinds. Along with the music, the mic captures one of the dignitaries asking, 'Who added the part about the All-Star rainout?'

Someone among the group following after Nixon – it's impossible to tell exactly who – answers, 'I did.'

The first man can be heard, just before the two move out of microphone range, saying, 'Nice touch.'

FORTY-FIVE

Aquarius Reef Base off the Florida Keys

It's the Fourth of July, eleven days out from the Dark Side liftoff, and Paul 'Ruddy' Kipling, Director of Training for NASA Extreme Environment Mission Operations (NEEMO), is finishing off the last of the microwaved hotdogs and washing it down with a Pepsi as he stands in front of the viewing port sixty-two feet below the surface of the Atlantic Ocean. Then he picks up his iPad and scrolls down to the weather report. A six-footer, Kipling wears, along with his scuba gear, thin-soled rubber bootees. In street shoes, his head would graze the roof of the huge diving bell.

The Dark Side crew, all of them in wetsuits as well, watch his face darken with the incoming weather. Through the large circular window, they can see the vast pile of what he's been calling 'moon junk' – weighted down with sandbags – that's sitting on the seabed six miles east of Key Largo. Strewn around like a watery NASA yard sale are portable life support systems, a 1960s-era TV camera and Hasselblad camera body, replicas of Neil Armstrong's and Buzz Aldrin's moon boots (the ones that made the famous footprints in the lunar dust), and a welter of large and small items, 104 things in all including the flag – everything the Apollo 11 mission left behind on the surface of the moon. Today, the flat Atlantic Ocean bottom, calm for the moment, is standing in for the Sea of Tranquility.

Astronauts Casselmann, Walsh, Maybin, and Modugno look on as Kipling turns his face from the lighted screen upwards. To the heavens he says, 'Christ Savior, please, now that you've given us a happy, healthy Fourth, no tropical storms. Not till tonight. Or better, tomorrow – lots of people topside will be watching the fireworks.' Looking back at the crew, he says. 'OK, now that we're covered, let's begin.'

Gesturing through the triple-strength window to the water beyond, he asks, 'Notice anything new?'

Casselmann, as usual, assumes the question was asked of him. 'Sir, I see numbered stakes buried out there in the sand.' He squints. 'That far one is number 102. Or maybe it's 103. Not clear which.'

Kipling beams. 'It's 103. Why do you think we put them there, Walsh?'

Robin thinks for a moment. And then she says, 'As visual aids, sir? So we can practice where everything goes, I'm thinking. Match the numbers on the debris to the numbers on the stakes. Because we messed up some the last time.'

'Some? I'll say.' Kipling looks at the other two. 'Anything to add, Jack? Cesar?'

They shake their heads no.

'Well, watch and learn anyway,' an irritated Kipling answers. 'You two will be making the second run this afternoon.'

He takes out his stopwatch.

'All right, let's review: We calculate you'll have an hour, tops, up there on Tranquility to park the rover, deploy the material you see out there in the appropriate areas, and vamoose, brooming all the extra footprints and rover tracks on your way back to the Starliner. Lastly, let's touch on the order you do all this in. What did we say the other day?'

Robin beats Casselmann to the punch for a change. 'You said, "Toss Zone last."'

'Exactamundo,' the trainer says, grinning. 'Which is Spanish, in case you didn't know, Cesar. OK, after you set up the flag and the science experiments, making sure you go easy on the seismic detector and get the retro-reflector array positioned properly, time will be running short. So, the name says it all: toss everything in the bins labeled – surprise! – "Toss Zone" at least a dozen yards off to the side, out of Chinese camera range.

'There'll be a couple days' worth of food packets, four armrests from the Lander – don't ask me why – an insulated blanket, and the rest. All the stuff NASA said fifty years ago that we left up there. Now . . . I know I'm forgetting something.'

From the grin on his face, it's obvious Ruddy (The Kidder) Kipling hasn't forgotten; it's just that he's reached his grand finale.

'Oh yeah, four urine containers, four defecation collection devices, and four airsickness bags.'

Maybin asks the question the other three are thinking. 'Empty or full?'

Kipling smiles, showing all his nice white teeth. 'It was supposed to take them three days, strapped in a lot of the time, just to get there. So, what do you think?'

The crew's collective groan is just what Kipling was hoping for. 'Actually, they'll be your own bags, unless you're planning to hold it in.'

He picks up the stopwatch again and shows it to Casselmann and Walsh. 'All right, you two, get going.'

He clicks the watch and they head off to the airlock.

He adds, 'Finish in under an hour and . . . congratulations! You get to go to the moon!'

They managed the whole thing in fifty-four minutes. The storm didn't hit until eleven that night.

FORTY-SIX
300 E Street SW, Washington, DC

Five minutes before the briefing that will lay out the particulars of another routine crew-cabin launch, the Press Room in the National Aeronautics and Space Administration headquarters is less than a third full. Which is just how Administrator Hahnfeldt and Director Hensen, sharing a quiet moment in his office next door, like it. Fewer questions.

From her wheelchair, Hensen notices the tense set of Alf's jaw as he looks out his office window. She's always envied him this office. Not so much for the view, which fronts on a similar bureaucratic pile that houses the Centers for Disease Control across E Street, but for the giant topographic map of the moon that covers the entire far wall across from his desk. It's wallpaper, specially ordered, and it shows the six Apollo landing sites dotted among the thousands of impact craters large and small that make up the familiar surface.

It's eerily quiet outside the office door. Once upon a time, the TV networks and therefore the nation trained their eyes on each move NASA made, their attention riveted to every space-related announcement. But that was before men walked on the moon. Today, with its budget whittled down by Congress and many of its missions outsourced to private carriers – and lift-offs to the International Space Station departing from Kazakhstan, of all places – NASA's scientific and research missions draw the same attention that basic research attracts in every other field: next to none.

Additionally, the Director is thankful for a piece of good news they received earlier this morning from Dr Sheth's research lab: his team has successfully cranked the rover's battery life up to nine and a half hours on a charge. Right now, her people are looking for a landing site a little closer to Tranquility, and if they can bring the charger with them and let it run while they scatter all the Apollo junk, maybe, just maybe . . .

Hahnfeldt's jaw is still clenched. T-minus ninety-six hours; he must be feeling the pressure the way she is. She rolls over to the window and pulls up beside him.

'Know what I'm thinking, Alf?'

'What?'

'If they held a press conference like this one across the street, the place would be packed.'

'Well, hell, Lila, it wouldn't be *like* this one. When Disease Control gives a briefing, they're usually in panic mode.'

She starts to angle her chair away from the window. 'I've never delivered a briefing document with so many lies in it before.'

'Just the one big one, really.'

'That supposed to make me feel better?' She begins to roll back toward the Press Room. 'Here goes nothing.'

Hahnfeldt follows her out the door. Moments later, addressing the eight or nine people who showed up and the live webcast camera in the back of the room, he clears his throat and begins. 'Good afternoon, ladies and gentlemen.'

While an assistant hands out the thin briefing document that they'll also post online, the Administrator speaks into the mic clipped to his jacket, trying to give his words a Leslie Nielsen, nothing-to-see-here spin. And almost pulling it off.

'As you will recall from previous briefings, NASA and our industry partners are targeting the return of human spaceflight from Florida's Space Coast in order to prepare the way to Mars.'

He looks around the room. Two people have their cell phones out, recording what he says. No one uses pencil and pad anymore.

'For the past several years, ever since we discontinued the Space Shuttle program, the agency has employed Russian Soyuz spacecraft to ferry our astronauts to the International Space Station. For various reasons, including cost – each seat on the three-passenger Soyez costs us eighty million dollars – that contract is set to expire in 2022.'

His face assumes a grim cast.

'And given the recent failure of a Russian rocket's booster stage to ignite after liftoff from Baikonur and the emergency separation and recovery of the crew capsule, with all hands safe, thank God, the current testing program assumes even greater urgency.

'These ongoing flight tests aim to prove that our domestic partners – Space X and their Crew Dragon spacecraft as well as Boeing's CST-100 Starliner – meet NASA's safety standards for what some people are calling "space taxis." A successful flight will enable us to certify they comply before sending men and women to the Station. And then on to the Red Planet for the proposed landing in 2025.'

He turns to Hensen, sitting beside him. 'Lila?'

The Director rolls her chair forward a little. 'Here in the US of A, we believe in competition: may the best man – or in this case, vehicle – win. We'd love it if both competitors passed these flight tests with flying colors, and they really *are* a series of tough tests. In April, an unmanned Crew Dragon capsule took off on a Falcon 9 rocket from Space Launch Complex 39A, the historic Apollo launch pad at Kennedy Space Center. It successfully performed a two-orbit flyby of the International Space Station and splashed back down in the Pacific.'

(So ends the truth-based part of the briefing, Lila thinks.)

'Four days from now,' she briefly looks at her wristwatch, 'correction: three days and twenty-two hours from now, Boeing will launch its own unmanned spacecraft.'

(*There, that wasn't so bad. I just put a 'u' and an 'n' in front of 'manned'.*)

'The CST-100 Starliner – "CST" stands for Crew Space Transportation – will ride an Atlas-V rocket into low-earth orbit from the Cape Canaveral Air Force Station. Then it will undergo the same two hundred and twenty checks of flight and safety equipment as the Crew Dragon before returning to earth.'

(*With a short stopover on the moon.*)

'Designed to ferry up to seven astronauts to the ISS and future space stations, the Starliner can be programmed to operate on autopilot all the way to its destination and back, completely autonomously, with crew intervention only if there's a glitch.'

She smiles. 'Which is why NASA has put out the call for would-be astronauts who know how to play canasta.'

She hears one soft chuckle in the entire room and it's from Alf. Good thing she chose rocket science over stand-up.

'But unlike the Crew Dragon, the Starliner's retro rockets and airbags are designed to enable soft landings on terra firma instead of the ocean. The launch will be available for viewing on www. nasa.tv, as will the descent and return to Cannon Air Force Base in New Mexico. OK, I'll take questions.'

The science reporter for the *Boston Globe* raises his hand.

'Yes, Arnold?'

'What's the purpose of the double-orbit flyby?'

'Good question.' She gives the man a nice smile. 'By the year 2023, we expect to have placed an advanced communications satellite in lunar orbit, much as the Chinese have just done with their *Queqiao*. Ours will also serve another purpose: to act as a pivot point for a lunar gravitational assist, a sort of slingshot maneuver speeding us around the moon and on to Mars. This week's flyby is an early practice run.'

An Asian woman she doesn't recognize is standing near the back with her hand raised.

'Yes, ma'am?'

'Diana Soo, *Asia Times Shanghai*. The timing of this "test" just a few days before the Chinese government sends people to the moon. Isn't it simply an attempt to draw the world's attention away from our historic undertaking?'

Hahnfeldt steps in. 'Absolutely not, Ms Soo. Nothing could be farther from the truth. Like billions of others around the world, we here at NASA will have our eyes glued to our TV sets. The President has already wished the Chinese cosmonauts a safe, successful flight, and we heartily concur.'

The woman remains standing. 'A follow-up, sir: Will you deny this is in fact a spy satellite you're launching into orbit?'

'A, a *spy* satellite, ma'am?'

'Yes, to spy on my people's moon mission.'

Hahnfeldt feels himself getting red in the face.

'I don't know where you got these ideas, Ms Soo. This test program was set up long before the Chinese postponed and then rescheduled their lunar effort.' He gives a forced little chuckle. 'Maybe they're spying on us!'

The rest of the questions, three of which come from online sources, cover more mundane topics. The briefing ends twenty minutes later, but the Chinese reporter's insinuations are on the record.

Rolling back the short distance to Hahnfeldt's office, it occurs to Lila that they should be congratulating themselves on their stroke of good luck. The reporter's talk of spy flights will undoubtedly go viral in the next several hours. Like a successful magic trick, the world's attention will be focused on one thing while Dark Side accomplishes another. Like hiding a secret in plain sight.

The elevator that will take her down to the lobby and her waiting car is just along the hall, but she wants to see that wonderful lunar wallpaper one more time. Following Alf through his door, she plants her chair where she can take in the whole thing. Then she lifts her phone out of her shoulder bag and clicks off a couple of snapshots.

While checking the focus of the last shot in the series, the Director has one of her eureka moments: Talk about stuff hiding in plain sight!

She rolls her chair closer to the lunar vista and scrutinizes it for a moment. Then she looks back at her boss and asks, 'You know the scale of this thing?'

He peers at the wallpapered wall over her shoulder. 'Not sure. Maybe an inch to ten kilometers?'

'Can you find out?'

She fingers a tiny pinpoint two inches away from the Apollo 11 site. 'And this black flyspeck here. I can't tell if it's just an ink droplet from the printing job or the shadow of a pit crater right where we need one, on the far side of the hills from Apollo 11. If so, I need to know how big it is.'

'Minuscule, I should think.'

She looks back at him again. 'If it's there, I need the exact measurements: Diameter, depth, distance from Tranquility Base. And this is important: I want to know the makeup of the strata at the bottom. Is it rock or dust?'

He picks up his desk phone and dials the number for his secretary, saying, 'Lila, is this another one of your crazy—'

And then into the phone he says, 'Mary Lou, get me Planning.'

Lila has wheeled herself as close to the wall map as her chair can get, so Hahnfeldt is speaking to the back of her head when he asks, 'How soon do you need this? Want me to email you when you're back in—'

'I need it now.' She swivels her chair around. 'Immediately. Put your best woman on it.' She smiles. 'Or guy. Someone smart and fast.'

Ten minutes later, Lila Hensen knows the nearly invisible depression on the map is thirty-five feet wide, only twelve to fourteen feet deep, with a floor made of basalt, the same hardened lava flow as the rest of *Mare Tranquillitatis*. And, best of all, in the lunar rover it's little more than two hours away from rendezvous.

She practically does a wheelie in her haste to get to the phone on the Administrator's desk. When the secretary picks up, she says with some intensity, 'Mary Lou, get me Boeing!'

FORTY-SEVEN
Level 9, Johnson Space Center

Of all the things astronauts do – the physical training, weeks and months of classroom work on everything from robotics to geology, and finally the grunt work involved in keeping the International Space Station up and running (unclogging backed-up space toilets, anyone?) – the thing most of them claim to like least is the PR aspect of the job.

After all, your typical astronaut prepares for his or her career in space by studying math or science in high school and then in college. Not many extroverts in that group. Pressing the flesh and smiling in the face of every tourist in madras shorts who can pony up $69.95 ($35.95 for kids four to eleven) for Lunch with an Astronaut on a Friday or Saturday isn't what the space jockeys signed up for.

But with the Apollo flights in the rearview mirror, the romance of the space travelers themselves is practically all NASA has left to sell. So, it's part of the job. And today, it's part of Cesar Modugno's job.

Normally, the Dark Side crew would be preparing to go into quarantine well before a lift-off. But because this is a covert mission, its members must go about their long announced and well-publicized tasks, like this meet-and-greet in the dining room today. Any cancellation or replacement would have to come with an explanation.

NASA describes Lunch with an Astronaut as 'a casual event that gives you the opportunity to hear first-hand stories from a NASA astronaut while enjoying a delicious meal prepared by our in-house catering staff. Come early or stay late for a special presentation by our guest astronaut. Presentations begin at 11 a.m. and 1:20 p.m. And, as a special memento of your visit, you will receive a personalized photograph from our astronaut. Be sure to bring a camera to capture the memory!'

The talk Modugno gave this morning was on 'Preparing for Space,' the same one he'll give ten minutes from now. He's peppered it with stories of his upbringing in Miami as the child of *Marielitos*, the immigrants who set off from Havana's Mariel harbor in small boats and rafts in the search for freedom in the 'boatlift' of 1980. Freedom that they found in the United States of America.

His PowerPoint visuals include snapshots of his parents, Julio and Carmelita, a map demonstrating that Mariel is the nearest stretch of Cuba to the US mainland, and the future astronaut himself as a little boy in Florida. One of those early pictures his dad took was of Cesar at Cape Canaveral, dwarfed by all the rockets.

He threw in a few of himself training to run cross-country along the beach when he was in high school. And then later, of more strenuous training sessions for triathlons as a post-grad at Miami-Dade. One of his favorite pictures, of the whole family taking the oath and becoming American citizens in 1988, went over big with the morning audience.

In preparing the slides he glossed over the broken ankle and torn ligaments as quickly as he could, ligaments that forced the big career changeover to test pilot and then astronaut. Lots of pics of everyone in monkey suits heading for the Space Station. Thank God for PowerPoint.

Now he's halfway through the after-lunch picture-taking with the paying guests. A family of five, all of them blond, poses around him while the teenage daughter takes the selfie with her phone on one of those extension sticks. Smile. Click.

Next in line is a big, muscled-up guy sporting one of those Houston Astros bucket hats with the circular brim, the kind fishermen like to stick their lures into. The headgear is neon orange and black, Astros' colors, and it's pulled down so far you can barely see the man's eyes.

When Cesar reaches out to shake hands, the guy takes his own hands out of his pockets. He's wearing latex gloves.

The man shrugs and says, 'Skin condition.'

Cesar pulls his hand back and says, 'Sorry about that.' Instead of a handshake, he touches elbows with the man. 'I'm Cesar. And you are . . .?'

'Gus Grissom.'

Cesar knows he must have a quizzical look on his face because the man hurries to explain. 'Angus Grissom. Not the astronaut.'

'OK, Angus. Gus. Do you have a phone, or should our photographer do the honors?'

The man smiles broadly. He has one black tooth right in the middle. 'Nah, just an autograph if you don't mind. Got my favorite pen right here.'

He reaches into his inside jacket pocket and takes out a six-inch-long gray metal cylinder. Unscrewing the top a little clumsily because of the glove, he extracts a fountain pen and takes off the cap. Then he hands Cesar the pen and the Lunch with an Astronaut menu. 'Next to your name. My kids will be thrilled.'

'Sure you don't want a photo? I'll be happy to.'

'Just "To Marge, Gus, and all the Grissoms" with your signature will be super.'

Cesar accepts the pen and the menu. Bending over the nearby lunch table, he's managed only the 'To' when he notices he's writing with green ink. Different. He notices something else: the man's pen is leaking green ink all over his fingers.

'Oh, I'm so terribly sorry.' The big man whips out a handkerchief and picks up the leaky pen. Then he grabs a napkin from the table, dunks it in a half-empty water glass, and offers it to Cesar. 'My bad.'

While the astronaut busies himself wiping the ink off his hand, the man returns the pen to its metal case and pockets it, leaving without his autograph.

Cesar, more confused than anything, will pose for several more pictures without feeling at all sick. In fact, he'll only become aware of an episode of double vision during his second 'Preparing for Space' talk, just about the time the picture of his family taking the Oath of Allegiance pops up on the screen.

That's how it is with di-methyl sulfate. An ocular reaction is often the first thing the victim notices. Carcinogenic and odorless, DMS is easily absorbed through the skin, especially when diluted in water. The compound makes its way through whatever tissue it encounters, including mucous membranes and the gastrointestinal tract. The respiratory shutdown is always fatal if even as little as a tenth of a milligram is absorbed.

Before getting into his rental car in the Space Center parking lot, 'Gus Grissom' tosses the sealed fountain pen container into a recycling bin. It's not until he's in the driver's seat and starting up the engine that he removes the loud hat. There's a garbage bin around back of a nearby Walmart where he can ditch the thing along with the gloves.

Shifting into Drive, the big man congratulates himself on never killing the same way twice.

FORTY-EIGHT
Leaving Ellington Field

t almost the precise moment Cesar Modugno is trying, without success, to wipe the fatal green stuff off his hands, Gary Stephens is booting up his NASA iPad in the van on the way back from the morning's Vomit Comet ride, his fourth go-round on the Zero-G roller coaster.

It's exactly ninety days since 'Bert Forrester' signed his white-board contract and became an astronaut-in-training. In that time, he's been down to the bottom of the Neutral Buoyancy Tank, kicked up Rock Yard dust, flown the flight simulator to both the moon and Mars, and handed in more than a dozen homework assignments on the subject of, well, rocket science.

This morning, the other ASCANs were sent their second ninety-day assessments. For Gary, it's his first report card, and he finds himself scrolling down through his raw scores with sweaty palms. Gary, as Bert, has strained to manage at least a thousand pushups and logged close to a hundred miles of plain old-fashioned road running on the margins of Space Center Boulevard. (Good thing he logged all those hours biking along the West Side Highway.) All to keep up the fiction that he's just another would-be astronaut, an 'eager beaver' who's dying to blast into space.

So, for all the definition the recent exertions have brought to his musculature, and even though he has no intention of making space travel a second career, Gary would still like to know if Bert Forrester has, in fact, been keeping up with the competition. He glances over to Carrie and Ralph, sitting across the aisle from him in the van. They have their heads together, comparing their own reports. Gary can picture himself with Robin that way. Robin—

'Curt, how'd you do?'

His daydream has been interrupted by Marty Bienstock, who's leaning over his right shoulder to look at his screen from the seat in back. Marty's been calling him 'Curt' ever since that evening in the Lounge. A real competitive jerk.

'Uh, gee, Marty, I haven't focused on it yet.'

He grins. 'That's *Dr* Bienstock, MD to you, Curt.'

'Oh, right. Lila said we had a doctor.' Gary won't give the man the satisfaction of correcting his name.

'*Lila*? You still brown-nosing the boss?'

He gives Gary a 'friendly' punch on the shoulder that's harder than it has to be. 'Hey man, just messing with you. I'm a doctor, you're a filmmaker; we're all credentialed up the ying-yang.'

Marty cranes forward again to look at the iPad screen.

'So, let's see what you got. It's your first scorecard! Don't you want to know where you rank? Me, I'm fourth, with a bullet. Up from eighth last time. Your number's down at the bottom on the right. You're dying to know, right?'

'Not particularly.'

'Liar.'

Marty, his face close to Gary's as he leans over the seat, is sporting a huge grin. 'If you thought college was a goddamn rat race to get into grad school – medical school in my case – wake up, bub. Scuttlebutt has it they're only taking three from our class. It's Compete or Die, man!'

He points a finger, the nail bitten down to the nub, at something on Gary's screen. 'Shit, they gave you a ninety-seven on the Comet! How'd you do that?'

Gary swivels to look at him, but Marty's face is uncomfortably close, so he has to pull back a little. 'I guess it's because I don't get airsick, or whatever they call it. "Space sick." I don't know what else it could be.'

Without asking permission, Marty uses his finger to scroll down Bert's iPad page. 'OK, an eighty-seven on the Rock Yard. That's more like it. I just got an eighty-nine.'

Gary pulls the tablet away from Marty. 'Mitts off, *Dr* Bienstock!'

'Touchy, touchy.' Marty actually clucks his tongue. 'None of us got a ninety driving around the Rock Yard our first time. That eighty-seven is like gold, man.'

Flashing through Gary's mind is the memory of that first day in college, when all the newly arrived go-getters went around comparing high school SAT scores. Never again. He places the iPad on his left leg, the one planted part way in the aisle, so the guy can't see it over his shoulder.

With that, Marty slumps back in his own seat as the van jounces over the rumble strips that guard the Space Center entrance. 'Have it your own way, bro.'

Carrie, in the far window seat, is looking at Ralph and smiling. Guess she likes her scores. Turning his own screen face up again, Gary scrolls down his report to where the trainers' comments are. Theo and Miriam wrote some nice things, and his Space Medicine prof gave him an 'Improving' grade. (His first test earned a thirty-eight, so anything after that would be an improvement.) Even the instructors who run the Clear Lake facility had something nice to say about Bert and his efforts on the Parasail and Land and Sea Survival courses: 'The candidate seems able to adapt to unknown challenges at a level that's well above average.'

The highest praise is from Steve Barkley, the flight simulator pro: 'Despite his complete lack of real-world hours in the air, Bert Forrester is a natural at the controls. His ability to work down his flight checklist while subjected to various levels of oxygen deprivation would be exemplary for even the most experienced—'

'Fuck! Everybody: Curt's third! Shit! Third!'

Instead of staying where he was, Marty repositioned himself so he could squat in the aisle to Gary's left and view the screen that way. Not bothering with the comments, he's jumped to the end.

'Third! In half the time as the rest of us! Can you believe it? You waltzed right in ahead of me, a doctor for Chrissakes, and made the cut!'

He fist bumps Gary's left hand, deliberately hard, with his own.

'Congratula— ow! Bro, that ring you're wearing just did a number on my fist.'

Gary looks down at the ring with the little diamond Carla slipped over his finger on their wedding day, the man's version of the one he gave her. And, as the driver brings the van to a stop and opens the door, any thought of Lila's encouraging words and Carrie's happy smile and the memory of the way Robin's hair smells all melt away.

FORTY-NINE

St Paul the Apostle Church, Nassau Bay, Texas

Ramon Diaz remembers to roll the collar of his white dress shirt down on his neck so it won't extend above the red cassock when he puts it on. Then he moves over to the tall cabinet to the left of the sink in the Sacristy. Ramon is usually the Cross Bearer, but he'll handle the incense for the first time this morning as a pinch-hitter for the head altar boy, Patrick, who's out with the measles.

He removes the thurible, the same one the Fathers at St Paul's have used forever, even before Ramon was born. Then he takes three lumps of charcoal from the bag on the bottom shelf the way Patrick always does and places them neatly in the censer. He starts them going with the prong of the electric charcoal lighter. Maybe even more than the red cassock, permission to plug in and handle the electric starter without adult supervision tells Ramon he's well on the way to manhood.

Because it's a weekday funeral Mass, it's just Ramon and a younger kid they drafted to be the Cross Bearer. That's the advantage of going to a Catholic high school like St Mary's; they understand what's required. Of course, the kid – Stephen something – is late. So, with the deacon out sick as well, Ramon will have to handle the prelims all by himself while the priests are getting ready in the robing room next door.

He runs down his mental checklist. Light a few votive candles. Done. Make sure the head usher has the programs for the service. Done. The picture on them, the soul they'll be praying for, is of an obviously Latino guy named Cesar Modugno. An astronaut, how cool is that? But the usher serving this morning, another guy from the Space Center across the Parkway, acted like he knows what he's supposed to do with them and he isn't even Catholic.

While Ramon is getting ready, Kirk Casselmann is handing out stacks of folded-over single-page programs to the others standing just inside the church's front doors: Jack Maybin, Robin Walsh, and – volunteered by Robin for the job – Bert Forrester, today's only Jewish usher. They'll each man one of the four doors to the sanctuary, already beginning to fill up.

Yesterday, the coroner released Modugno's body to his family for burial back in Miami, so this will be a Memorial Mass. The official verdict confirmed everyone's fears: he was poisoned, for reasons unknown, by a large someone wearing an Astros hat pulled down around his ears. The Johnson Space Center's surveillance cameras captured, mostly, the hat.

The FBI is said to be using their facial recognition software on the footage, but they've announced they hold out little hope of making an ID. They already know the credit card he used to pay for the lunch online was stolen from the purse of a Bayview woman earlier in the week.

Now, having helped a wheelchair-bound congregant find a place down in front and then setting the chair's brake while the elderly man barked instructions the whole time, Gary takes up his position by the door on the left closest to the altar. From this vantage point, he can see across the vast open space of the modern St Paul the Apostle Church, the place where Modugno worshipped every Sunday he was in town. Casselmann and Robin stand on either side of the double door at the rear of the sanctuary.

At this moment, Administrator Hahnfeldt and thirty of NASA's thirty-nine – make that thirty-eight – active astronauts are taking their seats in the front three pews of the place to the somber music of a piano, cello, trumpet, drums, and two guitars. Lila Hensen's wheelchair is positioned in the aisle on the far right and down in front. Only the ushers and the four Americans up in the Space Station are missing.

Located across East NASA Parkway in what is technically the suburb of Nassau Bay, St Paul the Apostle is all blond wood and windows, with lots of sunlight streaming through the stained glass. On a few perfect mornings, like this one, the five-paneled depiction of the Last Supper spreads its intensely colored reds, blues, and golds as a benediction upon the entire congregation.

Worshippers face the three-dimensional sculpture of the crucified Christ that hangs over the Last Supper windows. Directly above Jesus, the church's largest single window portrays the Dove of Peace ascending to the heavens, its image reflected all the way down to the polished wood floor of the nave's central aisle. The idea being, if you weren't a Catholic before you walked in, there's every chance you'll become a believer by the time you leave.

Taking their places behind the astronauts – the ones who've simply crossed the road and the rest who've flown in from various parts of the country – are members of their families, seven of the current astronauts-in-training, the supervisors and trainers, and anyone else from the Space Center who knew Cesar personally, as well as other churchgoers who wish to pay their respects.

The beginning of the music tells Ramon it's time. With the coals glowing, he removes the lighter and unplugs it, making sure the prong rests on the heat-absorbing pad as it cools. Then he reaches into the cabinet and takes down a new tin of incense, with the words 'Pontifical Church Supply' and a drawing of a medieval cathedral stamped on the front.

Because he's a fill-in, Ramon doesn't realize it's a different brand of aromatic resin from the one St Paul has used for benedictions, processions, and Masses since he's been assisting the priests for the past three years. Still, when he opens the lid, the mix of frankincense, myrrh, cedar, and whatever else they use has that familiar, wonderful smell. He takes a heaping scoop of incense from the tin and places it directly on the glowing coals in the censer.

Father Mangan gives him the nod and Ramon picks up the thurible by its golden chain. While waiting for the others to get in line behind him, he gives the thing and its smoking cargo a quick, practice swing, like José Altuve in the on-deck circle at Minute Maid Park. Just to loosen up the wrist as he waits for the choir to add their voices to the music.

As the singers are rising to their feet, the prickly man in the wheelchair signals to Gary. He says, 'I need the restroom.' No please, no nothing.

The men's room is placed to the right of the church's main doors, near the cloakroom. Gary lifts the brake and wheels the chair back out his door as the twenty blended voices begin the funeral hymn, 'For All the Saints, Who From Their Labors Rest.'

Happily, the man does not require Gary's help in the bathroom's stall. After a few minutes, he assists the parishioner back into the mobile chair, waits for him to wash his hands, and returns him to the spot where he was before. More instruction about how to set the brake.

The priests and altar boys are all in their places as the choir has moved on to another hymn. The aroma of the incense is nearly overwhelming here in the wheelchair area. The kid in the red smock must have really done a number with the stuff.

Gary is supposed to take his seat in the last row for the service. Instead, unaccustomed to the heady smell, he walks back up the aisle and out the sanctuary door, past the neat stack of extra programs he left there on the floor.

Outside, he shakes off his sudden lightheadedness. Is it because he's of a different tribe and unaccustomed to incense? Anyway, it's a beautiful July day. Maybin, too, is out there on the lawn, over on the other side near the parking lot, having a smoke with Marty Bienstock. Gary will never understand the siren call of cigarettes.

It's a shame Cesar won't ever again know this feeling of the sun on your face and the sound of the birds singing in the trees. But, Gary realizes, as he stands here far enough away from the smokers to be breathing in fresh air, the chirping of the birds isn't all he's hearing. The sound, unmistakably, is that of people coughing. A few at first. Now it sounds like dozens and dozens of people, back there in the church.

As he hurries inside, a few of the parishioners are already stumbling out, gasping for air. Inside the sanctuary, Gary can see the altar boy dressed in red has collapsed and lies unconscious near the left-most window of the five in The Last Supper, still gripping the chain he was swinging. An older priest has dropped into one of the nearby seats, on the verge of joining the boy.

No wonder everyone's coughing: When the kid dropped to the floor, the censer fell as well and scattered its contents. They're still smoking.

FIFTY

Union Station, Washington, DC

The Vice-President does not have his customary 'Uncle Hal' grin affixed to his public face. Instead, the frown that's been there since he picked up the papers at the newsstand in Wilmington only deepens as the first Acela of the morning pulls into the station and disgorges the early birds.

Tucking the *Times* and the *Washington Post* under his arm, the VP only has a few seconds to pay for a *Houston Chronicle* from the Out of Town rack in the news kiosk before getting into the Town Car Carmelo has waiting outside. Its headline reads, *NASA Director Dead, 63 Sickened by Noxious Fumes in Area Church.*

Otto is already ensconced in the back seat, looking straight ahead with a faint smile on his lips, the Buddha thing again. Thankfully, he seems to have abided by Hal's no-smoking-in-cars rule.

Hal holds out the *Chronicle*. 'Have you seen this, Otto?'

The old man turns to face him and answers in a rumble that seems to come from the back of his chest. 'It made the night owl editions online. You know me.'

'So, you're up to speed. Good.' Then to Carmelo, Hal says, 'Floor it. We're late as it is.'

The long black car peels out around the parking circle and onto Massachusetts Avenue. But, instead of making the usual left, Carmelo keeps going straight toward New Jersey Avenue and Georgetown Law School. Hal shoots his driver a questioning look in the rearview mirror.

'Pile-up on Louisiana, sir.'

'Gotcha.'

He turns back to Kurzweil. 'Any idea who'll be at this thing?'

'I gather POTUS and her people, you and me, Homeland Security, FBI, maybe others.'

Having said that, the Gautama turns away from his boss to stare out the passenger window. Instead of guessing what his advisor is thinking, the Vice-President decides to read the rest of the story.

'Lila Hensen, Chief of Astronaut Operations for NASA, died and twenty or more of America's astronaut corps were sickened yesterday by noxious fumes that engulfed St Paul the Apostle Roman Catholic Church in Nassau Bay. They were attending the funeral Mass being said for another astronaut, Cesar Modugno, who was murdered in mysterious circumstances four days ago.

'Thirty congregants suffered similar respiratory distress, caused in all likelihood by exposure to the toxins in the incense used as part of the Catholic Mass. The NASA chief, wheelchair-bound for more than two decades after a training mission crash, was seated near the altar and unable to make it out of the church sanctuary in time due to the crush of panicked parishioners trying to escape the fumes.

'On life support is Ramon Diaz, fifteen, an altar boy and honor student at St Mary's High School. Also in critical condition is Stephen Lavelle, another St Mary's student acting as crucifer. The two were taken to Texas Children's Hospital Emergency Center. Also in critical condition is the celebrant, Father John Mangan. He is in Houston Methodist St John Hospital in nearby Clear Lake.'

'Damn,' the VP says to no one in particular, 'Lila was terrific. I loved her.'

Hal flips the story over to the continuation below the fold. 'Preliminary indications are that naturally occurring mycotoxins in the mixture of ingredients used to create the incense in the ceremony may have been the source of the outbreak.'

He looks up from the paper. They're past the law school and turning onto K Street. Three more minutes and they'll be there.

He asks, 'Know anything about mycotoxins, Otto?'

'The word comes from the Greek. Toxins are, obviously, poisons. Myco derives from *mykes*, meaning fungus. Thought you might ask, so I looked it up before going to bed. Several different kinds of crops can develop a fungus or mold that gives off these poisons. When cattle graze on the crops, whole herds have been known to sicken and die.

'Church incense is made from the sort of gifts the wise men brought – frankincense and myrrh, which are really the sap, resins, harvested from trees and shrubs grown in the Middle East – and other materials like aromatic cedar. It could have been anything.'

Carmelo drives them on to the White House grounds. Hal releases his seat belt and jabs at the door handle before the aide outside can do it for him, muttering, 'Some fuckin' gifts. Practically all our astronauts are down for the count.'

FIFTY-ONE
The Director's Conference Room, JSC

Twenty-four hours after it happened, three Houston trauma centers and two additional clinics are treating the fifty-eight victims who succumbed in various ways to the incense cloud, with those closest to the altar showing the gravest effects. Besides Father Mangan and the altar boys, Administrator Hahnfeldt and nearly all of the NASA contingent, seated in the front three rows, were felled by the smoke. Four people are on life support and another twelve in intensive care. Five congregants, all located at the rear of the church, have been cleared to return to their homes.

The ushers at the doors in the back, Walsh and Casselmann, experienced different fates. Robin herded several children outside to safety and stayed with them throughout the ensuing chaos. The chief astronaut, though, saw his boss immobilized at the front of the church and rushed to her aid. With no thought for his own safety and the safety of his lungs, he barreled through the hysterical crowd with her chair.

It was too late. Casselmann was taken to Houston Methodist St John, where doctors wanted him to spend the night in an isolation room with floor-to-ceiling plastic sheeting to prevent any new airborne irritants from entering his lungs. But he checked himself out before anyone could stop him.

The upshot of all this is that Deputy Administrator Phil Beuerlein has flown in from NASA's Wallops Island facility in Virginia to take over the Dark Side command. He's on the video call now with the White House.

Joining him in the Director's conference room on the sixth floor are NASA's Chief Health and Medical Officer Harlan Park, three more heads of Johnson Space Center departments, and three of the four ushers at Cesar Modugno's funeral, who just happen to be the crew of the flight scheduled to lift off secretly from Cape Canaveral in thirty-six hours: Casselmann, Walsh, and Maybin.

On the wall monitor at the far end of the room in Houston, the President looks like someone working without any sleep. And she is. Flanking her are the Vice-President and their staffs, with Otto Kurzweil allowed to smoke his pipe by presidential dispensation, the Secretary of Homeland Security, the Administrator of the Agency for Toxic Substances and Disease Registry – a woman named Regina Perkins – and Leah Davis of the FBI.

'All right, everyone. I need recommendations. Can we still manage this thing on Thursday?'

Beuerlein looks at the others gathered around the table with him before replying. In that moment, a loud sucking sound comes from the other end of the table. It's Kirk Casselmann, who's just taken a quick pull on the kind of rescue inhaler asthmatics use. Before the Deputy Director can begin, the President, who was looking down at some briefing papers, butts in.

'Wait, Phil, what the hell was that noise?'

'It's Casselmann, Ms President, our Chief Astronaut Kirk Casselmann. He's set to pilot Dark Side. Or, at least, he was.'

With a confused look on his face, the Vice-President says, 'I don't understand.'

After a brief glance to his left at the Commander-in-Chief, he adds, '*We* don't understand.'

Beuerlein turns to Dr Park, a white-haired man in his early fifties with strong Asian features and a medical caduceus pin in his lapel. 'Harlan?'

The doctor says, 'I'm Harlan Park, Ms President, Mr Vice-President. As the Chief Medical Officer down here, it's my job – my responsibility – to certify an astronaut is medically ready to fly. Commander Casselmann did a heroic thing in trying to rescue the Director yesterday. But in the process, he inhaled lungfuls of the mycotoxins in the smoke. I'm afraid he's suffered second-degree damage to his pulmonary function.'

The President says, 'Then why is he here? I still don't understand.'

Dr Park says, 'He wants to go despite the damage. While my decision is, has to be, to ground the Commander, he insisted on going over my head.'

On the monitor the President says, 'Talk to me, Commander Casselmann.'

The man in question pushes his chair back and stands up, lowering the inhaler out of sight below the top of the table.

'Madame, uh, Ms President, I'm currently the senior member of the astronaut corps. I've trained to lead our Dark Side team on this mission for the past three months, to pilot the Lander and then drive the . . . the Rover . . . to' – Casselmann stops and tries to take a breath without anyone noticing, unsuccessfully – 'to Tranquility and plant our flag. I've worked all my life to walk on the moon. I'm not contagious or anything and I *deserve* this chance!'

With that he turns his head and, still standing, coughs into the back of his hand.

At the White House, Regina Perkins, the Toxic Substances lady sitting on the other side of the President from Hal, speaks up.

'Ms President, Harlan and I are together on this. Commander Casselmann deserves every medal you're going to pin on him for his heroism. But a CT scan performed at the hospital last night and a bronchoscopy Harlan did this morning – lowering a camera on the end of a fiber-optic line into the Commander's lungs – show twenty-three percent loss of alveoli function.

'The collagen and elastin in these tiny air sacs allow them to expand and spring back into shape, passing oxygen to the surrounding capillaries when you inhale and then expending carbon dioxide. While he will eventually recover, Kirk Casselmann is missing a quarter of his blood/gas regulatory system right now. It's our considered opinion that he is likely to lose consciousness during liftoff, or later, with potentially dire consequences for himself and the mission.'

'Then, thank you for everything, Commander,' the President says. 'You can stand down. There'll be other moon missions, I hope.'

'But—'

'When I say "you can stand down," sir, that also means you can sit down.'

Finally, reluctantly, he does.

'So, where does that leave us, Phil?'

'Ma'am, Robin Walsh here will assume overall mission command. She's flown twice to the International Space Station and is fully capable of stepping in.'

'Uncle Hal' beams an especially bright smile at her as the President says, also with a smile, 'Captain Walsh, Robin, you started all this. Are you ready to see it to completion?'

Robin gets to her feet as Casselmann, sitting in the chair next to her, shoots her a sullen look.

'I am, Ms President.'

'Good. That's settled. And I assume Captain Maybin will continue as well?'

As Robin takes her seat, Beuerlein nods briefly at Maybin before answering, 'Yes, ma'am.'

The head of the American government looks down at her briefing deck once more.

'This was supposed to be a three-person mission. With the late Captain Modugno unavailable, and so many of your people hospitalized, what is your reco, Phil? Call someone back into service?'

The Acting Director holds up the stapled sheets in his hand. 'If you flip ahead to page nine, you'll find our roster of recently separated astronauts, people who've flown in space within the past eight years. As you can see, two of those are currently serving in Congress, one in the House and the other in the Senate. With important votes coming up this week, we're told their absence would raise too many questions. Ellery would be ideal, but he broke his leg when his dune buggy flipped over last month. Rosenberg is out as well, just had an angioplasty. And Meriwether, well, we grounded him ourselves eighteen months ago. Section Eight.'

Taking the pipe out of his mouth, Kurzweil asks, 'Does that mean what it used to mean back in my day?'

'Yes, sir. Psych discharge.'

Exasperated, the President drops the papers she's holding into her lap. She says, 'Then you're saying we scrub the mission?'

'No, Ms President, I—'

'What about the Space Station?'

It's Cy Talbott, sitting two seats off to the President's left, who's spoken. 'Don't we have four working astronauts just sitting around up there? Couldn't you dock at the Station on the way to the moon and pick up the personnel you need?'

'I'm afraid it's not that simple, Mr . . .?'

'Under Secretary Talbott.'

'It's not that simple, Mr Talbott. Our guys aren't alone up there. The two Russians and the Norwegian would notice if their room-mates suddenly picked up and didn't come back.'

'Oh, I see. Sorry.'

Beuerlein flips to the back of the deck he's holding and is about to go on when a presidential aide appears on the monitor. She hurries over to her chief and hands her a note, which the President reads.

'There's just been an earthquake in Italy. Will everyone please "take ten" while I call the Prime Minister?'

On the Washington monitor, the President gets up and walks out of camera view. The Vice-President follows her. His advisor, Kurzweil, remains where he is, helping himself to another bowl of pipe tobacco from the pouch in his pocket.

The attendees in Houston allow themselves to relax a little without the President, all except for Casselmann, who immediately moves over to Dr Park to begin hectoring him some more about his medical verdict.

Robin stays where she is, leafing through the rest of the deck. The last five pages contain, surprisingly, the latest field test scores of the current class of astronaut candidates. Gary's report is in there, and it's a good one. In fact, it's a great one. Who knew?

With her speed-reading done and still no sign of the President's imminent return, she gets up for a quick visit to the ladies' room. Crossing behind Beuerlein puts her directly opposite the monitor. She sees – or thinks she sees – a look pass between the Acting Director and the pipe smoker. Everyone else in the conference room, all the NASA people, are either lost in conversation or flipping ahead through the briefing deck the way Robin did. She's the only one in a position to see the old man tamp the tobacco down in his pipe and then, looking up, nod his head to Beuerlein.

And only because she's this close can Robin see the man now running Dark Side give the slightest of nods back.

Two minutes later, from the last stall in the ladies' room, Robin uses her cell phone to dial Gary's number. He picks up on the second ring.

'Hello?'

'Bert, is that you?'

'Robin?'

'It's me. Can you talk?'

'We're just finishing breakfast. What's up?'

'When you're by yourself, call me back.'

'You OK?'

'Yes. Call me back on this number. ASAP.'

With Lila Hensen gone, only two women have their workspaces here on the sixth floor, so the bathroom should be safe enough. Her phone rings less than half a minute later.

'Rob, what's the deal?'

'Look, there's no time to explain. How adventurous are you feeling?'

'Me?'

'That other night when, you know, you, we, the conference table . . . afterwards you said some things about being together. The future. Did you mean it?'

'You and me? Our future? Of course I mean it.'

'Till death do us part?'

'Absolutely. Till death do us part.'

'OK, you're on.'

'Wha—?'

Robin ends the call just as one of the secretaries walks in. For the woman's benefit, she crosses to a sink and washes her hands before returning to her seat across the hall. On the monitor, the President, who's returned, faintly smiles in her direction before turning her attention to Beuerlein. 'You were saying, Phil? There's another option?'

'Yes, ma'am. We go with an ASCAN.'

'Ash can?'

'Sorry. "ASCAN." NASA lingo for *As*tronaut *Can*didate, ma'am.'

The Vice-President interjects, 'You mean a trainee?'

Beuerlein is about to respond, but the man sitting next to him answers first.

'If I may, Mr Vice-President?'

'And you are?'

'Theo Underwood, sir. I head up NASA's training program. Our trainees, as you rightly call them, often come to us with a wealth of private industry experience. Some fly for the commercial carriers, others are test pilots for Lockheed or Boeing who want to go higher than winged aircraft will allow. In our case, a lot higher.'

The President, her mood lightened considerably, steps back into the dialogue. 'Is there an ASCAN you'd recommend, Theo?'

Underwood says, 'That's the Acting Director's call, ma'am.'

On cue, Beuerlein holds up the briefing deck.

'If you'll look at the last five pages, we've attached their resumés and credentials.'

Robin watches the people on the monitor leafing to the last few pages.

Beuerlein says, 'Of our current class of thirteen, seven were seated with the others at Cesar's funeral. Though not life threatening, the respiratory issues all seven are having will keep them in area hospitals for the duration. They include our two highest-rated ASCANs, Carrie Hasegawa and Ralph Lucci.

'However, several of the next-highest rated candidates are available to serve as the Payload Specialist on this flight. These are people who, in most cases, have piloted jets in civilian life, though the Starliner pretty much flies itself. We propose making Dark Side's third crew member one of these.'

Otto Kurzweil asks, 'Who do you recommend, Director?" as he exhales a cloud of smoke.

'If you'll flip to page twelve, you'll find Martin Bienstock's info. *Doctor* Martin Bienstock. Air Force Academy graduate with honors who flew cargo on weekends for FedEx right through college. Then University of Oklahoma Medical School.

'Been in the program for six months, that's two full testing periods, on a space medicine path. His trainers give him high marks in the buoyancy tank, the altitude chamber, the Rock Yard – our name for the moon surface simulation area – and, of course, the flight simulator.'

Leah Davis, an observer up to now, says, 'I don't see a security vetting here for Mr, uh, Dr Bienstock. Do you know if there's been a background check?'

Beuerlein turns slightly to look at the FBI agent on the large screen.

'I'm pretty sure there hasn't been one, ma'am,' he says. 'For budget reasons, standard procedure is to run only those candidates who make it all the way through the two-year program. These are, well, obviously special circumstances.'

'Obviously,' Davis says.

Kurzweil slides a note to the Vice-President, who reads it quickly before saying, 'If none of the ASCANs, as you called them, have been vetted, then I suppose this Dr Bienstock is—'

'Excuse me, sir.'

His almost-daughter-in-law Robin is on her feet.

Hal gives her his warmest smile before saying, 'Yes, Robin? Or should I say Dark Side Commander Walsh?'

'Two things. First, I see here from these documents that Martin Bienstock ranks fourth in the candidate class.' She turns to Underwood. 'If the top two are in the hospital, may I ask who's third? And why you're not recommending her? Or him?'

'I'll take that, Theo.' It's Phil Beuerlein. 'The candidate who ranks third is Bert Forrester. Real name, Gary Stephens. He makes TV ads, he's never piloted an aircraft, and he's only been in the program for three—'

'Wait, "Gary Stephens?"' Underwood is mystified. 'What do you mean "real name?" And why wasn't I told?'

'Sorry, Theo. Need to know.'

Robin has remained standing. 'If I may continue, the scores given him by our professionals have placed Gary above Dr Bienstock. How do you account for that?'

Beuerlein says, 'If I were to be flip, I might say "beginner's luck."'

He flips to the Bert Forrester page. After a moment, he says, 'If you look at his individual scores, you'll see his ninety-seven on the Zero-G flights is what's lifted him up to third.'

'You're saying that's a bad thing?'

A flush of color reddens the man's cheeks. 'It's a very good thing. *One* very good thing. But, if you'll compare the two ASCAN profiles, you'll see Marty Bienstock scored higher than Forrester, um, Stephens, on the actual task he'll be assigned: distributing the material on the lunar surface.'

'One has an eighty-nine, the other eighty-seven on the Rock Yard. Is that statistically significant, sir?'

Now the cheeks are bright red. 'I won't argue statistics with you, Captain. It is what it is.'

'And the individual you've chosen to head up this mission – while a whiz at astrophysics and chemistry, if I say so myself – scored an eighty-two on the Rock Yard her first time. I'm sure an eighty-seven is the highest *initial* Area 268 score in years.'

'But—'

Robin keeps on talking over the Acting Director's interjection. 'I said there were two things. Gary Stephens has had an exhaustive vetting by the FBI. Isn't that right, Agent Davis?'

On screen, Leah Davis nods. 'Correct.'

Otto Kurzweil takes the pipe out of his mouth and loudly bangs the contents into the ashtray in front of him. 'With all due respect, Captain Walsh,' he begins in his rumbling way, once he has everyone's attention, 'Dr Bienstock's experience in the private sector must count for something.'

'I agree. That's why I'm proposing they both come with Maybin and me.'

There's a moment of silence as the two rooms, one in Houston and the other in Washington, take in her words. Then the President says, 'Would you please explain yourself, Captain Walsh?' The Commander-in-Chief has begun rubbing her temples with her fingertips, a headache coming on. 'Isn't Dark Side a three-person operation?'

'It was, ma'am, before Kirk here's fitness became an issue,' Robin answers.

Casselmann turns the look he's been giving everyone else and locks it on to Robin. She ignores him.

'As it happens,' she continues, 'the crew module we'll be flying is the Boeing Starliner. Unlike the Apollo capsules, the Starliner is designed like an SUV. It can carry a three-, four-, or even as many as a seven-person crew. When Cesar – with all his experience and training as part of the team – was our backup, three was the right number. Now that we need a replacement for Kirk, two heads are better than one. In my opinion, ma'am.'

The President switches from massaging her temples to rubbing her eyes. Her headache is only getting worse. 'Phil, what do you think?'

Beuerlein seems at a loss. 'Gee, I don't know, ma'am.'

And then, because Robin is looking for it, she sees Kurzweil give a quick, covert thumbs-up to the man on the spot while everyone else is watching the Acting Director dither in the conference room.

Just as quickly, Beuerlein seems to come to a decision. 'Yes, a four-person crew would work. We could be in and out of Tranquility that much faster. I second the Captain's motion.'

With her eyes closed in pain, the President says, 'Let's face it, everyone on the Washington end of this call is a total amateur when it comes to staffing a space flight. If I don't hear an objection from Houston, we're done.'

After a few moments of silence, she says, 'We're done. It's a go.'

FIFTY-TWO

The Canyon of Heroes, New York City

August 13, 1969

The stretch Chrysler Imperial convertible carrying Neil Armstrong, Michael Collins, and Buzz Aldrin is making pretty good time, all things considered. Sure, the Secret Service driver has to navigate through the tons of pages ripped from phone books, paper towels, shredded newspapers, and computer punch cards that people are raining down on the street, the car, and the passengers inside. More like snow, it's a manmade snowstorm in the August heat. On the other hand, the lights are green all the way up Broadway and Park Avenue to the UN.

Good thing, too, because this will have to be the quickest ticker tape parade in city history, faster than any marchers can keep up with. The moonwalkers are on a tight schedule: hop a plane for Chicago at 1:30 and another parade there this afternoon, and then grab a flight to Los Angeles for the big state dinner tonight, the third stop in what will become a forty-five-day 'Great Leap' tour that will see them continue on to twenty-three foreign countries.

It's crowded in the car, with the driver and a couple of bodyguards up front, the Apollo 11 trio sitting on the raised bench in back, and, in the middle, New York Mayor John Lindsay and UN Secretary-General U Thant smiling and waving to the crowd as if they, too, were just back from space.

It's crowded outside the car as well. Four million onlookers are jammed on to the sidewalks all the way up from Bowling Green, the spot where Peter Minuit pulled off his $24 heist of the island of Manhattan almost 350 years ago. Four million is more than all the crowds who lined all the ticker tape parades in the nineteenth century, starting with the extravaganza celebrating the unveiling of the Statue of Liberty.

What makes it extra dazzling for the astronauts is that they spent the last twenty days in quarantine – isolated first in the Airstream on the *Hornet* and then in Houston's Lunar Receiving Laboratory. No wonder Armstrong, when asked by a reporter on the City Hall steps how he felt about all the hoopla, responded into the microphone, 'It's wonderful, exciting. The best part is simply being here at all.'

Now, with the UN in sight and the last of seventeen bands along the parade route blaring, however inappropriately, the current Credence Clearwater Revival hit 'Bad Moon Rising', U Thant cranes his neck to look up at Michael Collins riding behind him and says something inaudible. Collins tries to lean down the better to hear, but is thrown a little off-balance by the speed of the Chrysler.

Instead, the Secretary-General half gets up from his seat, twists around, and shouts, 'The world thanks you, Michael!'

Collins, humble as ever, replies over the din, 'It was nothing.'

FIFTY-THREE
The Astral Lounge

'Are you crazy?'

Gary is on his second circuit of the astronauts' canteen, deserted at this hour in the morning while nearly everyone else is lying in a sick bay somewhere in the city. Robin sits at one of the tables calmly nursing a cup of coffee, which only adds to Gary's agitation. She considers his question.

'Maybe I am. But it was the only thing I could think of.'

'*Maybe*? There's no "maybe" about it. You're certifiable! An astronaut? I'm not even a real *trainee*. Bert Forrester is, and he doesn't even exist!'

'Please, Gary, come over here and sit down so I can explain.'

'I don't want to sit down.'

'Then, at least stand a little closer; I'd rather not shout.'

He walks over to her table and, realizing he's acting like a baby, sits down.

'Thank you. Now, let's start with a simple fact: Bert Forrester *does* exist. He's *you*. You're *him*. *You* got all those terrific grades from the people who train astronauts for a living.'

'But—'

'Shut up and listen to me. You're sitting next to one of the best, most experienced flyers NASA's got. I've lived and worked with these people for most of my professional life, so I know what it takes to ride into space. And, well, you're the real deal.'

'I direct TV commercials. For dog food.'

'OK, maybe you don't *feel* like an astronaut, but nobody gets a ninety-two on Land and Sea or a ninety-seven on the Vomit Comet who doesn't have the goods. Me, I received eight ninety-day reports in my two years of Comet rides, and I never got a ninety-seven.'

'Can I have a sip of your coffee?'

'Finish it.' She slides the cup over to him. 'It's cold anyway.'

He drinks what's left.

Then he says, 'All right, I'm listening. Why the hell did you volunteer *me*?'

'Something's going on. I'm not sure what but Cesar's death, a whole church down for the count . . .'

'An accident. A coincidence.'

'And you call *me* insane? Somehow, the fix is in. I saw what I saw in that meeting on six between the new Director and Uncle Hal's guy, the one we met up there in DC.'

'Kurzweil.'

'The pipe smoker. I don't know why, but they've gone to a lot of trouble to get your Marty Bienstock on this Dark Side ride.'

'*My* Marty Bienstock? I can't stand the guy. Still calls me Curt.'

'Good. So, if he tries anything, you've got my back.' She reaches over and rubs his hand. 'And after that, you've got the rest of me.'

FIFTY-FOUR

Cape Canaveral Air Force Station, Florida

T he first thing an onlooker would notice about the reconstituted Dark Side crew – if there *were* any onlookers in the middle of the night – is their spacesuits. New from head to toe, they're designed especially for use in the Starliner to be ten pounds lighter than the launch-and-entry suits worn by Space Shuttle personnel. Helmets and Reebok-style cross-training shoes have been incorporated into the design. Advanced materials and new joint patterns allow water vapor to pass out of the suit while keeping the air inside, cooling the wearer in flight. 'Touch-enabled' gloves make a real difference in manipulating materials. Finally, unlike the Apollo and Shuttle suits, they come in a color the manufacturer calls Boeing Blue.

One thing hasn't changed: each astronaut is equipped with a portable air conditioner that looks like an attaché case. Hooked up to the suits, they keep Mission Commander Robin Walsh, old hand Jack Maybin, and brand-new astronauts Marty Bienstock and Bert

Forrester reasonably sweat-free in the lingering heat of a July night in Florida as they make their way from the ready room along the gantry and up to the crew capsule high above the launch pad. Gary's still being called 'Bert' for security purposes; everyone assumes the crew's communication with Ground Control, though encrypted, may yet be the target of sophisticated hackers.

It's two in the morning. Only thoroughly vetted support personnel are working within the restricted zone surrounding historic Launch Pad 41 here at the Air Force Station. This is NASA's go-to spot – or rather, go-from spot – for all manner of uncrewed missions: the Viking robots that landed on Mars, the Voyager spacecraft that toured the outer planets, and the Curiosity Rover, currently traversing the Red Planet, all launched from here.

The four Americans find themselves crammed together, with all eight knees just about touching and the air conditioners wedged under their seats, in a loading pod designed for lifting cargo into the Starliner's hold. If there were windows in the pod, they could look across the Banana River at the Kennedy Space Center on neighboring Merritt Island. With a window on the opposite side of the pod, Robin would be able to see her mom's house across the water on Dempsey Drive in Cocoa Beach. Of course, even if there *were* any windows, they'd be covered over tonight. To preserve the *un*manned fiction.

Robin and Jack are sitting opposite the newly promoted ASCANs. Bienstock, apparently lost in his own thoughts, stares straight ahead at Maybin. Gary is lost in thought, too. What kind of lunatic do you have to be – a practically forty-year-old ex-photographer and ad guy – to be flying to the moon with under a hundred days of prep and exactly no days spent outside the earth's atmosphere? Robin keeps telling him there's a first time for everyone, but this isn't how Neil Armstrong did it.

The thought of Armstrong leads to thoughts of Army and the dognapping. Then, naturally, to Pippa, Roger, Gracie, and Ash. If this goes wrong, they'll be the only family left to sit *shiva* for him. *Wait*, he thinks, *this is getting morbid.*

Look on the bright side: If Dark Side comes out of this in one piece, he'll have Robin. And she'll have him. The thought of it allows his whole body to relax a little, his fists to unclench. Robin notices, and reaches across to squeeze his hand with hers.

'Hey, get a room!'

It's Maybin, grinning at the two of them. And then he follows up with, 'Or a capsule. I think I know where one's available.'

The joshing seems to snap Bienstock out of his reverie. He chimes in, 'If it's gonna be a four-way, someone's gonna have more than she can handle!'

Involuntarily, Robin pulls back a little.

Maybin jumps in. 'What the fuck, Bienstock?'

The new guy stammers, 'I just—'

Maybin actually puts a hand on the man's mouth. 'Not another word. Apologize to the captain.'

When Maybin withdraws his hand, an abashed Bienstock says, 'Sorry, ma'am. I don't know what got into me.'

She looks at him closely for a moment before saying, 'Accepted. Look, Marty, Jack, Bert, we're gonna be jammed together for nearly a week. Jokes are a good way to relieve the tension, but let's, uh, keep them G-rated.'

This cargo pod has already made a dozen trips up the seventeen stories from the launch pad to the newly repainted crew capsule atop the Atlas rocket. Under its two-part, breakaway nose faring, the capsule has had all the Boeing and US insignia covered over with sprayed-on, dun-colored camouflage, something Director Hensen ordered before she was killed.

First came all the mission-critical things the intrepid Americans will require for spending a week in space. The food alone, nearly a hundred fifty meals with drinks and snacks, required three separate trips up the sixty-meter, tail-to-nose length of the Atlas-5 rocket. No self-respecting quartet would leave home these days without breakfast sausage links, chicken fajitas, shrimp cocktail, beef brisket, mac and cheese, sides like Brussels sprouts and creamed spinach, even cherry/blueberry cobbler. All in ready-to-eat pouches or micro-waveable bags. And, of course, lemonade.

Then came the other stuff space travelers have to have: The hygiene supplies (mouthwash, toothpaste, etc.); recyclable waste bags for used food service items and others for human functions; and the 1.5-lb Personal Preference Kits that hold books, thumb drives, religious articles, and other knick-knacks, like a crew patch or pin. Bienstock has packed an Air Force Academy cap with a stylized eagle logo above the bill in his.

The largest item to be loaded on was the collapsible lunar rover, hinged at the center, with wheels that have their own drive motors and tires made of zinc-coated steel mesh. The state-of-the-art battery, too, can be taken out and hung on its own hook.

Last but definitely not least, it took several trips to haul up 103 Apollo leave-behinds and stow them where the crew can get at them for spreading on the lunar surface: science projects like the retro-reflector and the seismic detector along with the still and video cameras and all the other Apollo 'discards.'

The cargo pod brought up only 103 leave-behinds because the 104th is riding up to the capsule right now. It will be Robin Walsh's privilege, as Dark Side Mission Commander, to plant Old Glory on the moon, driving the one-inch aluminum tube eighteen inches into the surface (with a rubber mallet, if need be) before extending the fabric on its telescoping rods, and she's taken a proprietary interest in her task, not letting it out of her sight for the five hours of pre-launch prep. Even now, as the elevator slowly lifts the crew skyward, the cylindrical metal case of the Lunar Flag Assembly is wedged tightly behind her.

After another quarter-hour, the team finally settles into the Starliner. The first thing Robin does is place the LFA, gently and lovingly, with the other leave-behinds. Next, she calls up the space-craft's automated guidance system.

'Stella, turn audio links on.'

Robin came up with the name 'Stella' for the guidance system's interface – one that runs all mission functions as well as providing internet connectivity for the crew – back when Casselmann was still the mission's commander. She sold her suggestion to him and the others by calling up the 1952 Charlie Parker version of the pop standard 'Stella By Starlight' on her iPod and playing it for Kirk, Jack, and Cesar. Given that Mission Dark Side's space-craft would be bathed in starlight as soon as they left the earth's atmosphere, they'd made it unanimous and inputted it into the system.

The synthesized voice – Boeing has given Stella a warm, throaty one, not unlike Peggy Lee – says, 'Audio links on.'

Because the Starliner people have ceded control of the launch to NASA, Robin and Jack will spend the next two hours working with Stella and with Ground Control here and Mission Control in Houston.

For reasons of mission security, once the huge rocket lifts off all voice communication to and from the ground will cease.

Meanwhile, the two recently promoted ASCANs get to double-check all the Apollo leave-behinds in the cargo bay. They work from laminated checklists, like those washable placemats you come across in rural diners. Marty picks up each item in the hold according to its listed number and reads it out while Gary checks it off on an iPad.

'Number sixteen: Aldrin moonboots.'

'Moonboots, check.'

'Number seventeen: Armstrong moonboots.'

'More moonboots, check.'

'Number eighteen: Hasselblad camera body.'

'Hasselblad, check.'

'Number nineteen: LFA.'

'LFA, check. Wait, what's an LFA?'

Bienstock picks up the long aluminum tube from the stack of bins behind Bert and holds it up for him to see in the overhead mirror. 'Lunar Flag Assembly, LFA, the reason we're doing this whole thing, Curt. The sticker says it's a "sun-bleached American flag packed in its own extendible pole."'

At exactly the same moment, the two newbies to space look at each other. 'Cool!'

Stella says, 'Robin, execute visor configuration.'

It's T-minus two minutes, and the digitized voice can be heard clearly in the crew's helmets. To Gary's untrained ears, it's nice to know the spacecraft and its commander are on a first-name basis. He snaps his visor down along with the others.

Robin responds: 'Starliner visors closed.'

Several other voices chime in over the next ninety seconds with things like, 'Auto sequence start' and 'Range: Green.'

Strapped in behind Robin, Gary judders with the bumping and thumping of valves opening and closing as engine systems are pressurized, like the ogre from Jack and the Beanstalk waking up.

Soon a different voice in their helmets says, 'This is the Mission Director. You have permission to launch.'

Robin says, 'Starliner is go for launch.'

Stella says, 'T-minus nine . . . eight . . . seven . . .'

The first few of the twenty separate engines begin to light and there is a terrific low frequency growling far below them. That's when the shaking begins. The main engines get involved and the rumbling and shaking become even more intense as the whole vehicle strains to lift off the launch pad. Six hundred twenty-five thousand pounds of liquid oxygen, liquid hydrogen, and specially treated kerosene are on the verge of supplying a million and a half pounds of thrust. Seven seconds after the main engines light, the solid rocket boosters ignite and it feels like a huge kick in the behind.

The female voice in his helmet, calm as you like, finishes the countdown.

'Three . . . two . . . one . . .'

Gary takes a quick look at the others. Are they nervous? No way to tell.

'We have liftoff,' says the same warm voice.

Slowly, the massive rocket begins to move up and away from the launch pad. Before Gary can get used to the sensation, the Atlas-V begins to pitch and yaw. He can feel the G-forces building as it gains speed. Thirty-five seconds into the flight, Dark Side has reached and surpassed Mach-1, the speed of sound.

Soon, those gravitational forces are twice as heavy as anything he felt in the Vomit Comet and he's plastered to his seat. A good thing too; otherwise, the bang when the rescue system is jettisoned, and another when the protective nose faring comes off, would have him jumping out of his chair.

With the faring gone, light is streaming through the windows. Four and a half minutes in, the second stage separates from the spent booster and the G's drop dramatically. They go up again, though, when the third-stage engine lights. For the next couple of minutes, what feels like a giant gorilla is sitting on Gary's chest, making it difficult to breathe. Then, eight and a half minutes after launch – about the time it takes Mr Coffee to produce a full pot of hot java – a final loud bang announces the last section of the rocket is jettisoned and the gorilla magically disappears. Just like that, Gary is hanging upside-down in his shoulder harness. Nothing is pushing him back into his seat anymore.

Cue 'The Blue Danube Waltz.'

FIFTY-FIVE
Xichang Launch Center, China

'*Shénzhōu* 12, you are cleared for launch.'

Seconds away from achieving his lifelong dream, Chen Xu is a crazy mix of thoughts and emotions as he sits at the newly retrofitted and upgraded launch tower instrument panel and looks out at the very latest, most sophisticated Long March rocket ever produced. *His* rocket.

From this angle, he has a pretty good view of the world's most advanced crew capsule perched on top, the vehicle that will carry the three flagbearers – two men and a woman – safely to the moon and back. Crazy that it should be called *Shénzhōu* 12, he thinks, the 'twelfth divine boat.' By rights it should be number fourteen, seeing how thirteen space probes named *Shénzhōu*, both unmanned and manned of various kinds, preceded it. But no, Chinese science, even when it leads the world, has to take a back seat to fucking Chinese numerology.

'Four' is bad. Unpropitious. 'Four' sounds like the word 'death' in Mandarin.

Can't have that, even in the number fourteen.

Given that the number one is the sole digit associated with the water element – and, therefore, like a diver cleaving the waves, represents the ability to break through barriers on one's way to something better – and that 'two' sounds like 'sure' and 'easy' in Mandarin, the combination of 'one' and 'two' in the designation augurs a sure and easy breakthrough into space.

The number thing still burns him, even at this moment. But he was powerless. When a billion people believe something . . .

For some reason – maybe it's the bellyful of wonderful Sichuan-style pork working its way down his digestive system and producing an uptick of perspiration in his armpits – Chen flashes on a half-century-old memory playing in his brain. Mao's Great Leap Forward sent his parents, both teachers, to the hinterlands here from Shanghai to be 're-educated' in the Communist way. Backbreaking physical labor for both of them by day and then communal classes in history and economics at night.

The kids had it better. After lessons all day every day, they were herded back into the dining hall after supper for, sometimes, inspirational orations of poems praising the Chairman. Or there might be traditional music and dance presented by some of the professional performers who'd been dragged off the stages of Beijing and Shenzhen and trucked out to the sticks along with his mom and dad.

But every so often, once in a blue moon, they ran one of the old silent Hollywood films taken from the commandeered villas of the aristocrats up in the hills. Of course, they were screened first by the commissars for political correctness. Chen Zu's mind calls up the ending of one of those antique movies now. *Old Home Week* was the title. The hero, a nonentity for much of his life, returns to the home place he grew up in and, using just his brains, becomes the toast of the town.

Oh, crap . . . the countdown. Chen snaps out of his reverie just in time to speak into his microphone the words a billion countrymen have been waiting to hear. '*Wǒmen yǒu shēng kōng.*'

We have liftoff.

FIFTY-SIX

4230 Lenore Lane NW

Through the closed door of his den, Otto Kurzweil can hear Marianne and their guests still babbling away in the living room. Hell, it's after two in the morning, and the twenty or so invitees are all wide awake, yakking over the now-cold dishes of Chinese take-out she got at Mr Wu's down on Connecticut Avenue.

Before retreating to his man cave, as she calls it, Otto sampled a few of the choices. Damned if he can tell whether organic Chinese tastes any better than the plain old kind, but the beef and snow peas is still sitting on his stomach over an hour later. Who eats dinner after midnight? The Spanish, maybe.

He looks out the window beyond the HP's screen into the backyard. There is the cardinal, the bird's internal clock thrown off by all the unaccustomed living room and dining room lights streaming through the windows, still working the suet on its string. And there's Mrs Cardinal, down on the ground, gobbling up the morsels he's dropped. Just as Otto thought: eating this late is for the birds. And the Spaniards.

Begging off from the party, he's retreated to watch the show online. Maddening, these launches, they never go off on time. There was a twenty-minute hold at T-minus forty-five minutes and another at T-minus eleven. Now, with their act together at last, the Chinese are on the verge of making their dreams – and his – a reality.

The excitement, the vindication, is such that it makes him want to give out with a victory cry, a war whoop, *something*. Anything to express the sheer ecstasy of the occasion and the release of the weight of a half-century of planning and working for this very moment. Even though Marianne will probably come hurrying in all concerned the way she does, he decides it'll be worth it. And then . . . nothing comes out.

Strange. His throat feels all tight. Constricted.

Liftoff! The engines, released from the gantry that's falling away in perfect high-def glory on his vast computer screen, do their thing. He hears the big cheer from the friends and neighbors on the other side of the door as the huge bird takes off from the ground. This is it, he's close enough to *taste* it. Though all he can really taste is a metallic something mixed with the beef and snow peas.

In fact, as the CNN people, a whole panel of scientific and political talking heads, discuss the early seconds of the flight, the metal taste in his mouth is only getting worse. And there's a pain in his arm he didn't notice before. Both arms, actually.

But his arms, suddenly, aren't strong enough to push himself out of his desk chair. And they throb like nobody's business. With the throbbing comes one of his headaches. The irony is overwhelming: the supreme triumph of his lifetime has come at a time in life when he's too old to exult in it. Too old to even get up from his chair.

And then the light goes out.

FIFTY-SEVEN
206,000 miles above sea level

Robin and Jack Maybin are still discussing the Chinese liftoff two hours after the crew saw it happen, going on about the launch angle and God knows what else. In one of the seats behind them and with his helmet off, Gary is even now trying to recover from the Starliner's own launch. And that was more than twelve hours ago.

He isn't sick from the weightlessness. Rather, it's the 'new normal' of the thing. Unlike the alternating half-minute pinned-to-the-floor and half-minute free-floating periods of the Vomit Comet, the endless nothingness of space means you're either bobbing around the cabin willy-nilly or feeling the harness continually forcing your shoulders, and you, back down in your chair. At least on a transcontinental flight you can get up and walk around when they turn off the Fasten Seat Belts sign.

He's picturing the astronauts in Stanley Kubrick's *2001: A Space Odyssey*, the way they exercised by jogging inside their rotating space station. Like hamsters on a wheel, with the centrifugal force created by the rotation standing in for gravity. If only.

Instead of exercising his body, Gary is exercising his mind, entering his thoughts into Bert Forrester's iPad on its Notability app, using the stylus he picked up to draw the changing world around him. An hour or so ago he let go of the stylus and watched it slowly float up and away. The thing wound up hovering a couple of feet above his head before he undid the harness and let himself rise up to meet it. In a word, unearthly.

It's dinnertime on the Starliner. Lunch a while ago consisted of a few bags of snacks as everyone adjusted to their new environment. Now they're hungry for a real meal while they go over the details of their mission. Even though the speeding craft is self-navigating all the way to the moon – the celestial body looming ever larger in their windows – Robin and Jack have declared themselves too occupied with discussing systems oversight with Stella to prepare the food.

While they were doing that, the good doctor Bienstock spent time inventorying the items in his medical bag stowed in back, 'just in case,' before taking the first shift on food prep. For the last quarter-hour he's been assembling their individual meals from the myriad of freeze-dried food packets and Mylar beverage packs in the storage locker. He works according to each Dark Side member's culinary likes and dislikes printed on another plastic checklist.

After labeling the appropriate entrees, side dishes, desserts, and drinks with the name of the person they're intended for and then affixing the correct meal to the Velcro dots on the four serving trays (which also have Velcro straps to attach them to each astronaut's thighs), Marty taps Gary on the shoulder before sliding into his seat and snapping on his harness.

'You're up, bro.'

Thanks to their agreed-upon rotation, Bert Forrester will be this evening's chef. Leaving his seat, Gary uses the handholds built into the cabin's walls to pull himself over to the galley, where the shoe treads that are part of his onesie of a suit will allow him to stand comfortably in place on the special treaded mat.

Jack and Marty are having the BBQ ribs, Robin the haddock in cream sauce, and Gary the chicken Milanese. He was shown in training how to add the right amount of liquid – in this case, hot water from the Rehydration Station built into the galley – for each freeze-dried dish. And to do the same with the side-dish packets of creamed spinach for Marty and Robin and the two of creamed corn, his and Jack's.

Gary shifts over to adding what the Starliner calls 'ambient temperature' water to the various powdered beverages that come in the same kind of drink packs as Capri Sun. When they're filled, he'll puncture each bag with the sharp end of its drinking straw. Unlike the kids' drinks, these straws have a built-in plastic clamp you can squeeze to keep the fluids from floating out the business end between sips.

And then he notices something curious. An almost microscopic something is floating in the air at eye level. When Gary gets up close, he can see it's a tiny, liquid drop. The only reason it even caught his eye is the color: a sort of yellow-green. Floating three feet above the tray Marty set out for Robin, the floating artifact is a drop of her creamed spinach.

Gary places his thumb on Robin's side-dish packet and presses gently. Sure enough, another couple of tiny drops bubble up from a tiny hole in the bag. He grabs a paper towel from the nearby dispenser and whips the sheet of Bounty rather neatly around the airborne spinach drops before they can hit the ceiling and create a mess. Opening the disposal bin, he goes to drop the soiled paper in, forgetting that things in space don't drop. It stays in his hand.

He tries again, flipping open the cover of the bin and intending to close it fast after placing the balled-up paper inside. He notices something in the otherwise empty bin and picks it up: it's one of the Capri Sun straws. And the sharp end is colored an unmistakable yellow-green.

Strange.

Is the leaking spinach bag simply defective? Was it damaged in the loading process? Could Marty Bienstock have nicked it inadvertently with a drinking straw he then threw away? Gary checks the four dinner trays set out on the counter in front of him. Four drinks, four straws. The one in the trash is obviously an extra. Hmm.

He stands in the galley area, wondering what, if anything, to do. As he looks around, he notices the medical bag near his feet. It's slightly open, and he can see an eyedropper sitting on top of the other instruments and plastic vials full of medicine. An eyedropper, when 'nothing drops in space'?

Looking back and up at the overhead mirror to check that no one is watching, he bends down and opens the bag a little more. With the clean bit of the paper towel that's still in his hand, he picks up the dropper and peers closely at it: empty. Does Dr Bienstock require drops in his eyes? And how would that work, anyway?

He flicks the small plastic barrel the way they do with syringes on the TV doctor shows, and a tiny water droplet escapes the tip and floats upward, the same as the creamed spinach. This eyedropper was recently washed. Emboldened, he runs the length of the dropper between his thumb and forefinger. It's warm. The thing was recently run under the Rehydration Station's hot tap.

Gary flashes on what Robin said back in the Astral Lounge:

'They've gone to a lot of trouble to get your Marty Bienstock on this Dark Side ride.' And then, 'If he tries anything, you've got my back.'

And so she does.

He decides to perform a little experiment. Holding the straw from the trash with one hand, he inserts the tip of the dropper into the sipping end with the other. A snug, perfect fit. So, if there was something other than hot water in it a few minutes ago, a squeeze on the rubber end of the dropper would send that something down the straw with the clamp held open and into whatever the sharp end was poked into. Like a bag of creamed spinach.

Then Gary stops and shakes his head. Crazy. The trainers made a point of it, warning the ASCANs that extended exposure to the combination of microgravity and canned oxygen could produce a number of weird side effects in the brain. One of which, in a tiny percentage of subjects, is paranoia.

Still, if there's nothing wrong with Robin's bag of spinach, Marty will like it just as much as his own. So, Gary picks up the side dish from the doctor's tray and carefully peels his name tape off it, replacing it with the one that reads 'Robin' from the questionable bag. Then he sets her new spinach packet down on the Velcro holding dot beside the haddock on her tray.

Next, he takes the leaky bag and turns it face down, securing it to Marty's tray so nothing else will work its way out. When he's done, he affixes Marty's name tape to it with his thumb.

Better safe than sorry.

Marty dies twenty minutes into dinner.

At first, he's chowing down like the rest of them, even complimenting Gary on his skills in the kitchen. 'Delicious, bro.'

Gary thinks it's nice the guy has stopped calling him 'Curt.' And that dinner *is* delicious, though there's a trick to eating chicken Milanese from a bag. You have to undo the cross flaps and pick up just enough of the food on your spork so you can gulp it down before the chicken flies up and away. Close the flaps, swallow, open the flaps, pick up some more, repeat.

By the time Gary looks up, Marty is convulsing. He grabs the man's medical bag and races it up front to Robin, who knows about these things. Marty's eyes have rolled back in his head. She sorts through the vials in the bag, prepares a syringe, and injects the dying doctor right through his Boeing Blue suit.

Too late. She feels for a pulse as Maybin rips open the Velcro tabs holding the collar to Marty's neck so he can begin chest compressions. Several minutes later, after they both work on him, Jack gives up. He notes the time on his watch.

'T plus thirteen hours, twenty-two minutes.'

The four-person crew is now down to three.

'Let us say a prayer for our fallen comrade.'

Jack Maybin holds out one hand to Robin and the other to Gary. Looking at Robin, he says, 'You or me?'

'He was Air Force Academy. You take it.'

He nods. The three bow their heads over the body of Dr Martin Bienstock, still strapped into his chair. Jack Maybin makes the sign of the cross before launching in. Gary was a junior counselor at a YMCA camp in the Poconos, so he's used to the Christian form of prayer.

'O Lord, our comfort and help in time of need, You have shown us that death is but the gateway to a more glorious life, and that we must not fear its coming. We know, also, that neither life nor death can separate us from Your love. Assure us yet again that our comrade Martin Bienstock, departed, is not lost to us, but already sharing new life with You in the Kingdom of our Father, where we shall in Your good time be reunited. In Christ's name we pray.'

Four voices say the 'Amen' in unison, as Stella has joined in their prayer.

Jack raises his head but doesn't let go of their hands. To Robin he asks, 'Now what, Commander?'

She says, 'Given our orders to proceed under strict radio silence to rendezvous – and the fact that our mission won't conclude with a touchdown back home for another thirty-three hours at the earliest – our choices are lousy. We don't have the ability to perform an autopsy here in the capsule. Even if we did, the only person equipped to do that would be our medical officer, Dr Bienstock. And, while we have plenty of storage space, it isn't cold storage. So, Marty will begin to decompose in . . .'

She stops, not wanting to go down that road.

'Look,' she continues, 'We have another nine hours to rendezvous.

In the meantime, I don't think we should leave him lying right here. Can we lay Marty out on the other side of the galley?'

The men undo their harnesses and move over to Bienstock. The weightlessness makes it relatively easy to lift him with one hand and use the other to work their way to the rear with the handholds. Once they get there, they undo the Velcro utility straps on the dead man's suit and use them to anchor him to the floor mat under the lunar rover on its hooks.

Robin has been going through the man's medical bag, more carefully this time. One of the small vials catches her attention. She holds it up to the light. Then, working her way over to the corpse, she shows the others what she's found.

'Lidocaine.'

Jack looks up at the tiny 300-milliliter bottle. 'So? It's a numbing agent. I imagine every doctor has one in his bag.'

She holds the little glass container closer so he can see it better. 'It's empty.'

Jack and Gary stare at the empty bottle.

Robin continues, 'We all saw him going over the supplies in his bag, checking each medication. Who takes an empty medicine bottle on a week-long trip into space?'

Jack says, 'Stella, tell us how many milliliters of lidocaine are fatal to human beings.'

Stella answers instantly. 'Lidocaine is a local anesthetic that produces transient loss of sensory, motor, and autonomic function when the drug is injected or applied in proximity to neural tissue. It is the most common local anesthetic and used in almost all medical specialties. In a 170-lb man like Dr Bienstock, 300 milliliters would produce fatal toxicity. A smaller man and most women would require a smaller dose.'

After just a moment of hesitation, Gary looks up at Robin and says, 'He meant to poison you with it.'

Then it all comes out, the story of the creamed spinach, and how he switched the names on the bags.

'So, if anyone killed Marty Bienstock, I guess it was me.'

FIFTY-EIGHT

The cartoon mouse has his cartoon foot resting on a soccer ball. He's lecturing a cartoon duck. 'OK Donald, imagine this soccer ball is the earth.'

The mouse produces a tennis ball and begins tossing it to himself. 'Then, this is the size of our moon.'

He tosses the tennis ball in the air one more time but Donald Duck grabs it away and begins to frenziedly bounce it all over the place. At the same time, he's squawking excitedly and unintelligibly

A tall cartoon dog named Goofy enters the scene, dressed in a flannel nightgown and rubbing the sleep from his eyes. He takes the tennis ball from Donald and stares at it, uncomprehendingly.

Even as the duck goes ballistic over the loss of the ball, Mickey the mouse calmly says, 'That's the moon.'

Goofy is confused. In his characteristic slow Southern drawl, he says, 'Uhh, Mick, are you sure? Looks like a tennis ball to me.'

With Donald jumping up and down and Goofy scratching his head, the mouse looks off-screen. He calls, 'Help me explain, Dr von Braun!'

A handsome middle-aged human being enters their cartoon world. From his jacket pocket he produces his own tennis ball.

'Wait! I know this one!'

Gary and the others have taken a break from the sober effort of sorting out Marty Bienstock's poisoning to catch up with the progress of the Chinese space mission that's unwittingly following on the heels of Dark Side. Thanks to the Starliner's Bluetooth capability, they're able to surf the Web and tune into this wall-to-wall Aussie broadcast to take their minds off what happened.

With English-speaking Australia 2,500 miles closer to China than the US, it's no surprise the Land Down Under would make a big whoop-de-doo over every moment of *Shénzhōu* 12. And now, after lots of dry science-speak, the Aussies have had the good sense to cut to this sixty-year-old educational film – produced by NASA and the Disney organization – as a form of comic relief.

'Pop did that! I remember, my father directed that short! We have a copy at home! Wow!'

Robin and Jack are looking at Gary in wonder. Partly because he's excited like a kid, and partly because, well, what are the odds?

Gary says, 'Von Braun's ball has a rubber band attached.'

With that, Wernher von Braun shows the inked-in characters that his tennis ball has an elastic cord. He holds the free end of the rubber band in his hand and swings the ball in an arc, saying, 'The moon travels around us in a big circle called an orbit.'

Dr von Braun picks up the soccer ball from the ground and swings the tennis ball around it. A dotted line appears, superimposed between the two balls. The German rocket scientist is saying, 'The distance from the earth to the moon averages 240,000 miles. That's like flying ten times in a row around the earth at the equator.'

Mickey Mouse asks the German scientist, 'How fast does a rocket ship go in space?'

Von Braun stops spinning the tennis ball and kneels down to speak with Mickey eye to eye. 'Just to escape earth's gravity, you have to go more than 15,000 miles an hour.' He continues, 'Once you leave our atmosphere, there's nothing to slow you down. So, you keep on speeding along for the sixty hours it takes to get there.'

Goofy has wandered off-screen. Now he returns wearing the thick black eyeglasses of a scientist with a plastic protector full of pens in his nightgown pocket. He wheels in a chalkboard that reads, 'From the earth to the moon.' Then, picking up a piece of chalk, he solves a math equation: *Distance $\div$ Speed = 16 hours.*

He points to his handiwork on the board, saying, 'Sixty hours? I think your arithmetic is *way* off, Professor.'

The famed aerospace engineer straightens up and faces the animated dog. 'If the moon stood still above the earth, you'd be right, Goofy. But it doesn't.'

He twirls the tennis ball on the rubber band around the bigger ball once again. This time, a dotted line appears to start at the soccer ball, like a spaceship leaving earth, and travels in a curve, hurrying to catch up with the 'moon' that's moved on in its orbit. For every mile the rocket travels toward it, the moon is traveling nearly a mile as well. They finally come together well along the moon's orbit around the planet. The dotted line on the screen is now four times as long as it seemed to be before.

After the demonstration, von Braun says to Goofy, 'When Apollo flies to the moon, it will take them sixty hours just to get there. Understand?'

Goofy scratches his head. 'Uhh, I *think* so.'

The cartoon is coming to its big windup. Donald is sneaking up behind von Braun with a huge pair of scissors.

Excitedly, Gary says to the others, 'Here it comes!'

The pen-and-ink duck cuts the rubber band and runs away with the second tennis ball, quacking like a madman. Or mad duck. Von Braun, unperturbed, turns to the chalkboard and underlines the number sixteen before leaving Mickey and Goofy with his final thought.

'Today, it takes sixty hours to get to the moon. But with bigger rockets and smarter computers, we'll get there a lot faster. In the future.'

With the short over, the Australian space experts appear once more on the screen. Robin mutes the sound before saying, 'I hadn't realized it before, gentlemen. We must be living in the future.'

FIFTY-NINE

Washington National Cathedral

Carmelo nudges the Vice-President's limousine along South Road toward the entrance to the country's pre-eminent Episcopal cathedral. He's trailing at least a dozen cars, all inching their way together in a convoy ever since they got off Wisconsin Avenue, waiting for those at the head of the line to disgorge the notables who've come to pay their respects to Otto Kurzweil. And, not incidentally, get their pictures into tomorrow's papers.

Sitting in back next to his wife, Carole, the Vice-President is remembering his late advisor. The man's crazy form of speech that sounded like a volcano erupting. The way he banged his pipe down on an ashtray, emptying it, whenever he needed more time to think. The occasions when he acted as if his hearing aids were malfunctioning, though subsequently it was clear he'd heard every word.

'A penny for your thoughts.'

Carole is peering at him; he must have some sort of look on his face.

'Just thinking of Otto, hon.'

If the Professor was a believer, he never showed it. He certainly wasn't Episcopalian. But Marianne had called in a few favors from congregants – the main one being Hal himself – and was able to book the place this morning, just a mile and a half from the Kurzweil home.

By now, Carmelo has worked his way into the start of the wide turn-around area in front of the cavernous building. Hal would like to get out and walk the thirty yards to the doors, but Carole's shoes, from the look of them, aren't up to the uneven cobblestones that make up the plaza, so he sits and waits.

A tall black man with a shaved head, six foot four or five, is getting out of the car that's made it to the head of the line. The collar of his white dress shirt – expensive looking, like the cut of his tailored dark blue suit – perfectly contrasts with the man's almost blue-black skin. Hal can see he's caught Carole's eye as well. Kareem? Salim? He remembers the guy ducking under the transom to get into Otto's set of rooms in the Old Executive Office Building. Raheem! Works for one of the agencies.

Raheem closes the limo door. Then, before he mounts the sets of granite steps that lead to the double wooden doors under the tall central arch, he looks over to the passenger getting out of the next car down, a silver Audi. She's saying something to the driver – her husband? – before he heads off to park. She looks familiar; someone at State? No, Defense. It's Madelyn Connors, a mousy analyst type. One of Otto's groupies from Yale.

And then, only because he's peering at the striking, GQ-ready icon that is Raheem, he notices the black man smile at her, crook his index finger, and run it down the length of his nose. Unusual. And then she does the same gesture back at him. Is this the way government people greet each other these days? If so, nobody told Hal.

Inside the vast cavern of a church a quarter hour later, he and Carole are seated in the second row, behind the family. Across the aisle and half a dozen chairs in, the Connors woman is sitting with Raheem and her husband, also in the VIP section. She's singing lustily from her hymnal and dabbing at her cheek with a handkerchief, her mascara a little awry.

Hal's surprised to think the loss of crusty, forbidding Otto would bring anyone to tears, even a family member. The thought has him reaching into his breast pocket for his own handkerchief. Ever the politician, he uses it to wipe away a few non-existent tears for any observers with their camera phones pointed his way. Then he looks down at the printed Order of Service in his lap.

After Hymn 208, 'The Strife is O'er, the Battle Done,' will come the Very Reverend Holloman's remembrance of a man he never knew in life, and then Otto's estranged oldest son's, and then – he counts down the names in the program – seven others, all with government or university ties to the deceased. Finally, at long last, it will be Hal's turn. Fifty minutes at least. So, the Vice-President does what he always does on the rubber chicken circuit: he sets his features into an interested look and stops listening.

Half an hour later, he comes back to life. Something out of the ordinary just tripped his brain into action. What? The fifth or sixth eulogist, the Chief of Staff at the IRS – the program in his lap says he's Larry Wilbur, probably a Kurzweil grad student way back when – is unfolding his notes and placing them on the lectern. Nothing unusual about that; it must have been something before he got up there.

Hal is still thinking it through a few minutes later when it happens again. The man, Wilbur, has finished his praise of Otto Kurzweil and, walking back to his seat, does that same finger-scrape thing down his nose in the direction of Mrs Connors and the man with the shaved head sitting next to her, Raheem.

And then the light bulb goes off: It's the gesture Paul Newman and Robert Redford make to each other in *The Sting*. In fact, all the in-the-know characters in that film do the finger-down-the nose-thing, a sort of signal that the plot, the scheme to bilk Robert Shaw's character, is still on track. Hell, it's one of Hal's favorite flicks of all time.

And then it's his turn to move to the podium.

While he's up there talking, he's thinking about Otto (a little) and Paul Newman (a lot). Nine minutes later, he wraps up his prepared remarks and walks down the steps – slowly, must remember his heart is heavy laden – to return to his seat. He passes in front of the section across the aisle from his own, where the IRS accountant and the other two are sitting. On a whim, nothing more, he looks their way, smiles mournfully, crooks his index finger, and runs it down the length of his nose.

The surprise on Larry Wilbur's face is worth the price of admission. Well, the funeral was free, but still, the man is totally discombobulated. Hal catches the unspoken distress signal the IRS guy sends with his eyes toward the pair sitting a couple of seats on down the row. And they give the same confused looks back.

Good, they think he must be in on the thing. But, Hal wonders, in on *what* thing?

SIXTY

Aboard the Starliner

The conversation has taken a morbid turn, thanks to the question Robin asked of the others a minute ago. 'How old were you when you saw your first dead body?'

Maybin turns the question back on her. 'How old were *you*?'

Her eyes take on a faraway look, as if viewing her memory right then and there. 'My folks had a cabin cruiser. One Sunday, we planned a day on the water, so we got there early. A guy had washed up, shot through the head by smugglers, maybe, and dumped from a boat. He was floating face up under the wharf. Ugh.'

She shivers, and clasps her hands around her shoulders to stop the tremors. 'Sorry I brought it up.'

Jack shifts his eyes to Gary. 'Bert?'

Gary says, to no one in particular, 'My daughter, Jill, was nine when her mother, my wife, Carla, was walking her back from roller skating in Riverside Park. We lived a block from there. They were crossing the street when a drunk driver ran the light on Eighty-ninth, killing Carla and Jill. I got there just before they took them away.'

Robin reaches out and takes his hand in hers, giving it a sympathetic squeeze.

Jack looks at their clasped hands. 'I guess that leaves me. I was just out of flight school early in the Afghan War, assigned to airlift supplies to an FOB that overlooked the Korengal Valley, and—'

Gary asks, 'What's an FOB?'

'Oh. Sorry. Forward Operating Base of the coalition forces. This one later got the name Restrepo, after an Army medic who died there. Anyway, I made the drop and was returning when I took incoming fire from one of the hamlets that kind of hang off the mountainside. Well, naturally, I fired back. Dropped a bomb right down the well in the center of this scummy Taliban village.

'I was circling for home when my right engine flamed out. I'd been hit by one of their handheld rockets. When the fire spread I had to bail out before my plane crashed into the hillside. Broke my leg as I hit the treeline. My chute was tangled in the branches and I guess I hung up there the rest of the day and the night.'

Gary says, 'This is . . .'

Jack smiles ruefully. 'Yeah, the thing I'm known for. Anyway, they found me in the morning, the Taliban. Not a nice crowd. They were mad as hell about my blowing up their water supply. They brought me back to that bombed-out village and forced me to look at the people I'd killed. Nine or ten, mostly women, some old, some young. So, they were my first dead bodies.'

Gary waits for Jack to go on. When he doesn't, curiosity gets the best of 'Bert Forrester.'

'I've heard the story, of course, Jack. Everyone has. But, it was two years – wasn't it? – before you were rescued. What can you—?'

'Three years. Thirteen days short of three years. But who's counting?'

Robin asks, 'How did we get you out?'

'*We* didn't. *We* pretty much left me there to die, though you won't find that in the official version. I guess, when I didn't make it back, they thought I'd bought the farm when my plane hit that mountain. And since it was hostile territory, I don't think they even tried to find me.'

Robin and Gary wait for him to continue.

'Anyway, they finally set my broken leg and started moving me around all over the place, mostly at night. I was blindfolded a lot of the time, so I didn't really know where I was. And I couldn't ask because, in the beginning, I didn't understand what they were saying. Pashto, Dari, Urdu, what did I know? Eventually I picked up a few words, and figured out they'd gotten word back to our people that I was still alive, that they were trying to trade me back for some of the prisoners *we* had.

'All I know is, I finally was taken to a village where one of their commanders spoke English. He told me the coalition, the Americans, refused to swap prisoners. Wouldn't pay blackmail to free any *terrorists*. Not even for their own POW.'

Robin says, 'How can our government *do* that? What about "no man left behind?"'

Jack gives her a grim smile. 'Guess that's just the Marines. Anyway, Year Three saw me held way up north near Turkmenistan. Elements of the Russian army, commandos, were camped in the hills across the border. There's no love lost between the Russians and the Afghans; they fought a war for years before we took over. Learning an American was being held a couple of clicks away, one night they sent a squad over and raided the place where I was. Killed my guards and got me out of there.

'I was with them for a couple of weeks before they arranged my transport home. Just long enough to learn how to say, *"Das blagoslovit menya Bog za spaseniye vas."* That's Russian for "May God bless you for rescuing me."'

The story sends a chill along Gary's spine, but Robin seems to be fighting to hold back a laugh.

Jack sees it too. 'Something funny about what I said?'

She lets out the guffaw she's been trying to hold in. 'As a matter of fact, there is. You actually said, "May God bless *me* for rescuing *you*."'

'What? Really?' Jack's face turns a bright shade of pink. 'No, I'm pretty sure—'

All Robin can do is nod her head while tears of laughter well up in her eyes. She tries to wipe them away with the sleeve of her suit as she says, 'Oh my God, did you *really*?'

Gary is nonplussed, and embarrassed for Jack. He manages to ask her, 'You know Russian?'

She looks at him. It takes a moment or two before she's calm enough to say, 'The, uh, the whatzit . . . the International Station. You spend a few months up there working with their guys and you pick things up. I—'

Before she can say another word, Stella's synthesized voice – still sounding like Peggy Lee – announces itself with four simple words: 'Moon Approach systems on.' Gary can feel the braking rockets coming to life along with an instant shift in their angle of flight. The thrill of it sends another shiver down his spine. He thinks, *I'm going to walk on the moon!*

At the same time, the unspoken thought of another member of the Dark Side crew is: *Did I just tip my hand?*

Robin begins speaking to the guidance system. 'Stella, please go over your revised—'

The autopilot interrupts in the same neutral voice as before. 'I detect a problem, Commander. One of our braking rockets will not ignite.'

Robin begins looking over the braking switches on her console. In an equally calm voice, she says, 'I see it. Number three.'

She reaches for the section of the instrument panel where one of the little lights is out. She toggles the switch next to the light back and forth. Nothing.

'Is this possibly a delayed burn for some reason, Stella?'

'Negative. My error report tells me there is a faulty fuse. I will have to recompute our Moon Approach speed.'

Gary asks the others, 'What does that mean?'

But Stella, thinking the question is for her, answers. 'Nothing catastrophic, Bert. We still have seventy-five percent of our retro rocket capability. However, I will not be able to brake our speed sufficiently to place us in moon orbit without making one extra pass around.'

'Around what? The whole moon?'

'Yes, Bert. My flight plan had us dropping into lunar orbit in nine minutes, thirty-five seconds. Unfortunately, we cannot achieve a low enough trajectory to—'

Impatiently, Jack interrupts. 'How much time will we lose, Stella?'

'Nearly two hours. On the bright side, we—'

'Did you just say, "On the *bright* side?"' Robin's voice has an edge now.

Their autopilot doesn't seem to notice. 'On the bright side, we will make a pass directly over Tranquility Base. So, you'll be able to—'

Jack angrily barks at the Starliner's voice. 'This isn't a tour bus, Stella. Tell me how far the Chinese are behind us.'

In her unruffled way, Stella responds, 'Do you want that in kilometers or hours, Jack?'

'Hours, Stella.'

The computer says, 'I calculate the *Shénzhōu* will enter lunar orbit in seven hours, fourteen minutes.'

It's Robin who exclaims, 'So, now they're only five hours behind us!'

Stella corrects her. 'Five hours, thirteen minutes, and twenty-five seconds.'

Gary asks, nervously, 'If they're that close, Stella, won't they be able to spot us on their approach?'

'No, but it's a good question, Bert.' Maddeningly, the guidance system's voice betrays no sign of emotion. 'Spacecraft travel through the void between the earth and the moon at speeds of up to 35,000 kilometers an hour. You can't feel how fast we're going because there's no atmospheric resistance and no signposts whizzing by. Given that they're more than five hours behind us, that means they're about 180,000 kilometers away. So, no, they won't see us for quite a while.'

'What about their *Queqiao*?' It's Robin who asks the question. 'That satellite is already parked near the moon.'

Like the computer geek she is, like the *computer* she is, Stella warms to her task.

'Currently, there are four objects already in lunar orbit. The *Queqiao* arrived last month, joining our Lunar Reconnaissance Orbiter, which moves in a north–south polar orbit, and a pair of US Artemis satellites that were sent up a decade ago to record the moon's interaction with the sun.

'My programming has allowed me to, temporarily, place ourselves in the same known orbit as Artemis 2. That should convince the *Queqiao*'s instruments that we are an existing satellite and not some newcomer.'

Robin asks, 'Stella, what makes you think the Chinese will fall for it?'

'Because, Robin, *I* would fall for it.'

SIXTY-ONE
Room 414, Ulitsa Optikov

Three of the monitors in the empty room are turned off. The fourth, the one closest to the windows facing the parking lot, is showing the telecast of the Chinese moon launch with the sound muted. On it, Wei Fenghe, the commander of the *taikonauts,* a neologism that incorporates *taikong* (space) instead of 'astro' or 'cosmo', is demonstrating weightlessness by trying to capture a floating shrimp from his dinner with chopsticks.

The delicacy keeps sliding upwards and away from even his expert manipulation of the wooden instruments until Wei reaches out and grabs it with his hand. He pops it in his mouth and gives a wry smile for the three billion or so people watching around the world.

On the fifth monitor, Yevgeny Prigozhin, 'Putin's Chef,' is quizzing his Washington-based operative, Alexei Morozov, across from him on the sixth.

'You watching this?'

'Everybody here is.'

'Are the Chinese really this unaware of what's going on?'

'Totally, sir. And their on-board instrumentation is supposed to be top-notch.'

'Our agent still in play? My principal wants to know.'

'I have no way of knowing; Dark Side remains a stealth mission. Guess you'll both have to wait for the doctor to come out and tell us.'

'Huh?'

Morozov grins. 'You've got kids, right?'

'Two girls.'

'In the old days, the fathers weren't allowed in the delivery room. They had to wait until the doctor came out and told them what they had.'

'Oh.'

'Precisely, sir. No cigars until the doctor comes out.'

SIXTY-TWO
Aboard the Starliner

As they travel over it, outfitted now in their spacesuits, Robin, Jack, and Gary can see just how vast the Sea of Tranquility really is. On earth it would cover much of Western Europe, with Apollo 11's landing site sitting in the extreme southwest of the *Mare Tranquillitatis*, about where Bordeaux would be on a map of France. Because the unnamed pit crater Lila Hensen discovered – the tiny speck on the lunar map in the Administrator's office – is the same twenty-kilometer distance from Apollo's landing site as the great wine-making vineyards are from the city of Bordeaux, the crew asked Stella to call the spot 'Margaux.' Stella thought it was a woman's name, and asked who she was to be celebrated in this way. Marty had said it was Margo Channing from *All About Eve*.

'Approaching Base Margo; helmets on, visors down.'

She accompanies her announcement with a renewed application of the Starliner's braking system while simultaneously reorienting the spacecraft so the crew capsule is uppermost, the way it was during liftoff.

Now that they're directly above it and able to view the Margo crater on the monitor, it's frighteningly small. Robin asks, 'Are you sure we can fit in that hole, Stella?'

'Have no concern, Commander. My sensors tell me Margo's diameter is 5.4 meters across at her narrowest point. Since my specifications show I'm no more than 4.5 meters at my widest, we have nearly a meter to spare. Like parking a Chevy Suburban in a fifties tract-house garage: tight but doable. Or, more aptly since we're descending, like placing a teacup back down on its saucer.'

Jack, not entirely at ease, asks, 'What do you know about Chevy Suburbans, Stella? Or cups and saucers, for that matter?'

'From the ads on the TV programs you've been watching while I flew us here. Most educational.' Then her digital voice says, 'Prepare for landing.'

For the next few moments, Gary can feel the braking effect as the retro rockets drop the Starliner slowly into its 'garage.' There's a noticeable bump when the capsule comes to rest on its inflated airbags and the firing systems are turned off.

Stella announces, 'Attach oxygen tanks. Preparing to unlock main hatch and cargo hatch.'

The dust stirred up by the Starliner's descent has, very slowly, begun to settle. The bolts on the main door and the cargo hold slide open with a loud double thunk.

'Releasing gangway.'

Doubled back on itself during flight, the nine-foot-long metal walkway unfolds until it meets the mostly smooth surface of this part of *Tranquillitatis.*

Stella says, 'Margo's rock substrate was covered in a slightly thicker layer of sediment than estimated. Now that it's been blown away by my three retro rockets, we are sitting a little lower relative to the lunar surface than we anticipated. The good news: there's less of us visible to observers orbiting overhead. The bad news: my gangway will not fall into a level position. You will have to exert slightly more force moving the SEV out of my hold. So, please follow all instructions to the letter. Good luck.'

Jack and Gary take down the various parts of the lunar rover from brackets in the cargo area and trundle them up and out along the gangway. The moon's reduced gravity makes it a comparatively easy operation.

And because Maybin is in front, his are the first human boots to set foot on the moon since the crew of Apollo 17 departed in 1972.

Once they've taken a few tentative, bouncy steps in the micro-gravity and become used to breathing the air from their tanks, the two men take a moment to survey the rugged wilderness of the moon in all its forbidding glory. The rocks in the *Mare* have a slightly bluish cast compared to the rest of the lunar surface due to their higher content of non-ferrous metals – less iron, less red rust. Nearby highlands to the northwest prevent them from seeing their destination, Apollo 11's Tranquility Base, over a dozen miles away.

To the north and east of where they're standing is the vast crater called Moltke, well over a mile wide and perfectly round. Closer to hand, the camouflaged nose of the Starliner barely peeks above the lunar surface, like a brown speckled egg sitting in the nest that is 'Base Margo.'

Jack says, 'Better get a move on. We've only got ten hours of oxygen at the most.'

His voice has a slightly canned quality to Gary's ears, even though the helmet's built-in speakers are state of the art. Of course, part of that is the sound of that oxygen rushing in and his breath rushing out. He resorts to shallower breathing and flashes Jack the OK sign.

Lifting the rover's lightweight aluminum engine, one that weighs 220 lbs on earth but is less than 40 lbs now, from its wheeled sled is a relatively simple two-man job. While Jack runs down the check-list of assembly instructions on his plasticized card, Gary goes back down the gangway for the rest of the rover's parts. They'll need to completely assemble the rover before they can begin loading all the leave-behind items Robin has begun to gather. Including that all-important American flag.

When Gary comes back with an armful of aluminum rods, Jack stops what he's doing and says, 'Look, Bert . . . I mean, Gary . . . I'm sorry about what I said back there.'

Gary sets the rods down in a pile. 'Sorry? About what?'

'That woe-is-me tale about Afghanistan. I promised myself I'd never make a pitch for sympathy, and—'

'Don't be ridiculous. Robin asked about dead people and we answered. Besides if it helps any,' Gary smiles at Jack inside his helmet, 'I'm completely unsympathetic.'

Maybin grins back. 'That's a relief.'

Thirty-five minutes later, when the rover assembly is completed and the now over-engineered battery is hooked up for what should be not much more than a two-hour trip to the site, Robin helps them lug all of the individually numbered Apollo articles from inside the Starliner to the SEV.

The one item that doesn't have a number, Marty Bienstock's already-decomposing corpse, is also carried out across the gangway and laid on the nearby ground made of rocky material that was 'splashed' out of Margo eons ago by the asteroid that created it. They promise each other to do something of a more reverential nature, some kind of burial, on their way back.

For the next half hour or so, the three of them place camera bodies, food waste bags, and the rest of the Apollo detritus in the newly erected jungle gym of a cargo carrier, covering the whole thing with a roll-down canvas top that's camouflaged to look like the lunar surface, the same as the Starliner's nose. Having accomplished the job, Robin is able to get behind the wheel and, pressing her gloved finger on the little black key fob's button, fire up the rover only seventy-four minutes after landing.

Before starting out, she says, 'I miss Casselmann telling me what a lousy driver I am. And Cesar coming to my defense.'

The three of them share a somber moment before Robin steps on the accelerator. The rover lurches ahead, kicking up a storm of lunar dust from the wheels in the lowered gravity, some of which settles on the cargo in back.

Jack says, 'Is it too soon to tell you what a lousy driver you are?'

SIXTY-THREE

The White House Treaty Room

'How are you holding up, Alf?'

The President, on the phone, is sitting beside her husband, the only civilian in the group, in the second-floor residence of the White House. They share the beige couch that faces the fireplace in this historic room that once served as our sixteenth President's pass-through from his library to what is now called the Lincoln Bedroom.

Three others with knowledge of Mission Dark Side are there for the viewing session as well: The Vice-President, Under Secretary Cy Talbott, and the FBI's Leah Davis are sitting in the overstuffed chairs that form a U with the couch. A huge bowl of buttered popcorn rests on the padded coffee table in front of them. The Chinese are still flying to the moon, but silently; Hal muted the large flat-screen TV so POTUS could call the hospital in Houston.

Hahnfeldt, on speakerphone, replies, 'Not doing very well, I'm afraid, Ms President.'

'Oh? Is it the breathing?'

'No, that's much better, thanks. It's the lying down on the job, so to speak. I should be back at Mission Control where I can do some good, instead of watching it from inside this plastic cocoon.'

The President tries for some humor. 'Now you know how *I* feel. People say we live in a bubble here in Washington, and they're right. I don't drive my own car, spend my own money. I didn't even place this phone call, an assistant did it for me.'

'At least you get to do your job, ma'am. I'm out of the loop in this medical warehouse. Like some football player on injured reserve.'

The Vice-President leans toward the phone. 'Alf, it's Hal. Forget the injured player stuff. You're the manager. You helped pull this whole team together. Besides, with our people doing their silent running, you'd just be watching and waiting like the rest of us. So, rest up and hustle back up here as soon as you can. We're gonna celebrate Dark Side's success the moment we know they've pulled off the sting.'

'That's very nice of you to say, sir.'

The rest of the group sends him their well-wishes before the President puts the phone back down in its cradle. Hal, though, is thinking about the word he just used. The 'sting.' Like the movie. And scraping a finger down your nose. Is that what we're doing? Or, is someone running a sting on *us*?

The President is saying, 'Isn't this the craziest thing? We're sending Robin, Jack, Marty, and Gary to the moon, and we won't even know they've made it safely until they get back.'

Hal says, 'We'll know it sooner than that, once Chinese TV gets into camera range and we see that flag up there.'

Leah Davis asks, 'How soon will that be?'

The Veep picks up the remote and turns the TV sound back on. Judy Woodruff is interviewing someone who wrote a book about the moon.

He lowers the volume. 'Guess it's still the pre-game show. That last segment, when they had Chet Predovic on, he estimated a couple of hours to go. Before we called Alf.' He looks at the First Couple. 'Want me to find another station? Maybe CBS or CNN has a better fix on the time.'

The President says, 'No, stay with PBS. We help underwrite the place, may as well get our money's worth.'

Cy Talbott has a concerned look on his face. 'Ms President, what if they don't make it? What if there isn't a flag? We have time scheduled with the press in a while and—'

'I've got it covered, Cy.' She gestures over to a manila folder lying on the Treaty Table, the large Victorian desk where President McKinley signed the peace agreement ending the Spanish-American War. 'Jotted down a few words, just in case.'

The President's husband, famous for having no official opinion about anything and saying even less in public than Margaret Thatcher's spouse, Denis, did, clears his throat before addressing his wife.

'Dearest, there's this thing online. A few kooks have found a loophole, sort of. Since the last Administration pulled us out of the space treaty and Congress hasn't yet re-ratified, they're calling on us to declare the moon *American* property. Because of the flag. Despite what they think the Apollo crew said and did fifty years ago in the name of mankind.'

She gives him one of her sardonic grins. 'They *are*, are they?'

The First Husband, as usual, is all earnestness. 'Yes, and they want you to do it before the Chinese plant *their* flag next to ours a couple hours from now.'

She says, 'Any of these kooks have a name?'

He smiles a bit. 'Guess.'

'My predecessor?'

He smiles a bit more. 'Bingo, hon!'

SIXTY-FOUR

On the moon

Fifty minutes into the trip, either Robin's become a better driver or the moon's surface is now a lot smoother. Probably both. At least, that's the way it feels to Gary in the rover's back seat.

Once they got past the highlands and headed northwest, the Apollo gear sitting in the racks of aluminum piping behind him and over his head stopped threatening to fall and crush him with every jounce.

Heading north from the moon's equator as fast as the SEV will go – that failed fuse in Stella's system having cost them two hours of their head start on the Chinese – the Sea of Tranquility is just that, tranquil, with its ancient basalt free of dust and rocks most of the way. Unlike its Rock Yard equivalent, thank God.

One drawback: the vehicle is now out of Stella's range. Without geo-synchronous satellites overhead to map their route the way they do on earth, the Starliner's guidance system was able to beam out a sort-of GPS substitute for the route to the Apollo site, one they could pick up on the Apple Watch embedded into the sleeves of their suits. But with the hills in their rearview mirror blocking further transmissions from the capsule, Robin and Jack, navigating for her, will have to make do the old-fashioned way, with a map of the area on the Apple screen.

Jack says, 'Four minutes to rendezvous. The countdown function on my watch says we'll be in Chinese camera range in ninety minutes or less.'

Robin says, 'Gonna be tight.'

Tranquility Base, when they pull up and park, looks just like the rest of the moon. Rocks, some dust, a few rises and dips in the ground, with the Little West Crater, only thirty meters across but very deep, sitting nearby. Not only will they have to scatter 103 items around the area before planting Old Glory, they'll have to create the same pattern of footprints in the dust that Armstrong and Aldrin were supposed to have made fifty years ago. Like following the steps on one of those Arthur Murray *How-to-Cha-Cha* charts.

Familiarity with the reduced gravity means it takes them less time to unload the leave-behinds. Before there's any flag-raising, though, Robin will have to follow Aldrin's path southeast of the rover and deploy the passive seismic experiments package and the laser-ranging retroreflector in the positions in which they appear in the manufactured photo on NASA's website. The two-foot-wide reflector panel studded with a hundred little mirrors is designed to bounce a laser pulse sent from earth straight back where it came. Like hitting a ball into the corner of a squash court.

But first, she needs to don the replicas of Aldrin's moon boots, so she can create that iconic footprint in the dust a billion people have seen around the world.

Meanwhile, Jack has the tricky job of inflating a replica of

Apollo's Eagle Descent Module with a tank of compressed air. A full-scale Mylar and plastic model that stands eleven feet high when blown up, it will look OK from a distance, if it hasn't developed any punctures on the way here. Of course, should one of the *taikonauts* decide to take a selfie with it, all bets are off.

Gary, the greenhorn, drew the short straw and got several large pieces to scatter, along with a bunch of stuff, some of it disgusting, for the Toss Zone. So, when his initial tasks are done, Robin hands him the key-fob starter and he drives the SEV west for about a minute. Pulling up to a little depression in the ground, he places the TV camera and the Hasselblad body on the surface beside a couple of film magazines.

It takes a dozen back-and-forth short trips on foot to litter the Zone with the two A7L portable life support systems Aldrin and Armstrong wore, the armrests from the Eagle Descent Module, tools of various descriptions like a bulk sample scoop, tongs for picking up moon pebbles and rocks, wrenches, filters, brackets, and a US Army trenching tool. Finally, he unloads the actual trash: urine containers, the elaborately named 'defecation collection devices,' and the airsickness bags from the Starliner. It takes him the better part of three-quarters of an hour.

With the *Shénzhōu* almost in view, Gary unbuttons the rover's built-in, camouflaged tarp and drapes it over the SEV and its now-empty aluminum monkey bars in back. Then he lowers the rear bumper's metal drag mat and drives back for the flag planting, sweeping away his tire tracks as he goes.

The others, their own tasks just completed, are waiting for him. As Mission Commander, Robin has the honor of planting the flag. She picks up the metal case holding the Lunar Flag Assembly and opens it, pulling out the three-by-five-foot, garden-variety flag. It's tightly wrapped around its telescoping aluminum flagstick and held in place with three strips of adhesive. The fabric is specially treated to look bleached by the sun's all-but-blinding rays.

'Now that we're actually here, I guess we should say a benediction. Something significant.'

Jack Maybin smiles and eyes the watch built into his sleeve. 'Significant and quick. We've gotta get this done and head for those hills over there. I make it no more than forty minutes before we're on global TV.'

Robin looks at Gary and, pointing at him with the still-furled flag, says solemnly, 'You're the one who started us on this journey, Gary. *You* say something.'

Surprised, but happy to be acknowledged this way, he thinks for a moment and then, keeping his eyes on the banner, says, 'I'll simply utter the words that were supposed to be spoken here half a century ago by Neil Armstrong: "We come in peace for all mankind."'

'Cut!'

It's Jack Maybin. He's holding the zero-gravity camera they brought with them up to his eyes, like a movie director.

'Sorry, Gary. Give me another take while Robin plants the flag.'

There's an object in Jack's other hand. It looks like a gun.

'And while you're at it, the scriptwriters have come up with a little rewrite. Your character now says, "I claim this moon for the United States of America."'

Robin stares at him a long moment before saying, 'What? You're claiming the moon? Really?'

Jack grins. 'Not just me. Now that the space treaty has been taken out with the recycling, it'll belong to a whole bunch of Americans. Green cheese and all.'

'And your claim is based on, what? That you've got a gun?'

His grin broadens. 'Not just any gun. A plastic, 3D-printed gun. And plastic bullets. Very effective on the firing range. Breezed through the metal detectors. Now, the flag, if you don't mind.' He looks at the watch on his sleeve. 'I'm in a hurry.'

She makes no move to plant the flag. Instead she says, '*I'm* in a hurry? You're planning to . . . what? Shoot us and leave our bodies here at Tranquility for the world to discover?'

'Then, let me rephrase: *we're* in a hurry. Nobody has to die as long as you accept my little script change. A couple of words said over that flag you're holding and the whole place is ours.'

Gary is standing off to the side, midway between them, the one with the gun and the one with the flag. If he tries to rush Jack, he'll never make it.

Robin is as calm as ever. 'You said "ours." I thought it was *our* government that left you to rot in Afghanistan. Why would you—'

'Hey, sweetheart, just because a few sons of bitches in Washington didn't think I was worth it, that doesn't make me any less an American.'

She says, 'And Marty Bienstock, was he part of your *American plan?*'

'He was the cameraman. I was going to play the hero.'

'And me, what was I supposed to play?'

'Dead.'

There's a sheepish look on Jack's face. 'I disagreed with that part, but I was outvoted.' He grins. 'Lucky for you, Marty's vote no longer carries any weight.'

He takes another glance at his sleeve. 'OK, prelims are over. What does Nike say? "Just do it."'

'No, I don't think I will.'

Still recording her with the camera in his left hand, the man takes a step forward and gestures menacingly at her with the gun in his right.

'Don't you get it?' Jack says, a little feverishly. 'This is for us, the good ol' US of A! Truth, justice, and the American way! The tide of history is on our side.'

'The laws of chemistry are on mine.'

Calmly, Robin makes a sweeping gesture toward the brightly lit lunar landscape. 'Any idea how hot it is out here without an atmosphere?'

'What's that got to do with anything?'

'You can't tell it inside your spacesuit, but the temperature where we're standing here in the sun is over one hundred degrees Centigrade. Not Fahrenheit. Centigrade. Water boils at a hundred degrees. Plastic melts. Or, at least, it starts to.'

Considering the Chinese are minutes away, Gary marvels at Robin's sangfroid.

Jack waves the gun at her more emphatically. 'Melt? Not this baby. Look at it, solid as a rock. And what about our visors? They're plastic, and *they* still work.'

'Our visors are a polymer-copper blend, Jack. They'd never make it through a metal detector. Did you sleep through Astro-science class? And even if that gun in your hand *could* work when it's exposed to extreme, momentary heat, we've been out here for a couple of hours.'

She takes a step forward.

'No plastic bullet on the verge of melting can withstand the 30,000- to 50,000-PSI the firing pin will exert on it. Go on, pull the trigger, you've got a gummy bear in there. I bet nothing comes out.'

Jack looks over at Gary.

'Your girlfriend's crazy, you know that?'

Gary says, 'Crazy, maybe. But she knows her chemistry.'

'Fuck it,' the gunman says. 'Guess I'll have to be the hero after all.'

Jack aims for her heart and pulls the trigger.

Nothing.

'Told you.'

Jack is stunned to find his gun hasn't fired and Robin is still standing there. So, he's unprepared when she takes two quick strides forward with the flagstick held out in front of her like a spear. With all her weight behind it, the point buries itself in his suit, piercing his body a couple of inches below his heart.

The metal rod in his chest isn't what kills him. What kills him is pulling the metal rod *out*.

He drops the camera and the plastic gun and uses both gloved hands to rip the flag away. The effort leaves a hole in his Boeing Blue outfit bigger than a .45 caliber bullet would make. It depressurizes his suit – the air rushing out into the vacuum of space – so fast he doesn't have time to cover it with his hands before the lack of oxygen to his brain has his head reeling and his vision fogging up. He falls to his knees, his blood trying to follow the air out into the lunar void.

The last thing Jack Maybin knows is the sensation of the saliva on his tongue boiling away in the lunar heat.

Robin picks up the fallen flag, still taped around its aluminum pole, and dusts it off, the granules hanging in a tiny cloud where she does it. There's a red splotch of Jack's blood at the tip.

Turning to Gary, she says, 'Grab the camera, will you? We've still got a TV thing to film, and, well, who better than you? Oh, and let's have the gun, too. We don't need anybody tripping over it out here.'

She stabs the flagstick into the ground, saying, 'Sweetheart, do you *really* think I'm crazy? I hope not.'

He puts the plastic gun in the PPK attached to his suit, next to a just-in-case protein bar and the key-fob starter for the rover that's parked ten feet away.

'Crazy? No! I think you're amazing.'

She gives him an odd little smile. 'Remember when I called you from the bathroom in Houston? I asked if you'll love me "till death do us part?"'

'And I said I will. I meant it. I *mean* it.'

'Then, I have a story to tell you.'

'A story? Now? With the Chinese practically—'

'Yes, it has to be now. It'll explain things. Back in Mom's house, in Cocoa, there are a bunch of framed pictures on the piano.'

'Pictures on the piano? Correction: You *are* crazy.'

Robin continues as if she hasn't heard. 'Did you notice one of a baby?'

He thinks back for a moment. 'Yes, a baby in a blanket. At an airport, I think.'

She says, 'That's the one.'

'Are you trying to tell me *you* have a baby? If you do, I under—'

'No, sweetheart, I don't *have* a baby. I *was* the baby. *Am* that baby.'

Gary's totally confused. 'Everybody has baby pictures. I have mine somewhere.'

'But yours weren't taken in front of the International Arrivals building at Miami's airport. Like mine.'

He blinks. 'What are you saying? You're adopted? What possible difference—?'

'The difference is my birth mother was Russian. My adoptive parents, too: Artur and Kristina Wolski. They got out in the fifties and settled in Florida. Anglicized their names to Art and Chris Walsh. *Capiche*?'

'And my family's from Romania, originally, I think. Who gives a crap?'

'Our government does. Or to be precise, *your* government does. Russian spies are, like, a no-no.'

'What are you saying? Your dad was a spy?'

'No, my *mom*'s the spy, the sleeper agent, to be technical about it. She trained me, so that makes me one as well.'

Gary wants to say something, but suddenly his mind doesn't seem to be working.

Robin is picking at the tape that's keeping the flag furled on the aluminum pole in the ground, but her gloves aren't making it easy.

She says, 'Have you got fingernails? I can't seem to—' and then the tape gives way, loosening the fabric.

As Robin begins to pull the free end away from the pole, she says, 'Can you set the camera on something? We should grab a couple of selfies.'

Gary hears the words in his helmet, but he can't make sense of them.

'Hey, Gar, chop chop! We don't have all day!'

Somehow, he manages to mumble, 'I thought you said you're—'

'A Russian spy.' Her sly smile is visible through her visor. 'Come to think of it, I *did* mention it just now.'

'Then . . . you didn't learn Russian from those cosmonauts, like you said.'

She gives him a grin. '*Dumayu, ya solgal.*'

'Which means?

'"I guess I lied."'

With that, she unfurls the American flag all the way. And there, rolled up inside the Red, White, and Blue, is another banner. The colors are the same, only it's the flag of the Russian Federation: horizontal blocks of white and blue over red.

Robin balls up the Stars and Stripes and, lifting a nearby rock with her toe, crams it underneath. She straightens up and extends the horizontal bar of the Lunar Flag Assembly, clicking it and the Russian flag into place. Then she drives the flagstick further into the ground. Gary is unaware he's holding the camera, immobilized by disbelief.

In mock petulance, Robin says, 'Do I have to do *everything* around here?'

She comes forward and takes it from Gary. Then she steps back and, with the Russian banner in the background, she holds the camera out in front of her and snaps a couple of shots.

'This would be easier with a selfie stick.' She giggles to herself. 'So, love of my life, want to join me in a group photo?'

He's still frozen in place.

Robin steps toward him again and puts her hand, tenderly, on his shoulder. 'It's OK, you don't have to. It's a lot to take in. Anyway, in a couple of minutes, hi-def pictures of the thing will be all over Channel Seven or whatever channel they've got in China.'

Still mentally fogbound, Gary asks, 'Was . . . this your plan all along? Kill those guys and plant that flag up here?'

'It was my mom's plan, actually. In the beginning, we just wanted the old thirty-five-millimeter Apollo films my dad helped your dad make. Leak them to the press, give America a black eye with the fiftieth anniversary coming up. But Charlie wouldn't do it. Said it wasn't patriotic.'

She smiles that sly smile again. 'Your old man was the original patriot, carved from Plymouth Rock. Still, patriotism is sort of in the eye of the beholder, isn't it?

'After Congress pulled the US out of the moon treaty, Russia and a couple of other countries pulled out as well. And then it wasn't about black eyes, it was about a second, secret race to the moon fifty years after the first. A race to own the greatest strategic military asset ever. And all that molybdenum and crap that's right here under our feet.'

With that, she stamps her foot on the ground, creating a second little cloud of dust. And another of those Aldrin boot prints.

Gary feels his brain searching for answers, but all he comes up with is a single question.

'You and your mom, *you killed my dad*?'

'Us? Absolutely not! I swear! There are some *really* crazy people in America, right-wing nuts who pretty much had the same idea we had: Plant the flag, own the moon.

'Jack was their boy. Marty . . . Marty was *your* doing. Much appreciated. Now, help me with Jack's body. I'm thinking nobody wants three people from China to find a corpse in the Sea of Tranquility. We've got to give him a sendoff.'

Gary helps Robin load the dead man into the rover's cargo area.

'Drive us over to the Little West Crater,' she says. 'We'll dump him in there.'

Like an automaton, he does as he's told and presses the starter button on the key fob. Moments later, having maneuvered around a few rocky outcroppings formed when a meteor created this particular hole in the moon, Gary halts the rover atop a little rise. They find they're facing planet earth across the 240,000 miles. It really is blue.

Robin gets out and lifts Jack's body, weighing twenty-eight low-gravity pounds, all by herself from the back of the rover. Then she walks the corpse over to the edge of Little West.

Gary gets out and joins her. 'You said a sendoff. Shouldn't we say a few words?'

She looks at him through her polymer-copper visor.

'Gary, don't take this the wrong way, but you're soft. Gentle, which is good, but also soft. All Americans are soft, sentimental. "Say a few words." Jesus H. Christ, he tried to kill me back there! And we're totally out of time!'

Then, relenting a little, she says, 'OK, the Air Force prayer Jack said over Marty's body back in the Starliner? About entering into new life with the Father?'

She stands Jack's body up at the precipice.

'Well, ditto.'

She gives Jack a push and sends him hurtling forty meters or more down onto the rocks in the darkness of the pit.

The astronaut's body makes no noise when it hits the bottom. Without an atmosphere to transmit the sound, the shock of what Robin did is multiplied by the eerie silence of Jack Maybin simply disappearing into the void.

Shock works in different ways on different people. It affects Gary now by freeing him from the fugue state his mind's been in ever since Robin revealed her true colors.

He turns away from the crater's black nothingness, Jack Maybin's final resting place, and finds himself staring instead back at the earth. In its rotation, the North American side is facing them. Washington, New York . . .

Robin takes a step over to him and puts a gloved hand on his shoulder.

'I know this is hard, Gary, so much stuff all at once. When you come to understand love of country isn't just an American thing . . . I mean, the United States is no more exceptional a place than . . .'

He isn't listening. Instead, he's hearing the phrase he uttered just moments ago playing in his head. Neil Armstrong didn't say, 'We come in peace for people who believe the same things we do.' He said, 'We come in peace for all mankind.'

And didn't someone call the earth a big blue marble? All seven billion of us rocketing through the heavens together?

She's saying, 'OK, you're right, Gary. There *is* a greater love than country. The love between two human beings. In our case, a woman and a man. If you love me, sweetheart, *really* love me the way I love you, that's the only thing that should matter.'

Her words bring up a crazy image: he's snuggled beside Robin in the rover, gazing at their planet through the windshield the way a pair of teenagers parked at some lovers' lane back home might stare at the moon. So far, it hasn't been a very romantic place.

He turns back to find her looking at him, all concern.

'Gary, honey, are you all right? We have to get out of here.'

No, he's *not* all right. Not by a long shot. And, of all things, it's her use of the word 'we' that upsets him the most.

Now, the woman he loves is pointing emphatically at the Apple watch built into her sleeve. 'T-minus-zero, darling! We're out of time!'

There it is again, that 'we.' And, just like that, he makes up his mind.

He says, 'We have to go back.'

Finally, she relaxes. 'All right! Starliner, here we come!'

'No, I mean we have to go back to the flags.'

He takes a single step toward the rover, saying, 'Make it right. Do what we came here to do.'

She puts her hand back on his shoulder, more heavily this time, holding him there. 'But, we *did* what we came here to do. What *I* came here to do.'

Peeling her hand off his shoulder, he repeats himself. 'We have to go back.'

She sighs with finality. 'All right, sweetheart, I understand.'

She starts to unzip the Personal Preference Kit on her belt, saying, 'I guess we've reached the moment when the Russian girl and the American boy have to go their separate ways.'

She reaches into the PPK and brings out something that glints in the harsh, unfiltered sunlight: A large plastic knife with a serrated blade.

She looks down at the thing in her hand. 'Jack brought a plastic gun. Wrong kind of plastic.'

Then she looks back at him, a strange smile playing across her face. 'I really *did* love you.'

Gary tries to think. And then he makes the smallest of gestures, a move for the PPK container on the far side of his belt from Robin.

She takes a menacing step forward. The two of them are standing together at the crater's edge. She says, 'You'll have the biggest memorial plaque I can afford. Bigger even than Yuri Gagarin's.'

He's groping inside the kit with his clumsy gloved fingers, feeling for the rover's key fob. Then, finding it, he presses the Start button.

The SEV comes to life. Parking brake off, it begins to slide down the rise in the ground toward the crater, toward them, like the Smart Car it actually is, rolling down someone's driveway.

It's moving slowly, barely gathering speed as it crunches the dust and gravel under its treads, silently.

Gary can't keep his eyes off the knife in her hand.

She's says, 'Cool, don't you think? It's based on a knife my adoptive father had. Loved to go fishing in the Everglades, showed me how to gut them. Fillet them. Of course, the Sea of Tranquility hasn't any fish.'

Just then, she notices something in the far distance behind Gary. A light, a blip, coming from the darkened, shadowy horizon.

'Well, how about that? The Chinese are here!'

Gary turns to look at the speck of light. Then he turns back.

Still looking at the pinpoint of light, Robin says, 'If this were a Western, they'd be the cavalry.' She gives a little laugh. 'Whoever heard of the cavalry speaking Chinese?'

Bringing her eyes back to Gary, she lifts a hand and actually caresses his helmet, saying, 'It'll be quick. Like Jack. Only faster.'

And then she starts to thrust the blade forward.

The rover can't be going faster than four miles an hour when it hits Robin Walsh – Robin Wolski – from behind. On earth, a bruised hip, maybe a bruised back. But in one-sixth the gravity, the collision sends her sailing off her feet and over the edge of the crater.

To join Jack.

Gary presses the Stop button on the key fob, braking the rover two seconds before it would have gone over the side after Robin. No time to rue what he's just done; he has work to do.

Getting behind the wheel, he drives back to Tranquility Base at top speed, pulling up at the flagpole. Stepping down, he grabs hold of the Lunar Flag Assembly the way Robin did, only this time *removing* the Russian flag, which he drops into the rover.

Then he goes back, rescues Old Glory from under the rock, gives the artificially sun-bleached banner a shake, and slides it over the flagstick. When he lifts the crossbar and clicks it in place, the American flag on the moon looks the way it does in all of his dad's mocked-up pictures.

Picking up the camera, Gary clicks off a couple of shots. The second one shows a beam of light in the upper left corner. Gary moves his eye away from the viewfinder. The Chinese are getting closer. He's got to get away.

Jumping into the rover, he guns the dune buggy, knowing any movement will attract attention on the *Shénzhōu* in less than a minute. Where to hide?

With the steel mat in back literally covering his tracks, Gary drives like a madman, returning to the 'splashed' rock formations around Little West Crater. If he can get there in time, maybe the camouflaged SEV can hide him from prying eyes. Maybe.

Fortunately for the last surviving member of the Dark Side mission, the craft from Asia is designed to park on the moon like the Starliner: feet first, with its retro rockets kicking up the loose material on the surface. Even though he's still forty meters from the safety of the rocks, the momentary dust storm effectively should cloud the *Shénzhōu*'s cameras on board until it settles.

Gary pulls up and turns off the rover. He's facing the flagstick with the American flag sticking out straight and proud. And now, he has to wait.

SIXTY-FIVE

It takes the trio of *taikonauts* a maddening three hours to pull off their stunt for global television. First, the hatch opens. Then it closes. Then, with the first explorer to emerge making a big deal about taking a step on the lunar surface, he (or she, Gary can't be sure from this distance) turns to film the hatch slowly opening again. The other two climb down, one at a time. That's twenty minutes right there. Are they allowing for TV commercials in-between?

Gary can feel himself getting hungry. He reaches into the PPK and pulls out the protein bar. And then it dawns on him: he can't take off his helmet to eat it. Bummer.

Meanwhile, the newcomers do everything, seemingly, in triplicate. Including, finally, each visitor has to personally pound in the flagstick they brought with a little rubber mallet. And then there's an intricate little dance, as slow as an underwater ballet on earth, as the trio poses in different combinations around the Five-Star Chinese flag when it's finally sitting alongside the Star and Stripes.

Are they done yet? Not even close. Armed with cameras, the three set off in different directions. One goes over to the science projects Robin set up and films that. Another seems to be photographing the Aldrin boot print.

Uh-oh, Gary thinks. Is the third *taikonaut* moving over to the plastic model of the Eagle? Is he (she?) going to touch it? If so, all bets are off. But no, thank God; he's just taking its picture from thirty feet away. Even better, nobody's wandering over in the direction of Little West Crater to blow his cover.

He's been hungry, starving really, for the last hour. And worse, much worse, it's been so long since they left the Starliner, he has to use a defecation collection device in the worst way. Too bad he threw them all into the Toss Zone.

To take his mind off the signals his body is sending him, Gary tries to imagine what the TV viewers back home are making of this. Clearly, a billion Chinese must be delirious with their country's technological achievement. A handful of Americans in the District of Columbia, centered around 1600 Pennsylvania Avenue, should be breathing a lot easier, too, while another handful knows something went awfully wrong with their plans.

Finally, what must it be like back in Moscow, in the Kremlin, to be watching in high-def the crew of the *Shénzhōu* cavorting around other peoples' flags?

Bet Mrs Wolski in Cocoa Beach is packing her bags right now.

And then the on-location segment of the Chinese TV show comes to an end. Good thing, too, as Gary's oxygen monitor shows little more than nine percent of breathable air left. The three pioneers climb back up the ladder and pull it up after them. After a final, interminable wait, they blast off from the surface.

And Gary Stephens is, once again, the only human being on the moon. Correction, the only *living* human being.

It's been nearly eight hours since he and Jack cranked up the SEV's engine. The battery life, what was the estimate? Ten hours, between the driving and the heat? Less. Nine and change? Gary would cross his fingers if they weren't encased in two sets of gloves. It's gonna be tight.

Um, wasn't that something Robin said today? The thought of her stabs Gary with an almost physical pang. He thinks of the three of

them – Marty back at the Starliner, Jack and Robin right here –
asleep on the moon for all eternity.

And then he snaps out of it. If he's going to keep on being the
moon's only living human, he has to get going. So, he hits the rover's
Start button, praying it still has enough juice.

It does, thank God, and Gary drives away from the crater, from
Tranquility.

The hills they passed on their way here make a nice landmark
on the trip back. Once past their barrier, Stella's GPS shows up on
the rover's dashboard. He's able to home in on the Starliner. In
another thirty minutes, the camouflaged nose sticking up from its
crater tells Gary he's almost there.

You can't run out of gas in a car that doesn't run on the stuff.
An electric car just stops turning its wheels when the battery dies.
No sound, no movement, no nothing.

So near and yet so far. Gary gets out of the rover and checks the
monitor on his oxygen tank, the one that goes from green to yellow
to red. It's flickering on red. He'll have to hoof it the rest of the
way. And quick.

One more silver lining: you can hop a lot faster and farther on
the moon than you can on earth. Gary overdoes it a couple of times
and loses his balance, but he's able to right himself and make it to
the Starliner's gangway in one piece.

'Stella, open up!'

He looks down and sees Marty's body there, awaiting a burial
that's never going to come. 'Stella!' he wails. Is the guidance system
even on? Is it able to hear him over his intercom?

'I heard you the first time, Bert.'

Even as the outer door of the airlock system begins to come
open, Gary can feel his oxygen supply becoming sketchy. He takes
a breath and holds it as he hurries across the gangway and through
the threshold.

In his ear he can hear Stella say, 'Equalizing pressure.'

Standing in the space between the inner and outer doors of the
airlock, he has the chance to look at the oxygen monitor built into
his sleeve. No more flickering; it's a steady red.

'Hurry, Stella.'

'We can't rush these things, Bert.'

'Sure we can, Stella.'

And then, a few excruciating seconds later, the second, inner door opens and he tumbles into the capsule before it closes behind him.

Unperturbed, Stella says, 'Welcome back, Bert. How far behind you are Commanders Walsh and Maybin?'

Before he can answer, Gary has to unscrew his helmet. He wrenches it off and takes a deep breath. Then he gets to his feet, not an easy proposition in the close quarters of the airship. He eases into the seat he occupied before. With difficulty he's able to work off first one glove and then, hurriedly, the other.

Now, how should he put this? 'Stella, Robin and Jack have decided to stay.'

There's a pregnant pause before the system says, 'There's a change of plans?'

'Yes, Stella, a change of plans. Now, take me home.'

'Aye aye, Captain.'

With that, the engines down below ignite, and the Starliner, on autopilot, slowly leaves the moon for earth.

Liftoff is a maddeningly slow process, especially with 'the call of nature' yelling at him to get out of his suit. When the craft finally levels off, he gets up. There's a spare collection device lying against the far wall.

Twenty minutes later, he wolfs down the protein bar from his PPK. Food, real food, can wait. He's got more than twenty-four hours to go before he sees another human face. More than that before he's back home with his family. Pippa, Roger, Ashley, and Gracie. Home with the people he loves.

SIXTY-SIX

Nearly all the residents of the Royal Freemasons' Benevolent Institution, just off the A32 here in Dubbo, are in their places in the community room. Even a couple of the dementia patients have settled in with their helpers from the memory support unit to watch the return of the Chinese mission to the moon on Australian TV.

Immediately after finishing lunch in the dining room, Una Ronald hurried as fast as a ninety-two-year-old can hurry and parked herself right in front of the home's sixty-inch flat-screen TV. It can be a little dicey, when you're saddled with more than a touch of macular degeneration, trying to make out what's going on from off to the side of the screen, so she's right in the center. Fortunately, her grandchildren have driven over with their kids to sit with her. They'll fill her in on anything she misses.

Thinking of misses, the image of Jock rolling away in bed flashes through her mind from half a century ago: He missed the moon then, and he's missing it now. Or, is he here in spirit? The youngest, Georgie, sitting two seats down, is the spitting image of his great-grandad, so there's that. She looks over at the pre-teen. He's drinking a Coke, and she smiles a little secret smile. A can, not a bottle.

Half a world away, Pippa and Roger watch side-by-side in their darkened family room. It's after two in the morning, and Gracie, Ash, and Army are all asleep on the flokati rug at their feet. Gracie is snoring a ten-year-old's snore, which brings a smile to Pippa's face. The twins insisted on staying up way past their bedtimes 'just this once,' but they conked out over an hour ago.

Like Una Ronald, Pippa's thoughts are on a missing someone. Two someones: Gary and Pop. Charlie wouldn't have wanted to miss this for the world, retired or no. And Gary, where in heaven's name is he? She hasn't heard from him in over a week. Hope he's watching this thing, so they can talk about it later.

And, as a matter of fact, he is. Thousands of miles behind the Chinese – and with thousands of miles still to go before Stella does a couple of spins around the Space Station on the way home – Gary is doing what those future travelers will do when they convert this craft to the 'space taxi' it was intended to be: he's watching what the world is watching on YouTube. And he's thinking he'll have plenty of time to do some grieving when he gets home.

Stella's voice interrupts his thoughts. 'If you don't mind my asking, Bert . . .' She stops, waiting for him to answer.

He says, 'No, Stella, I don't mind. What is it?'

'Commanders Walsh and Maybin and the change of plans. Did they die? Is that why they didn't return to me?'

'Yes, Stella. That's why.'

After a moment, the Peggy Lee voice says, 'You must feel terrible.'

Gary says, 'Yes, I do Stella. I feel terrible.'

Stella says, 'So do I.'

At least, Gary *thinks* she said that. Now that it's so quiet, deathly quiet in the Starliner, maybe he imagined it. What kind of lunatic consoles a computer? What kind of lunatic is *consoled* by a computer?

Really, what kind of person – one who once found true love and had it taken from him – imagines he can ever find another human being to love just as much?

The kind who believes it when he says, 'Till death do us part.'

ACKNOWLEDGMENTS

My thanks to the people at Severn House for publishing this book. Thanks to Kate Lyall Grant and her whole team of editors, designers, and marketers, especially Carl Smith, Natasha Bell, Emma Grundy Haigh, Piers Tilbury, and Michelle Duff. Thanks also to my agent, Mark Gottlieb of Trident Media Group, for placing it in their capable hands. An especial shout-out to my wife, Ellen Highsmith Silver, for putting up with my lunacy for more than fifty years.

Thanks as well to Neil Armstrong, Buzz Aldrin, and Michael Collins for taking their 'one giant leap for mankind.' I've been thinking about what they did, and the skeptics who doubt they did it, from the moment the crew made it back safely to earth. (Yes, I'm that old.)

Since then, I've read a bunch of books by the doubters, among them *Moon Landings: Did NASA Lie?* by Philippe Lheureux, *How America Faked the Moon Landings* by Charles T. Hawkins, and *Dark Moon: Apollo and the Whistle-Blowers* by Mary Bennett and David S. Percy. While some of their claims are hilarious – I'm not a doubter myself – it got me thinking about how the US could have pulled the thing off just two and a half years after the crew of Apollo 1 burned up, horrifically, on the launch pad in Florida.

We've just survived the hullabaloo of the 50th anniversary of the touch-down at the Sea of Tranquility. Any moment now, the Chinese will send an unmanned rocket to the moon to retrieve lunar rock samples, with a manned launch to follow. I've just speeded up their timetable.

Thanks for reading . . .

Mitch Silver, Greenwich, Connecticut

Summer, 2019